Cho...

A story of how p... transformed a boy's life with easy steps and inside secrets anyone can follow.

Dr. Jim Kay

Copyright © 2020 Jenna Say Quoi, LLC

All rights reserved. No part of this publication may be reproduced, distributed, or transmitted in any form or by any means, including photocopying, recording, or other electronic or mechanical methods, without the prior written permission of the publisher, except in the case of brief quotations embodied in critical reviews and other noncommercial uses permitted by copyright law.

Dedication:
My daughter, May, inspired this story. I care for her deeply and hope she gets what she needs out of reading it.
To my wife, Jenna, son Noah, and other daughter Catera. You provided me with the time and opportunity to complete this book.
To the 5,400 students I've taught, who deal with parts of the problems the two main characters face.

Discover other titles by Dr. Jim Kay:

Financial Wellness: Prepare for retirement and the unexpected. Become financially healthy and positively change your life.

Fast FIRE: Rules for personal finance to quickly become Financially Independent and Retire Early

Sudden Wealth: Forever wealth from specific investment advice and psychological strategies

When Pat was a teen, he accidentally kills a father of two children. He is overcome with grief and has to learn how to deal with his anxiety, depression, and post-traumatic stress. An unlikely friend, in the form of his high school finance teacher, helps him refocus his internal turmoil. Doc gives him straight-forward, specific advice as to where to invest to become a multimillionaire. Pat learns from his teacher: investment tips, tricks, and timings to make the most money possible. This refocus allows Pat to heal himself emotionally and become rich. Follow the life of Pat and learn exactly how he got past his troubles and how you could become a multimillionaire.

~Specific recommendations as to what to invest in, along with when and how.

~An incredible story that teaches personal finance, as well as strategies to help deal with PTSD and anxiety.

~Not many novels try to tackle how to deal with emotional loss. This one does this as well as how to deal with the trauma of accidentally killing someone.

~A personal finance story of a boy going from nothing to everything.

Choices

A story of how personal finance transformed a boy's life with easy steps and inside secrets anyone can follow.

The advice and information in this book are from research and exchanges with individuals and experts in their field. No identification with actual persons (living or deceased) or products is intended or should be inferred. The stories, characters, and entities are fictional. This book gives a broad overview of finance. The author and publisher are not offering legal, accounting, psychological, or other professional advice. No representation or warranty of any kind is offered or should be used or construed as an offer or recommendation for any security. Investors should seek such professional advice for their particular situation. No assumption of liability is made as to the accuracy or completeness of the material. Furthermore, the content may include inadvertent technical or factual inaccuracies. All advice is subject to individual situations and financial fitness for individuals or institutions. Liability of loss is the sole responsibility of the person using this guide. Invest at your own risk.

Intro:

No one's life is perfect. We all have problems. We all have our ups and downs. We have all seen successes and failures. Our goal is to do things right and make progress. For you to be successful, you don't have to be born at the right address or with money to make a success of your life. You already have the desire. You only need the knowledge. You want straight answers with clear guidelines. You want inside information. You want the secrets the rich use to become even wealthier, and you want to know how to protect your money.

Content

Chapter 1
- What is your money comfort zone?
- Are you willing to invest in the future YOU?

Chapter 2
- How much do you need to earn to put save 10% for the future?
- From where does the power to change need to come?

Chapter 3
- What is the easiest and surest way to become wealthy?
- What obstacles do I need to overcome before I start investing?

Chapter 4
- What are the best investments?

Chapter 5
- What budget is the best for the lazy?

Chapter 6
- What do I do if I have debt?

Chapter 7
- What fund do I use for my 20%?

Chapter 8
- How do I set up a stay out of debt fund?

Chapter 9
- Why should I focus on meaningful goals, things that matter?
- How do I determine if a purchase fits in with what matters most to me?
- What's more important to me having more or building relationships?
- Why am I unhappy with my situation?
- Why focus on things in my control?

Chapter 10
- How can I limit my opportunity costs and invest the money?

Chapter 11
- How do I build my credit rating?
- Why should I build my credit rating?

Chapter 12

    Is homeownership a good investment?

    What is the maximum house payment I can afford?

Chapter 13

    Which homeowner's insurance policy do I need?

    Is an umbrella insurance policy worth the money?

Chapter 14

    How much term life insurance do I need?

Chapter 15

    What do I do with an inheritance or large cash prize?

Chapter 16

    What trends do the rich follow I too could use and make more money?

Chapter 17

    How do I time the market and prosper during turbulent times?

    How do I create a stream of income, like the rich?

    How much money do I need to retire?

    How can someone who hasn't saved money retire?

Chapter 18

    When is it time to call in an investment professional?

    How do I choose a professional who will work for an hourly rate?

Chapter 19

    Should I move to a place with a lower cost of living?

Chapter 20

    Should I branch out into riskier investments?

Chapter 21

    How do I leave a legacy?

Chapter 22

    How do I teach someone all the investment strategies to become rich?

Chapter 1

What is your money comfort zone?
Are you willing to invest in the future YOU?

Pat

Age 13, income $0/year; 10% fund $0; 20% fund $0; Stay out of debt fund $0

I remember running. I looked back, surprised not to see the police chasing me. Surely a few of those cops could have climbed the embankment and caught up with me. Before I turned left, onto the street where I lived, I looked again. No one was behind me.

I didn't slow down. I had just done the stupidest thing and had no idea how to handle the situation. I was only 13 years old. Surely other teens have done bad things before, but this was a life-changer.

I reached the steps to our apartment. I knew no one would be home for hours. I unlocked the door and ran to the room, my brother and I shared. I hid in the closet. I've dealt with pain before, even broke a bone once, but I never cried as I cried in that closet. Tears came from my eyes like a broken pipe in the ceiling.

I don't know how much time had passed, but it couldn't have been more than 30 minutes. I heard the door open. "Police!" My heart raced. How did they find me? Why did I have to go over that bridge? I thought if I could just stop crying, they won't hear me. The closet door swung open, flashlights from three directions shining on my red face. I remember it like it was yesterday. The cop in the middle leaned in and grabbed my left arm, lifting me like he was angry with me, mad for what I did. He had every right to despise me. I knew how bad it was merely by the lady's scream. He spun me around and had handcuffs on me before I could wipe the newly formed tears from my eyes.

As soon as we hit daylight, I saw my mom. She was crying, pleading. People were standing around, filming me with their phones. Four cop cars, all with lights on surrounded the auto shop we lived above. The cop who was angry with me gently guided me into the back of the police cruiser. All I could think of during that ride was, 'things couldn't get worse.'

Doc

My students call me Doc, and it's not because I'm a medical doctor or a therapist. I treat financial ailments, and I've been on this path long enough to understand that a lot of people don't know enough to utilize their earnings and cash flow better. I've lived most of my life trying to bridge this void. No one listens. But occasionally, I find a man diligent in his ways, and he ends up sitting amongst kings.

I understand the appetite of man to pursue the satisfaction of his immediate wants. How easy it is for someone to spend all their income, and trod down the path of wastefulness, creating potholes of financial ailments. However, when I find someone who has even a small desire to save for tomorrow, I share a simple way for people to invest. I help everyday people become wealthy. To make this happen, I would share simple, time-tested strategies along with secrets and little-known market timings to help people become financially independent faster.

I am a finance teacher at Greenville High, one of the best schools in Portland, and I've had all the support and motivation I've needed to embark on my journey of instigating proven investment techniques. I have an overwhelming desire to ultimately make the world a better place one student millionaire at a time. One of the joys of teaching is when I get positive feedback from students or their parents. In some cases, I stay in touch with former students as they learn to live their own lives. Patrick Fitten, or as I called him Pat, was one such student.

When I first met Pat, he was a scruffy teen with more bone than muscle, and his hair was usually messy, but stylishly. It was apparent he only owned a few outfits, and he sometimes wore them unwashed. A couple of years before meeting Pat, I had taught his older and more popular brother, Chad. It was clear Chad had no interest in financial literacy, even though he always did well in class. Chad was the kind of kid who wadded his way through the turbulence of life without a clear cut plan. And I've noticed over the years, this way of living has become a popular worldview amongst the youth.

Pat was usually quiet during class. When no other kids were around, he would open up. During the time Pat was a student of mine and used to come in after school where we did most of our talking. Looking back at the situation, I realize Pat didn't have much support at home as he was growing up. He wanted someone to talk to, someone who took an interest in him. His brother, Chad, seemed to care genuinely about his younger brother. Chad was the one who brought Pat to me, having pushed his younger brother to take the class.

When Chad was my student, I learned he and Pat lost their father. His dad was a bricklayer who even had his own small company. The company consisted of odd jobs here and there that did more than pay the bills. Pat's dad had a great work ethic that supported an upper-middle-class income. His dad's long hours allowed Pat's mom to stay home with their three kids, Chad,

Pat, and their older sister, Nicole. I knew Chad as he was in my class, but over the years of knowing Pat, I'd only met Nicole a couple of times.

About two weeks into the semester, when I first taught Pat, he came in after school while no one else was around and sat at one of the computers near my desk. He seemed nervous. Rather than speaking, he opted to browse through random websites. The silence was deafening, and after a while, I finally talked to him, "Chad is your brother, right?"

Pat glanced over at me, as if not sure what to say at first. "Yeah… He told me to take your finance class. He thought it would be good for me after-" He didn't finish his sentence. Instead, he went back to the computer.

Like most teens, he was quick with the mouse. He was flipping from page to page. Knowing what he was looking for and barely giving anyone page more than a glance. It seemed like he was trying to find coupons for coffee houses in the area.

After a brief silence, I stood up from my desk and walked closer to Pat's computer, sitting backward in a chair a few desks away.

"Patrick-"

"Pat," the boy corrected.

"Pat. What's your story? Why did Chad want you to take my finance class?" I was direct and to the point. I saw no need to dodge around the subject.

His head dipped downwards, his eyes sliding off his computer as they focused on some distant spot on the carpet. No tears came from his eyes, but I felt the anguish rising from his skin. He looked up and met my eyes, and I suppose something clicked within him, something that made the teen open up to me.

"Before moving to this school district, my dad got sick and couldn't work anymore. We had some savings, so at first, it seemed like no big deal. Three kids and their mom could get by for a few months without any problems, right? Well, soon enough, his medical bills started coming in, and my dad wasn't getting any better. He had no disability insurance, not even a part of his income was coming in. Almost a year had gone by with Dad in the hospital. Thankfully, during that time, friends and family were more than willing to help. Meals were coming in, and people were picking us up from school so my mom could be with my dad in the hospital. But still, their help and kindness wouldn't be enough because she desperately needed money to pay the bills," Pat said.

I already knew he had lost his father. It didn't seem to affect Chad all that much, or perhaps Chad's relaxed demeanor was simply an act. On the other hand, Pat was outwardly upset.

Pat rolled around in his chair and fiddled with the keyboard, then continued, "We were flat broke. My sister, Nicole, suggested to our mom to take out a second mortgage on the house. To get by until Dad was feeling better and working again. It paid the everyday bills for a few months, but not my father's medical bills. We had medical insurance, but each new test they ran would cost us more out-of-pocket money. We started getting picky about which tests they were running. That was the only way we could try to save some money. Mom pushed the medical bills aside and turned to survival mode – first, buy food for the kids; second pay the utilities; third pay the mortgage," Pat explained.

My heart ached for Pat's suffering. I didn't know these details while I was teaching Chad. I leaned forward in my seat, crossing my arms on the back of the chair. "What happened?" I asked.

After a short pause, Pat began to tear up. He wiped furiously at his face. "My dad died on a Friday in early November. The illness overcame his body. Since he didn't have life insurance, we had two mortgages we couldn't afford. Mom got a job, but since she'd been out of the workforce for so long while raising the kids, her pay was low. It was too low to support our middle-class lifestyle," he said.

"Is that how you ended up here?" I asked.

"We filed for bankruptcy and moved out. My mom tried to get an apartment in the same school district, so Chad and I could finish. Nicole had already graduated high school by then. Mom couldn't rent a place because of the bad marks on her credit report or something. It probably would've been too expensive anyway. We ended up moving to this town so we could live cheaper. We found a small place above a mechanic's shop. The owner of the auto repair place felt bad and let us rent it for less than usual," said Pat.

The pieces of the puzzle were finally coming together for me, and as Pat stood up, I understood the weight he carried on his shoulders.

Pat

Age 17, income $0/year; 10% fund $0; 20% fund $0; Stay out of debt fund $0

When I came into Doc's classroom that afternoon, I wasn't expecting any more talk then a few basic pleasantries. People pretending to be nice to me was wasteful. I just wanted to find some coupons so I could justify buying myself a coffee after I left.

As I was talking with Doc, I remembered my dad. His smile, his rough hands - weathered by concrete. All of what had happened, I just lived for years with all that inside me. I never talked to anyone about it except talking with Chad on a rare occasion.

Briefly, my thoughts turned to Mom. She was still living in denial, never mentioning her husband, my dad. My mind raced to the friends I use to hang out with in middle school. I hated the fact it was hard to make friends as an underweight freshman, never mind one with a dead dad and no money to go out with friends. Thoughts were always swirling through my head, regret, disappointment, but most prominent was the uncontrollable anger. Here I was, though, sitting with a 'magic finance doctor' or whatever he called himself, and for the first time in a while, I felt as if someone was listening to me.

As I continued pouring my heart out, Doc looked at me with weathered eyes that seemed to understand and sympathize all on their own. I was sharing what seemed like my life story. I guess it was. I was only thirteen when I caused the accident. How much more would I have experienced before that?

I continued to tell Doc everything. "We went from a great house to me, sharing a room with my brother above some dude's auto shop. Ma worked long hours, so we rarely got to see her."

The memories from that time in my life bounced around the echo-chamber of my thoughts, I remember how exhausted I was physically yes, but also mentally, I was tired of living in the hell that my life seemed to be. I was burned out. Fatigued with self-pity and worry.

I realized I was staring off into space once more, my eyes scanning over a Star Wars poster on the wall over and over again. I snapped back into reality and saw the look on Doc's face, and he seemed concerned. I paused. Never detention, they had wanted me to meet with a counselor. At the time, it seemed like a stupid punishment, but they were only trying to help. I didn't think I needed help, especially not from someone who was paid to pretend to care. They were wasting their time on me. I didn't open up or anything. Instead, I mingled with the sickening thoughts that festered in my mind.

There wasn't even a slight chance that I would have been willing to open up to Nicole. She was my spiteful sister, who would do things that convinced me she truly hated me. I felt deep down; she blamed me for the predicament of the family. She always tried to make me feel worse about myself than I already did. I did love her, but she found a way to remind me of the terrible thing I did.

The words poured out of my mouth, words that I had kept inside for so long. A fountain of confession spurted like a geyser, and it felt good to let it blow. "I was thirteen, walking over a bridge, it was still under construction or some crap because the wall was only a few feet tall, there was a big orange barrel in my way and I just kinda got pissed at it you know?"

I didn't have to look up to know Doc was listening intently.

"So I pushed it, I pushed it over the edge of the bridge, it was too easy. I mean, it was heavy and all, but I was a skinny kid, and I could do it. It fell off the bridge and-" I stopped mid-sentence and looked up with a few tears stinging in the corners of my eyes.

Wiping the tears, as they rolled down my cheek, I looked back down at my hands and focused, telling the story that the police had told me years before, "there were a few cars involved, minor injuries, a broken wrist, and one casualty."

I was barely able to choke out the next words, "I killed the father of two baby girls." I continued as Doc listened, "The barrel hit a car directly on the windshield. A man was driving. The Police said he probably didn't know what hit him as he died instantly because of the head-force trauma. This father of infant twins was gone, just like my father was no longer around for me."

Doc kept staring at me. I'm sure he'd heard about the accident. It was on the news and in the papers. The reports talked about a teen causing a horrific accident and the death of a driver. That teen was me. I did it.

Doc had a stoic look on his face, not sympathy, not disgust either, these were just data pieces to him, bits of a very complicated formula, but he didn't have all the data he needed. "What happened next?"

The next moments were a hell that I had to relive every single day of my life. I knew all the details by heart. I had recalled the memory daily. Stupid. Thoughtless. "I wasn't sure what to do, I saw that some cars had piled up, but I would never have imagined someone was-" I shook my head a bit, "I just started walking, I made it to the other side of the bridge, and looked down at the mayhem I had caused. A woman walked up to the first car damaged and opened the door. The scream that woman let loose. I can still hear the ringing in my ears from that scream. I can't even imagine what she saw, but whatever it was made her open her mouth in terror, she ran back toward her car and made it about halfway before collapsing. I stood and stared as more people stopped, more people took out their phones, it somehow felt like an eternity had passed, but it was probably just a few minutes. The police arrived. My ears were ringing. I could barely hear the officers shouting up to me. That's when I started running, I ran and ran until I felt like I couldn't run any further and then I ran some more. I made it to the little apartment on top of the mechanic's shop. I slammed my door shut and crawled into the space under the shelves in my closet."

The next part of the story was much easier to tell, "The police entered the room. I was crying, and the cops cuffed me."

Doc

I started doing the math in my head to figure out Pat's age when he caused the accident and then how old he would be today. I met Pat two weeks after he got out of juvenile detention and was on probation. "I can see you've been through a lot. Why do you think Chad recommended you take this financial literacy class?" I asked.

"I just never want to feel like that again," Pat responded quickly and without hesitation.

"Like what?"

"Mom had no choices. We lost the house because of the bills and no insurance. We had to move because we had no other choice. I had no choice but to go to juvie. We had no choice of changing hospitals and getting better care for my dad, and maybe he would still be with us if we had." Pat stopped talking. His lean face was shaking. "I've never had any choices. Everything has always been out of my control. I see no choices for my future. I'll always feel this way like I'm drowning in remorse, there's no choice." Pat seemed like he was about to start crying again, and I could feel how frustrating his life had been.

I softened my voice, "and you think money could have fixed that? Could money have given you choices?"

Pat slammed his fist on the table, making the keyboard jump. "Money sure would've given my dad a better chance. The money would've kept our house. The money would've kept my mom from having to work. The money would've kept me from walking across that bridge and doing something so freaking stupid," he sounded angry now, tears welling up in his eyes, but these were tears of fury, not self-pity.

I brought my eyes down, and rubbed my thumb against my palm, taking comfort in the light scratch. "Pat, most people are a lot like you." I paused. "People develop money habits, good or bad, based on a large event or how their parents handled money. Most people don't have a big event in their life that would alter how they think about money as you do. They develop a pattern of spending and saving based on two main factors, their economic upbringing and things their parents insisted were important."

Knowing people like to stay in the same spending patterns as they grew up was an essential lesson for everyone to learn. Those who don't understand themselves, make financial mistakes. If they don't understand that their upbringing strongly influences adult-spending habits, they will continue to make financial mistakes their entire lives.

Pat questioned me, "I don't know where you're going with this, Doc. I understand how parents could influence their kids' money habits, but what about how the," he paused, searching for the words, "economic upbringing? And what does this have to do with me getting money?"

I wanted Pat to understand, with only his mom's income, things had to change. If he continued to spend money like a middle-class teen, he would never be rich, never have the luxury of making choices. He needed to realize he was at rock bottom. His spending habits would have to change.

"Adults raised with a certain amount of money, in certain neighborhoods like to stay in the same situation. If they suddenly find themselves outside of that comfort zone, they sabotage themselves to get back to their comfort levels. Rich people will be overly generous or reckless with their money, losing it. People raised with money, but can't afford the lifestyle, live beyond their means. They go into debt to continue to hang out with those people who have money. Do you ever see those people who don't have a bunch of income, but their friends do?" I asked Pat.

Pat answered, "Yeah, they continue to go out and spend money, shopping, and eating out, just like their rich friends."

"Do you see those people who are wealthy, but drive an older car, live in a house well below their means? They want to continue to fit in with how they were raised." I said.

Pat added, "I see what you mean. People strive to stay in a similar friend group they were brought up with and didn't feel comfortable until they get to that spot."

"Pat, one exception. People who grow up dirt poor and then find fortune. They typically want to show it off. Prove to everyone they made it. Prove to themselves, they'll never go back to the poor house again. As they try to prove their worth, they overcompensate with a bunch of high-end cars. Multiple watches that cost more than some people's income."

"Yeah, I can believe that. I've seen ballplayers living that lifestyle." Pat made a gesture of shooting a basketball toward the trash can. "I guess both are true. If someone grows up with enough money to feel comfortable, they feel compelled to stay in that situation. The guy who grows up poor has something to prove." Pat wrapped it up.

"Living outside your comfort zone is the first hurdle you have to get over. You have to realize you no longer live a middle-class lifestyle. You have to know the amount of money you're bringing in now, doesn't afford the lifestyle in which you grew up. You live above a mechanic's shop. Your mom doesn't have the income for you to go out and hang at the mall with your friends. Because at the mall, you'll end up spending money, or look poor in front of your friends. Realize the power your upbringing has on your feelings about spending money. Live within your real means. Don't try to live the lifestyle you became accustomed to, the status your parents could afford for you." I said.

I knew Pat wanted straight answers, but this was important. For Pat to be a financial success, he would have to realize he can't afford luxuries beyond his income. He needed to figure out his financial comfort level and then stop sabotaging himself to stay there. Pat had to realize he was no longer middle-class and change his spending habits. He would also need to protect himself from overdoing it once he had money. I concluded with, "I see students who are accustomed to a lifestyle, their beginning salary could never afford."

Pat

Age 17, income $0/year; 10% fund $0; 20% fund $0; Stay out of debt fund $0

Doc explained getting over my comfort level. I guess all that made sense. If your parents brought you up in a middle-class household, you would want to drive similar cars, live in a decent house, go out to eat as your parents did. Even if you don't have the same income, your parents had. To get to that comfort level, drive the car, eat out, live in a decent place, you might put yourself into debt.

I was thinking about what Doc was saying. Moments passed without either of us talking, I couldn't take the silence, "It'll all work out. You'll see. I'll be a huge success and make it big. I'm not saying I'll win the lottery, but through my talent, I'll strike it rich!" I was adamant. I knew I wasn't an idiot kid. I was pretty good at school. At least in July, I got straight A's. Then again, I was stupid enough to have to go to jail in the first place, and those A's were in the juvenile detention, not the brightest of Oregon there.

In Doc's response, he wasn't as agreeable as I thought he'd be, "Pat, I have faith in you, but the chances of making it big are slim. The chances of having one of your talents shine to the point it makes you millions are so small; you can't count on it. I do want you to count on building your job skills along with your work ethics so you'll earn an above-average salary. Having a high income or even two incomes will make becoming wealthy that much easier."

I could see Doc's point. I hear students in school talking about how they think they'll make it big. High school basketball players, 5 foot 11 inches, thinking they'll play professionally. Students were failing Mrs. Galloway's language arts class and dead set on being professional rappers.

I retorted and pretended to act angry, "Thanks a lot Doc. If my talent won't get me out of this mess, what will?"

"First, realize you deserve the vision of the future you want. You are going to be around 10, 20, 30 years from now. You care about the person who will be YOU in the future. You want your future self to have all the things your present self dreams of having. To get all the things your future self wants, set a plan in place to get you there," Doc said.

At first, I was thinking about me in the future. What I wanted to have, who I wanted to become. As my thoughts were racing about how the money will buy me choices, I realized no one was talking for a couple of minutes. This time, I used the silence trick on Doc, and it worked.

"Picture yourself in the future. Today, you didn't do anything to make your future a better place. All you did was buy stuff to try to bring you happiness today. You wasted your money on consumables instead of saving money for your future self." I pictured the bag of chips I bought from the vending machine—what a rip-off. Doc continued, "You're like the others, sabotaging yourself to keep what you believe is comfortable, trying to stay in the same friend-group as you were raised. At this rate, your future will look like this: you're in a house that costs money as upkeep. You get a small check from the government, but not nearly enough to enjoy life. You pay your utilities. You buy some basic food. You can't afford anything else. This doesn't sound like the future you want for yourself, does it?"

I pictured myself in my 30s, still living above that mechanic's shop. I knew I was exaggerating the terrible vision, especially when I imagined Chad there with me. Two middle-aged men, eating chips we bought from a vending machine.

Doc continued, "Pat, I used to live in Maine. There, I knew an older woman who didn't plan for her future. She got enough of a check to pay for basic living, a few weeks of food for herself, and enough to buy enough food for her three cats. At the end of the month, as she waited for her next social security check, she couldn't afford to buy food for herself. She ate cat food." Doc paused; my eyes got a little larger to express my shock. "The last week of the month, she didn't have enough money or food to feed herself, so she ate cat food. I don't know about you, but I'm not sharing the cat's food." Doc took a breath, and his tone changed. His voice got lower, and he talked slower, "Pat, I can't bring your dad back. I can't remove your remorse from killing that man on the highway. But I can help you make the right choices with your money."

"Doc, I can't make my mind up about which shoes to wear in the morning. I just want straight answers. Can you tell me the best course of action? I'm going to be rich. I am not going to be forced down one path because of a lack of money. I'm not going to be eating cat food, alright." I wanted his help. I was guessing this guy was the closest thing I could find who might be able to get me out of this life.

"Look, I understand you want straight talk, but if you're going to be successful, we've got to start from the bottom and work our way up." Doc looked down and noticed my worn-out tennis shoes, "In this case, maybe not exactly from the bottom," Doc said. I didn't laugh. It wasn't funny, but the jab did lighten the mood between us. After that, I told him I had to go. Once out of his room, I pulled out my cell phone and jotted down some notes from our conversation. I don't know why, but I didn't want Doc to realize I was taking notes about our conversations. It just seemed weird, I guess.

Doc

I remember the evening I got home after talking with Pat for the first time. His story was tragic. I was sure he was dealing with emotional issues in which I wasn't qualified to help. As I was getting changed out of my school clothes, I was thinking of the best thing I can do for Pat is to talk with him and tell him the truth about investing. Give him clear answers to make him wealthy. Even tell him about inside secrets the wealthy use. I figured he would need a distraction that would inadvertently be beneficial to him. And I thought about how I could help, the little things I would teach. As my mind was racing about the order I would tell him these things, the phone rang.

"Doc, this is Henry Townsend. We met in . . ."

I interrupted, "Berlin. Where I was a guest teacher for some financial principles."

"Yes, that's right. I don't know how you were at presenting the financial stuff, but I do remember how well you could hide."

I laughed out loud, remembering how we met. "How have you been?"

"Great. I left the German police force and went private. I've been doing private investigative work and writing books. How have you been?"

I had seen his books but never read any. They were popular mystery crime books. I never put the two together that those books were written by the same Townsend I met in the park in Berlin. "I've been alright. Still teaching young people how to be rich."

"That's great. Still givin' it to 'em straight?"

"That's how they want it, so that's what I'm doin'," I responded.

Henry got a little quiet, "Doc, I'll be straight with you too. I need your help. I'm launching a book tonight. I need someone to introduce me and help me with book sales while I sign autographs."

I walked downstairs and put my hand over the mouthpiece of the phone. Henry was still giving me the details as I asked my wife if we had any plans for tonight. After she answered no, I responded to Henry, "Text me the details, and I'll be there. I'd be happy to help you out."

The room was light, and the environment filled with all sorts of reporters. Henry was a readable writer. He had a bunch of books written, and a few of those had hit top seller lists. I was glad I was there. I found that when I go out of my way for someone, something significant happens in my life. Maybe someday Henry will do a favor for me, or perhaps someone I talk with tonight helps me in some way. I didn't talk about this principle with students. It would come across too odd, 'Be nice to people, and they will be nice in return.'

As soon as I climbed the podium, Henry signaled for me to take the mic.

"Good evening, thanks for the time you could spare with Henry this evening." My nervousness started to fade. I could talk in front of students all day, but this was different. "I met Henry first in Berlin…" I said as I could only hear the clicking of cameras in the large auditorium. Flashes of light were distracting me—a scene I never faced in a classroom. Soon the light bursts slowed, and I was able to focus again.

"It's kinda a funny story how the two of us met and a bit embarrassing on my part. I was in Berlin, teaching college-aged students. My students stayed late one night for a project. We were all pretty stressed, so we went outside, walked from the campus to a neighborhood park." I looked past the spotlights and could tell people were listening. They were interested in the story. Or more likely were interested in when I was going to get off the stage and bring the main attraction, Henry, up.

"For some reason, the students and I started to play hide-and-seek. Picture this, one grown man and a bunch of college-aged kids running around a German park hiding behind trees, buildings, laying in the grass. What we didn't know is a resident thought we were vandals or had just robbed a store. She called the cops. Henry Townsend gets the call. Instead of running in with sirens blaring, Henry here comes in stealth mode, lights off. He doesn't even close his car door when he gets out. Henry slid up next to me and freaked me out. I was hiding behind a bush, and he was a cop."

"'Playing hide-and-seek?' Henry asked. I didn't know what to say. I thought I was going to end the night in a German jail. I said, 'yeah, I'll tell them to stop.' Henry grabbed my arm and pulled me back down and said, 'No, we need to win this thing first.' Henry played hide-and-seek for the next hour. Two grown men and a bunch of college kids running around a park." The audience started to laugh a bit. "Now, you know where Henry Townsend gets his inspiration for his best-selling mystery crime novels." The crowd roared even more now, knowing Henry's writing style. "Please give a warm welcome to the author . . . and hide-and-seek expert, Henry Townsend!" Henry came on stage, and I handed him the microphone.

Pat

Age 17, income $0/year; 10% fund $0; 20% fund $0; Stay out of debt fund $0

I got home and was getting ready for bed when I realized I was feeling a bit better. I had been with Doc and knew that at least someone cared about my life and how I'll turn out. Since I caused the accident, I had trouble getting the memory of that horrible day out of my head. My mind would flashback to that day I killed someone. His classes and us talking took my mind off those horrible thoughts. Lilly also helped. I met her the first day I got to Greenville high. We were in Mrs. Galloway's language arts class together. She invited me to sit with her during lunch. At the time, we weren't dating, but I sure did want to, even after she spilled my coffee cup all over my shirt.

Tomorrow, I was going over to her place to work on some homework together, really a kind of project for Galloway. Lovely Lilly had brown hair, cut short. A fair complexion and a smile that would crinkle her eyes. Her eyes were brown, on the edge of being hazel. Looking back at it with adult eyes, I realize now; I just wanted someone to love me. I wanted a girlfriend who would talk with me. Someone who would help me deal with my problems—someone to take away the nightmares. And there were moments when I thought I saw too much in Lilly, but a part me felt she could help, and her friendly and hearty smiles harmonized with this selfish need within me. It was challenging to relate to anyone after my coming out of jail, but not Lilly. She had gotten a hint I just got out of juvie, but I don't think she knew what I'd done to get in there. I didn't bother giving her details, at least, not yet.

I loved speaking with her. I had lost all the friends I had. Everyone who knew me before going to juvie never wanted anything to do with me. The psychiatrist, who spoke to me after I got out of jail, advised it would be best if I made new friends. "It will be difficult to get your old friends back. Get new friends, people who wouldn't bother about your past. However, create a bond with your new friends before you tell them about your past; that way, they would have seen your true nature without a bias." I still remember his words in my ears. It was still fresh, just like the scream from the woman at the accident I caused.

I fell asleep more quickly than usual that night. I kept thinking about what Doc and I talked about. I kept thinking about the few notes I put in my phone. As my mind focused on breaking free of my desire to keep spending like a middle-class teen, I drifted off to sleep.

Lilly

There was something about Pat I couldn't wrap my head around. He was unusually quiet in class, but there was a cool vibe about him that increasingly attracted me to him. Behind the tousled hair and angular frame, something legendary was simmering, and I could sense it. I remember the first day Pat was coming over to my house. My mom was home, and I told her we needed to clean up before a classmate was coming over to work on a project. I didn't tell her I liked this boy. I did ask her to hurry up. Mom was doing the dishes as I was cleaning Legos off the floor. I was probably a bit rude to my mom. I would spend all day at school, holding it in. When mom got home from work, I would let it all out. I would tell her my frustrations. How people at school made me mad. I felt comfortable complaining to my mom. She probably felt all I did was complain, but I didn't. I kept things together until I got home. Day after day, mom would just listen to me. She never tried to solve my problems or fix my distress. She quietly listened and asked clarifying questions. It made me feel better to have someone who cared about me . . . well, just listen.

As I scooped Legos, I thought about Pat. I felt Pat was my soul mate. Don't ask me how I knew. Only time would tell, and I had all the time in the world for Pat's heart to belong to me, as surely as mine already belonged to him.

When Pat got to my house, I realized he was wearing the same outfit he had on the first day I met him. The one I stained with coffee. For some reason, I liked his disheveled hair and thin build. He was cute. Every day we ate lunch together. We talked about nothing in particular, but he was charming. It's funny, he wouldn't talk much during class, but get him alone at lunch, and he would open up. Well, as alone as a school cafeteria can be. We sat at long tables, nearly every seat taken. It's funny with hundreds of seats available, and everyone sat at the same place day in and day out. If someone tried to move chairs, people would wonder why. 'What's wrong with that girl? Does she hate us or something?' It's also odd how people will get the same food day in and day out and have the same complaints about it. Me, I didn't complain at school, but Mom would get an ear-full at night. One complaint I didn't have was because I brought my lunch, something healthier than the soy-crammed 'meat' they provided.

We sat at the kitchen table after I introduced him to my mom. She made us a snack, and we got to work. We finished the project quickly and spent the evening talking. As dinner was approaching, my mom asked Pat if he would care to stay for dinner. I remember the innocent look on his face as he looked to me for approval. I nodded, and he told my mom he could stay. Pat texted someone, and we all had dinner together—meeting my family for the first time.

Pat's Notes

I deserve the vision of the future I want. To get all the things I'll want in the future, set a plan in place to get me there. Don't count on it all just working out or making it big.

Don't waste money on consumables/things to try to bring happiness, instead save money for the future me.

Realize what my money comfort level is and break free from it, so I can live the life I can afford.

Work on job skills to earn more income. Use two jobs to make a strong enough income to invest and become wealthy.

Chapter 2

How much do you need to earn to put save 10% for the future?
From where does the power to change need to come?

Doc

October in Portland is a chilly, shivering month. The wind coming into the northwest, beating the rugged, rocky coastline, is constant. The chill is only outdone by the low clouds, the fog reminding us how lonely life can be. The low, rolling mountains imbued with wisps of grey mist. It was 7:50 in the evening when I dawdled down Iron Mountain Blvd. Introspective, and drenched in the quiet that pervaded the road. It's okay for my students to call me Doc, and when they do, they expect the exhibition of uncanny intelligence in managing their finances. It's one way I give back. I can't help myself. I want to help. When I see a young, disheveled boy slipping through the classroom door, expectant, sullen, and depressed, I understand that there is yet another kid who was trailing down a hill headed toward mismanagement. Perhaps, with a bit of knowledge and some investment secrets, they can have sure footing when they're walking up or even down those hills of life.

I know when students see me, they have their reservations. What could a man like me do to change their state? First, I make them feel at home and give them the freedom to make rational decisions. What I teach isn't complicated, it's nothing special, a few diligent steps can change a person's life. Man, in his shackled history, has never fared well being forced to follow rules that don't make sense. If you want a student to make an important decision, then it's common sense not to impose it on him. It is how I have succeeded. I make them understand their current state, how living paycheck to paycheck is one month away from being homeless. They convince themselves their future is worth a bit of sacrifice today. Once they see the value of having money, a lot of money, they start to listen. They want to know more, they want to change, they want to be successful. Perhaps it is fair to agree that despite my best effort, I won't reach everyone. Chad was an example—it's expected. Only no one asks the Doctor, where he draws his motivation. It's a selfish world, isn't it? People may not be born with baggage, but along the way, demons jump on our backs. Some are hard to shake. I help others because, at one point, I failed to be there for my friend.

I have been filled with the sound temperament to continue on this path of frugality and wealth building. Sometimes I find myself hindered by the thoughts of purchases, buying luxuries. Failing to explore the good-life might be a tragedy. What is the reason for saving, investing, putting off big purchases, when there is no guarantee you would see the next day? What is the purpose of saving when there is a world to explore? These are usually my distractions, and perhaps in this worrying state, I would find myself mingling with thoughts that are not mine—thoughts that negate the very foundation upon which my convictions are built. I try to think about the happiness my one indulgence brings. Money spent on one hobby or interest is affordable and even healthy. Living like a hermit so that I can say I'm wealthy later doesn't allow me to enjoy life. Those who have many interests and spend money, not on one, but many things find their finances stolen by greed. They don't reach happiness. Their insatiable desire to consume drives them to see the next toy, phone, outfit in hopes of bringing joy, but soon that happiness fades into spending money as upkeep for that once favored indulgence.

When I do find myself online shopping or thinking how old my car is, I rely on patterns of behavior. Instead of shopping, I people-watch at a bar close to my house every Saturday. I do not go there to drink, far from it. The only drink I take is my dark, bitter coffee—the recipe of angels. Only I visit a bar every Saturday to replenish my goblet of inspiration. It is in these rare places, I get an eventful glimpse of the weakness, the frailty lurking within people. I have to help—to teach. But resolve to use the stimulus back in the classroom.

The tall, wobbly street light uttered a dim, orange glow, and I found myself listening to a measured platter of my feet on the cement, watching how easily my shadow stretched into the distance. How easily my shadow got to the road, my feet had not yet reached. They got to my future destination before I had even made it there. Perhaps that night's shadow was representing how bad decisions travel to the future before we've resolved our feet to make the journey. Bad choices are why I visit these bars. They offered me the liberty to see disenchanted people, trampled upon by the sad shadows of over-indulgence and wastefulness. Now they try to drink the pain away, reveling in maniacal laughter for a few hours of what they believe is joy. Only the pain, the shadows, the mistakes of the past, they all return in the morning.

Four minutes into this journey, and I could see a sign that exuded a blue, red, green shifting colors: MAYHER'S PUB

A wispy undergrowth ran through the other side of the road, and in that shifting darkness, a man was tossing something into a small sack. He went about it in a deft, quick tirade. One that splintered into fastening a twine around it, and bolting away through the undergrowth that ran steeply down the other side. I shook my head and transcended back to the thought of fast traveling shadows in the dim glow of the streetlight. You could find the shadows of wastefulness in the wino who made a tunnel his home, matted hair, dirty clothes, forlorn look, stricken by a web of devastation and grief. You could find them in the drug-addicted who made a bed out of forsaken clothes and slept on bridges or wherever they embraced the caresses of their high. These shadows are darker in some people, but they are in everyone. People make choices, to live well or spend well.

When I got to the bar, Mister Jones, the owner, greeted me. He was a heavyset man who hadn't shaved in a few days and walked in the gait of an arthritis-stricken man. Two sturdy men flanked him, and when Jones saw me, he asked, "Hey! Doc. You revisit us?"

"I thought I could whine a few minutes of my time in here, catch up on a little dose of inspiration," I replied, smiling and studying the sizes of the quiet men tarried on his sides.

"Isn't that why they all come here?" He asked as he nudged one of the men rooted to his side. The man uttered a burst of theatrical laughter.

"People come here to reminisce and sleep in the sea of nostalgia. They get a reprieve from the sickness that lurks in them. The world is so hard and full of terrors. We are here to escape the problems of adulthood in an attempt to return to a carefree time," I replied, solemn and sober. Jones' face was contorting into a grimace.

Jones responded, "I am the undisputed manager of grief. My clients are discouraged, the crestfallen. And since they keep coming, I'll keep taking their money." Once again, Jones nudged the bouncer next to him to elicit agreement. I don't think he was listening. "But Doc, sometimes I wonder why you would even come here. I study people, and a man like you doesn't belong in a place like this. So why do you come anyway?" He asked, putting a leg on a low chair, keeping his gaze on me, like a child, expectant, hungry, interested. Silence briefly stood between us like an old, stuttering grandma, with tales to tell, life to invoke, but too little time, too many constraints.

"Let's say—there is a peace I find here: an inspiration, a tinge of contentment. There are a few things I find in a bar that I may not find anywhere else," I replied finally, with a smile.

"Hmmm," he retorted, rubbing two fingers on his chin

"Doc, it seems for a guy like you, for all the good works you do in this town, you come here to find solace in the path you have chosen. You come here to see the things you don't want in your life. Are you trying to find contentment in the devastation of others?" Jones walked away, not allowing me to respond. He savored the look on my face, my innocuous exhibition of apprehension. He waved wearing a simpering smile, and for a moment, I found myself harboring the first trace of resignation. It was selfish of me to find inspiration in the tragedies of others. They were people who needed help, people who drew closer and closer to the thoughts of suicide. It seemed I was riding a subliminal chariot down their griefs, savoring it, dancing to the clinking rhythm of glasses that had the same tone as shackles, almost to my intoxication.

What would become of my selfish habit if there were no drunks in Portland? Could I survive without watching those who wasted their money on what they thought was a grey goose luxury? My needy, wistful face quickened into a smile like those who slugged larger and larger gulps of alcohol. Mister Jones had a point, and I briefly found the combination of selfishness and exploitation wrong. The constellation of my escapades mingled with the thought of going back home, but a mesmerizing boldness came to me in the form of two questions:

What would become of a guy like Pat if I were not stronger?

What would he do if I were not bolder, stable, fresher?

If I could not be strong, it would mean I had inadvertently resolved to sacrifice the potentials of students like Pat. Boys who couldn't envision the route to their dreams. I had to be strong for my students. And perhaps it was easy to think drunks would be drunks. It was easy to visualize drunks running toward their outstretched shadow that had reached their future long before they even made the journey. Except, that night, my mind said I could help, I could influence the status quo, and that night I decided I would alter my routine. While I feed off their gluttony, I would keep a keen eye on the citizens of Maher's Pub. I would try to help one person. I would work, and of course, it is not an indication that I would succeed, but I would try.

Maher's Pub had a run of sofas that formed a semi-circle around the bar. The bartenders lurked on the other side, amid glass-paned cupboards crammed with different brands of alcohol. Drinks that gave people a temporary vacation from life. A trip that only cost a few dollars. A holiday that didn't require travel—an escape, forgotten about tomorrow. Stools, tall and thin, stood at the front of a high cubicle where waitresses went in and out. Sofas laced around the edges, where a throng of girls donned in miniskirts, revealing their lingerie when they started to sashay, looking for who to devour. To the right was a squadron of brawny men, tasked with the responsibility of instigating peace. One of the men gave me an appraising, dutiful look, and nodded when he reached his conclusion. I plopped down on the red sofa, and took off my glasses, wiping the lens that had become foggy. A small-framed man scuffed away from the high stools and sat next to me. There was grime on his head and goatee, and he wore a red tee-shirt with an inscription that said:

MEMENTO MORI

It was an appealing conflict, and I narrowed my gaze at it, infected by the perception that sometimes the answers to a man's misery sits close to him. In the little things, in the form of an innocuous inscription that reminds us to live life to its fullest each day. I wanted to engage him in a conversation, but it seemed it was what he wanted. It was apparent—the entire scene was something he had conjured up when he said:

"Hello, sir."

I pretended not to hear him, feigning concentration at the hushed conversation of the brawny security guards. The man kept quiet for a little while, and moments later, he gave my arm a nudge, a slightly painful one.

"Hello, sir. I was greeting you," he stammered, with a fake smile.

"Oh," I replied, giving a feigned smile that could only conjure the idea of my doziness. I knew right away; I'd need an excuse not to talk with this drunk. Most Saturday nights, I only speak with the waitress who brings me my black gold.

"Good evening Mister..."

"Frank," he retorted.

"My name is Frank. And you don't need to introduce yourself. I know you, Doc," he concluded, smiling the smile one gave in familiar terrain. This time sincere.

"Well, my works precede me."

"Could you maybe spare me three dollars for a drink," he blurted with his head tipped to the right in an attempt to favor my decision.

I was mingling with the faintest hint of astonishment, when my waitress, Angelina, greeted me.

"Hi Doc," she said, stooping toward the red couch. Her pencil-arched eyebrows close enough to realize they look like they are in a continuously surprised look. Maybe she was trying to make her eyes look more significant, like a movie star from 30 years ago.

"Should I bring your usual? Black coffee? Or would you want something different this time," she joked.

"Coffee would do Angelina," I replied, lowering my eyebrows in a subconscious attempt to bring hers to a human level.

Silence momentarily sat between Frank and me, and this time, it came in the form of a nostalgic mother who was short of words. Frank gave me a condescending look from beneath his loomed head, and that look said, please remember what I have asked you, don't make me ask again. I looked away towards the cubicle, watching Angelina, make the little journey toward me. She still had a continual look of surprise. She had measured calculated steps. She set the tray on the adjoining table.

"Thank you," I said.

Frank watched me take a sip of my coffee, watching the cup bend, and drip off its content into my mouth.

"Could you give me the three dollars?" he asked, this time his head was cocked upward, his eyes steady.

"Why do you want to keep hiding in the temporary courage of alcohol? Why won't you face your problem head-on?" I asked, taking another sip of coffee.

Frank gave off a scowled look that splintered into a more rheumy, watery-eyed guise. He had resolved in his mind that I was not his problem, no matter how much revulsion he had in his heart, he knew I was only doing what I knew how to do best: help.

"You won't understand Doc," he said, tears welling up.

"Life has screwed me so hard. So damn hard. I don't even have a place to crash. But I used to have a life, you know. I was surviving. I had a job at a grocery shop and lived with my longtime girlfriend in her late parent's house. I thought THAT was the bottom of the barrel. It had to get better. I was wrong. And life is unfair," Frank was sobbing a hushed, adult sob.

"One day, the manager of the grocery shop thought I was stealing some of the goods. I mean, there were a few of us working in different shifts, and somehow the manager thought it was me. He thought I had the face of a thief. Most of my coworkers were college students trying to get a few bucks to keep them going, and somehow, the manager didn't think it could be any of them. I was the only one he suspected. The only one capable of being a thief. Can you imagine?" he asked, raising his face at me.

I didn't respond. I only shook my head, and it was enough incentive to make him continue.

"He convinced himself, it could only be me—a local. One day he told me to find another job. He sacked me. Initially, I wasn't bothered. I thought I could quickly get another gig, but it seemed he put in a bad word on me. I tried in vain to get another job. Two months later, my girlfriend threw me out. She said, 'I was becoming a liability.' And she 'had enough liabilities in her hand to worry about taking care of a grown, idle man, who wouldn't find a job.' I left and thought it would work out, you know. I could apologize to her a few days later, and we could start new, then move back in. When I went back to her place three days later, there was another man there. Would you believe it Doc, she could not wait for a week before replacing me," Frank was wiping the tears with one arm, head still loomed down.

I took another sip of coffee, and I found it difficult to cut a swathe through the predicament of Frank. It seemed for him; open doors were simply thresholds to newer horrors. And it saddened me, but it was the nature of my job. Frank was now sitting upright, waiting for my response, the magic that permeated from my lips. Magic, he's heard about, that created high school rags to riches stories. I sensed Frank's anticipation, but a part of me thought he was not ready. A hunch, an intuition that virtually had no evidence. This perception struck me despite the look on Frank's face, the soberness of his story, the inscription on his shirt that translated to 'Remember Death.'

"How long did you work at the grocery shop?" I asked, starting the process to teach Frank about finances.

"Four years," he replied.

"How much did you save?"

"I never really had any savings."

I shook my head. It was a familiar story—stories of men who worked hard and saved nothing. Afflicted with the belief they would keep working, and if they kept working, they would keep surviving—nothing more, nothing less.

"And why did you not make any savings or investment?" I asked, swiveling to his direction.

He shook his head and looked up at the ceiling as if trying to summon the pages of a distant memory.

"I have to admit that the money was too small. It was barely enough for us to get..."

"Nothing is too small," I cut in, interrupting him. "No salary is too small for you to make a saving or an investment. Do you know that, on average, those people in the United States who make less than $13,000 a year spend 9% of their income on lottery tickets?"

Frank was introspective for a moment, and it seemed he had now summoned the pages of his memory and was gently reading through it, thinking of the dollars he spent on a dream.

"Well, I have to confess I was a little naïve. See my girlfriend, Lisa is a woman compelled to spend everything she makes and everything I make too. If she didn't manipulate me, I would've saved a few bucks," Frank shook his head, contending with new traces of tears.

"What do you mean by you were 'manipulated'?"

"My ex-girlfriend's needs always increased with each pay-raise. Working overtime gave her an excuse for us to go out to eat. The promise of a holiday bonus gave her an excuse to put large items on a credit card."

I had been captured in the subtleties of Frank's story, secretly falling under the influence of the recounting of wastefulness. Frank's story was no exception to the norm. When a person tells a story of how he failed, they must pepper-in a plot that excuses him of the blame. It's a shame, but people feel as though they have to give in to keep the peace. They don't stand up for themselves or what they think is essential as they believe the repercussions could be terrible. It sounds like this is what happened to Frank. He didn't stand up for his future, and he still ended up dumped. What he feared would go wrong went wrong nonetheless, and he had no money to fall back on. Without money, his choices were limited . . . like Pat's family.

"I understand you, Frank," I said, placing a hand on his shoulder. It was my subliminal way of empathizing with him, connecting with his predicament, giving him the impression it was something that resonated with me.

"You had little choices with your girlfriend. I suppose she must have been a nagger. The kind that would only want things to go her way. The kind that treats you like an ignoramus whenever you tried to give your opinions on vital issues," I said, keeping my gaze at him.

"I swear it feels like you have met my ex-girlfriend. It feels like you were there behind the scenes, watching the torments she inflicted on me," Frank confirmed, this time with dry eyes. I tapped him on his shoulder, trying to re-cloth some pride on his naked shame.

"But Frank, you should have seen this coming. You should have bought some choices. You know what buys choices?"

"No," he replied.

"Money, Frank. If you had put away just 10% of your income into an investment over those four years, you could've felt power over the unfairness of your girlfriend. It was a sacrifice you needed to make. If you had only thought about your future choices, if you were inclined to not be at the mercy of your lady's whims, you wouldn't be looking for a three-dollar drink. Things would have looked up for the better if you bought yourself a few choices."

His head loomed down, crestfallen. His look made it appear that he thought hindsight truly is 20/20. He looked up at me, and for the first time since we began the conversation, Frank had the face of a determined man. He straightened out the traces of intoxication that lingered on his face, resolving each muscle to become firm and ambitious. He looked at me, a new version of Frank, reconciliation wafting up from him. I was impressed.

"What am I going to do now?" He asked, with steady, enquiring eyes.

"I cannot go back to my ex-girlfriend. I heard she's now married to the man I saw when I went back to try and reconcile with her."

"Who said anything about going back to your lady? You have to choose between life and death, Frank. If you go back to your past, you choose death. You have to start fresh. You need a new life without the weaknesses in which you're currently contending. Like your shirt says, 'live every day to it's fullest. Do your best work today because tomorrow isn't guaranteed.'"

"Okay." Frank looked down at his shirt with a puzzled look on his face, like he didn't realize his shirt said all those things and chose not to ask, "But how do I go about it? How do I start this new life?"

"I am going to give you $50 to get new clothes. I want you to believe in yourself. You can do it. Tomorrow afternoon, come over to the school. I'll put in a good word for you, and try to get you a job."

"You would do that?" He asked, embracing me, a web of exuberance fell over the two of us on the sofa.

"Yes, I would. But most importantly, you have to decide you want this. You have to dispel the desire to revert to your past."

"I would," he replied.

I brought out my wallet, counted $50, and handed the cash to him.

"I want to believe in you, Frank. Do not fail yourself."

He thanked me, ecstatic, genuinely happy, and he left the bar in long, ambitious strides.

The time was edging past 8:55 when I took a final slug of coffee, in one large gulp. I gave Angelina a signal, and she charged down from the cubicle. Moments later, she was carrying the silver tray off the table, along with the bill and tip I had left her. She smiled a bartender's gracious, hearty smile, and scuffed away. A collection of diverse people now filled the bar. Some came to drink, those who came to socialize, and those like me, who simply needed to refuel. I needed fuel to teach - a little inspiration to perpetuate dipping motivation.

When I got up to leave, a lean, skinny man was shouting at the top of his voice. Words couldn't be distinguished over the background noise. His high-pitched chimes quickly got the attention of one of the security guards. One of the big guys, who were with Jones earlier, walked over to this skinny guy yelling at one of the ladies in a miniskirt. I couldn't hear what was said, but I saw the 130-pound customer grab the security guard's black tee-shirt. The muscle-bound peace-keeper initially allowed the customer to scream at him, spittle squirting out with every word, drenching the employee. Without a word, the big guy carried the tiny nuisance up by one shoulder and threw him outside. A peal of deserving laughter broke out in the bar, a tone upped by the ambivalent embrace of alcohol. The man laying on his back took a brief moment to inhale the humiliation. He nurtured the thought of making one last dart at the security guard who stood at the threshold, surveying him. The only dart he could afford was the one that took him down the road of redemption, away from Maher's Pub.

I gave the security guard a friendly nudge; he shifted one way and made enough room for me to pass. As I exited, I caught the eye of Jones. I gave one last wave, one that implied, 'I got what I needed from Maher's Pub once again.' I was trudging down the road, succumbing to the cold embrace of the night. Deciphering the rhythmic chirping of crickets, and for a moment, I thought they were a nightly choir that sang for the insomniac and the rest of the children of the night. I was happy because, in one night, I had got my fix of observing the wastefulness of Portland and set the pace for the impending healing of Frank. I had achieved a lot in a few hours, and I thought it was worth celebrating, worth dancing over, and I made a few moves down the road, tried to do the moonwalk, and a poor attempt at the cupid shuffle. Moves I would not be inclined to do amid the studious spears of peering eyes. It was in this generous insanity I discovered I had forgotten my eyeglasses at Maher's Pub. I had taken them off to wipe off the fog, and I had forgotten to put 'em back on. I had only been walking for a little longer than a minute, and after a brief moment of pondering, I decided to go back. It would be a decision that threw me down a path of anger.

A part of me starred on in disbelief. The other part, the clairvoyant part, already saw it coming. I dawdled back to the bar, still holding on to my optimism, the belief that today had gone a little better than I had planned. When I got into the bar, Angelina was having a conversation with the security guard, and the skinny nuisance had come back. He was sprawled on the floor, gobbets of vomits littered around the edges of his lips. He seemed unconscious, and perhaps he had eaten a few slabs of punches from the security guard's fist. Only the nuisance wasn't the only one who was back. Frank was back. He was rooted to the sofa, back reclining with three empty bottles littered the table ahead of him. He was staring up like he had starred when he summoned his pages of memories. Only, this time, it wasn't nostalgia he was invoking. Frank was invoking the ghosts from his past. Moments ago convicted to change, now sat in the shackles of his past. Frank was trying to drink away his problems, his misery. A man—trying to bring back a tiny piece of lost joy.

Like a wisp of madness capering around the edges of my eyes, laughing at me, instinct told me to stay quiet. If a man wanted to change, he would first help himself. A man who was incapable of helping himself stand up from the simmering broth of his tragedy would also be incapable of change. I had known this. I had nurtured it with my students. It had been a way of life for the teens I taught. Only, sometimes, a man feels inclined to tweak the script, help someone in the hopes they follow through with the advice. And what do they do?

Frank spun a story, most likely true. That story bought himself an opportunity, a choice. He had a choice to invest the money into clean clothes to get a job or continue living the same as he had for years. The fifty dollars enabled him to find a path to the past, as a dog returns to its vomit.

I took my glasses from the sofa, where I had left them. I left the bar, wondering how long Frank had lingered outside, waiting for me to go. How long he had lurked in the darkness, obsessed with the thoughts of having another reprieving sip off a bottle of alcohol. My journey down the road and back had only lasted for a few minutes, and in that space of time, Frank had gulped down the contents of three bottles. He didn't see me come, and he never saw me leave. It brought back a quote Mrs. Galloway once used in a staff meeting, 'There's no art to find the mind's construction in the face.'

When I reached Chandler Rd., I was infected with a mixture of anger, disappointment, and surprise. I no longer felt I had done well this night. My mind went racing 3,000 miles away, to a time I was still in college. I could feel the blood of my roommate, Eddy.

Chapter 3

What is the easiest and surest way to become wealthy? What obstacles do I need to overcome before I start investing?

Doc

The sky had resolved itself to a translucent blue with white rolls of clouds amid the orange glow of the narcotic sun. I was standing by the glass-paned window of my classroom. Seemingly immersed in the beauty of the well-trimmed foliage of the outside lawn. In the field, a soccer team had their routine practice. I could hear them shout their unfeigned screams that exemplified the passion of soccer. Most of the students had gone home, and for a moment, I thought about Eddy. I dropped a steel door on that thought and focused on the impending appointment I had with Pat. I watched him charge across the parking lot. He passed the condensers for the air conditioners toward the outside door next to my classroom. I was going to give him a brief breakdown on becoming rich. I had bought us a couple of non-diet sodas from the teacher's vending machine, and before Pat had to come down the hall, I met him on the stoop that led to the unswept flight of stairs. He waved at me. I lumbered down the black steps and took him for a walk around the school building.

"Pat, I'm going to give it to you straight . . . If you want the choices money can give you, you'll follow this one piece of advice. When you get paid, before you spend any money, pull 10% out and invest it in an index fund following the stock market," I said, while he kept his gaze at me, and it seemed he was trying to soak in the little words I had uttered. I kept quiet, and in that short silence, we walked our way through the school building. We rounded the corner, and Pat looked at me with a puzzled face—a curious face that wanted more.

"What else? Surely that can't be it," he said as he unscrewed his Coke to take another swig.

I shrugged my shoulders, "That's it. I've just given you enough advice to make you a millionaire. We can stop talking here. Or later, I can tell you inside secrets. I can even tell you exactly which funds in which to invest. I can let you in on how to time the market, tricks the rich use to become even wealthier, and how to take advantage of stock market cycles. These things will help you make even more money, protect what you earn, and retire with a steady stream of income with extra money coming in so you can live the life you want to live."

Pat looked back over to me, "The first part is so simple. I can follow that. I can live off 90% of my income. That's still plenty. Yeah, let's talk another time about other things. I've got to go home now," he said. As Pat walked around the corner, I could see him putting notes into his phone, or maybe he was texting.

Lilly

When I got home from school, I had the faintest hint that a few things were not right. The living room table had been dragged one way, in combination with this, and the TV had disappeared from where we usually kept it on the square shelf in the living room. I knew my family had been robbed. My mom was still at work. My heart was running up my chest. I had intended to prepare dinner, but I felt my strength vaporize, float away in a puff of smoke. My fright that began with only a slight trepidation was now making me wide-eyed and vigilant. Panic struck, I froze. The first positive thought that came to me was to put a call through to Pat.

"Pat," I began, crying.

"My family's been robbed!"

"What happened? Are you still in the house? Get out. If they're still in the house, they'll do anything to escape without witnesses," Pat was saying, and I could sense the nervousness in his voice.

"What's that noise?" I had heard something upstairs. I ran out the front door, but not before resetting the alarm. I was starting to remember. The alarm was off when I got home. I didn't think so much about it because sometimes Mom forgot to set it. I turned it on and watched the countdown. If someone were in there, the motion sensors would set off the alarm within 90 seconds.

While in the yard, I was panting. "Pat, I have been robbed. I have been robbed. All my mom's stuff, gone!"

Pat

Age 17, income $0/year; 10% fund $0; 20% fund $0; Stay out of debt fund $0

When I heard the shaky voice of Lilly, I knew I had to help. She was feeling a pain she had never felt. A revulsion for those thieves swept over me. Her words echoed in my ears and energized me to make things right. I got a shirt and ran down the steps of the apartment. I ran in long, deft strides, and for a moment, my mind had traveled back to the day at the bridge. How I was scared for my life. And for the first time since that sad day, I found myself going faster than I could have ever imagined. I was genuinely scared for Lilly.

A rush of anxiety slipped in my head like a bad dream creeps under the covers. I started to focus on Lilly and helping her. It didn't help. I landed in a yard, shaking. I couldn't control it. My mind was racing back to the accident, back to me killing a father, a man who thought he'd be seeing his family that day. The vision replayed in my head. I could see myself pushing that huge barrel up, over the wall, watching it fall, watching it hit the windshield, the woman's scream, and in that insane moment, it seemed the peals of techno music was screaming into my head. It was noisy in there. Only moments later, I was encouraged by my passion for Lilly. It was her I thought about, and it seemed for that split moment her thoughts invoked a cushion to my afternoon horrors. I also thought about Doc and his 10% theory of investing. It was starting to make sense. I was beginning to sense if I wanted to recuperate from this sad memory, I needed to concentrate on the things I loved. The memories of the things I loved.

Laying in the yard, I began chanting. I must have sounded crazy, "10%, 10%, 10% . . ." It went on and on, but it also allowed me to regain composure. Focusing all my attention on this one detail allowed me to get up. To help Lilly. When I finally got to Lilly's house, I saw the police and a few concerned neighbors. They all had different stories to tell. The police were friendly, and they took note of the items stolen from the house. They were proud of Lilly for getting out of the house and setting the alarm. Only Lilly had descended into a hypnotic spell of nodding her head to every question.

"Ma'am, are you sure you don't want to see a doctor?" One of the police officers asked her.

I convinced her she didn't need a doctor. After the police went through the entire house, I took her in and made her some coffee. I couldn't understand why her mother wasn't home yet. I didn't ask. I'm sure she heard about the robbery and her daughter's state-of-mind.

An hour passed before Lilly's mom came home. I offered to spend the night to make sure they were going to be alright. Both of them kindly turned it down. I didn't like the idea of leaving them in the house alone.

I tried to convince her and her mom to let Lilly spend the night at my place above the mechanic's shop, "She can sleep on the couch. My mom will be there. It will be better for you than spending the night here." She paused as I spoke to her the second time.

I almost convinced her to come over when her mom said, "Pat, you're a great guy, but we'll be fine." She was decisive, and I knew this would be the final word.

On my way home, I felt happy she called me to help. It made me feel valued, like a boyfriend.

Things got back to relative normalcy. School bells seem to help with routine. Days later, during class, Doc kept looking at me. I think he wanted me to chime in or something. I didn't know if he knew about the robbery. Talking up in class wasn't for me. I paid attention but never spoke up. I found Doc again in his classroom after school. "Hey, Doc, what's up?" I asked. I was trying to impersonate Bugs Bunny, but I think I messed it up. "Last time we talked, you said I should save 10% of my income. I've been thinking about that and looked into it a bit. I'm worried about a couple of things."

I sat down on the same chair I sat the other day when I told Doc my life story. Doc asked, "What's your biggest stumbling block? What's in your head that's stopping you from investing in the stock market?"

"Doc, I'm not an expert, and I worry about putting my money into something when I'm not an expert."

I was hoping Doc would understand. I was also hoping he wouldn't say something like 'that's what my class is for, young man.' I didn't mind his class. It was good. I needed someone to show they cared. Nicole, my sister, cared but was also mean to me. I could tell she held terrible feelings for me. Sometimes my sister would start to say something and then stop. I felt she was thinking about how I killed that man. Maybe she was thinking about those twins who no longer had a dad. Either way, she made me feel bad. My brother, however, was great. Even though he was a bit older than I was, we would still go out and do things. We liked the same movies, for the most part.

While I was mingling with the thoughts of my life, Doc spoke up, "Pat, investing is easier than you think. If you put your money into an index fund, your expenses will be low, and you'll follow the trends of that index. You aren't trying to beat the market. You aren't moving your money in and out. You're investing each month into a few funds," Doc explained.

"That does sound more simple than I thought. Following an index takes away the need to be an expert," I replied. I didn't know I could simply put my money into a fund or two and be following the stock market. I remember hearing Doc talk about mutual funds in class. He even mentioned a couple of investment firms. I was thinking about how I'd tweak the notes on my phone. The new focus to distract me from my thoughts. 'Invest 10% in an index fund'.

I was repeating it in my head when Doc asked me again, "What other hang-ups do you have?"

I paused my chant, thought for a second, and said, "Where I'm from, if one person comes into money, it's expected they share it with the others. Almost like it's wrong to have more money than others in the family or among close friends," I said. I knew something was wrong with that kind of thinking. However, I wanted to be sure I had the right ideas and stood for the correct principles. I also figured if Doc continued to talk with me after this type of comment, he did care.

Doc

For a moment, I was thinking about Frank at the bar. How he had the firm excuse of having to succumb to the spending habits of his girlfriend. People always had a reason, and lame as some might seem, their excuse was valid to them. It was something they savored, and I hoped I could talk Pat out of his impending weakness. A handout didn't help Frank, so I conjured up an analogy.

"Pat, can you picture yourself with one leg in quicksand and the other leg on the sidewalk of your neighborhood? When you come into a bit of money, you're putting that one leg on firm ground." I stood up to show what I meant.

I had one leg on a chair, like a raised sidewalk. The other leg was still on the ground near my desk. "You have a chance to pull yourself out of the quicksand. When you toss your money at other people in the quicksand, you aren't saving them. They never get out of the muck. They use the money and continue the same pattern of behavior. In effect, when you give your bit of extra money to those friends and even relatives, you're tossing your money into the quicksand pit. You're putting your raised leg back into their wasteland." I thought of Frank and the bottles on the table. "Not only are you sabotaging yourself, but you're also enabling your loved ones to stay where they are, do the same things they've been doing, and never learn they have the power to get out of the pit. If they discover you have a bit of extra money or a windfall, tell them, 'I already have a plan for the extra money.' They'll relate to this. They'll know the feeling of having money earmarked for something specific."

Pat looked back at me as I changed seats to sit closer to him. He seemed to have a slight sense of anger on his face. "Doc, you know my story. We had money at one point. We were comfortable. The doctors took it all away. One illness and our lives are changed. I have a terrible feeling; I need to spend the money, not save it. So, no one can take it away. Since we talked last, I got a job. I make an hourly wage and tips on top of that. I work hard for that money. I show up on time. I don't complain to the boss. I don't take long breaks. Nicole feels the same way. If we work hard for the money, we deserve to spend it the way we want." he said.

"No matter what our plans are, things happen. Plans don't always work out. I have a neighbor friend. The husband sold windows, and his wife was a schoolteacher, modest incomes. Even with two kids, both of them put money away every month, 10% just like were saying. They became multi-millionaires. When they were in their late forties, the wife became sick and had to retire early. Within two years, the husband's company changed hands, and he found himself fired. As all this was happening, the younger kid moved back in after college. They didn't plan for all that to happen 20 years ago. I'm sure they envisioned their life a bit different. Because they had some savings, they were comfortable dealing with the wife's illness and job losses. The money gave them choices," I said.

Pat added, "I couldn't imagine what would have happened if they hadn't been saving money. The guy selling windows would've had to find another job so he could afford the house and medical bills. I guess they would've sold their house to help pay the bills," Pat said.

I continued, "That's right. When people choose not to save, they take away their options. You said you want choices in life. So, start by choosing to save 10% of your income and put it into an index mutual fund," I checked my thermos to see if I had any coffee left at the end of the day. One sip would've been a sweet treat. It was empty, as expected.

Pat stood up. "I think all this makes sense. I'll talk with my family about it. Thanks again, Doc."

After that, I didn't talk with Pat for a few days. He came to class, did his work, and kept quiet. About a week after our last conversation, he came in before school, carrying a disposable coffee cup. "Doc, you drinking coffee?" He looked in my cup. "I like it black too. Do you add sugar?" he asked as he held up his coffee.

"No, just dark and bitter," I said.

Pat forced out a small grin before looking down in disappointment, not in my coffee choice, but something else. "I didn't want to tell you but thought you deserved an honest answer. I've decided not to follow through with the investment stuff. I talked with my sister, Nicole, and she's right. Rich people got that way by taking advantage of people like me, poor people."

I paused, took a sip of coffee. "I hear what you're saying. You feel the rich don't deserve their money because to get there, they used people. Think about my neighbor. He sold windows. Sure he made money selling those windows, but if he sold them at a price too high or the quality was terrible, would people still buy his windows?" I asked.

"No, I guess not. People would go to a competitor," Pat replied.

"Pat, don't get me wrong. We both know some people lack ethics and will take advantage of people, but most millionaires got there through saving as you can do. Another group of rich people got there by creating their own company and providing a good or service people wanted. They hire and pay people to help them with their company. If those people don't want to work there, they can leave. That's not taking advantage of people, now is it?" I asked.

Pat responded, "I guess not. I've met a few of those wealthy people who own a company or made it big in some way. They're down-to-earth, easy to talk with. It's as if they have nothing to prove, no one to impress, and no need to brag. The owner of the mechanic's shop, where I live, is rich. You wouldn't guess it from looking at his place or even at him. He's covered in grease. His place is always dirty. I found out he was rich from my sister. She somehow found out. He's easy to talk with and doesn't waste his money on luxuries. Well, besides tools. He has a lot of tools in his garage. He was lucky. He got a great site a long time ago. All the rich people I know seemed to have luck on their side or some skill I don't have."

I thought about it for a few seconds before responding. I rubbed my chin, realizing Pat and a lot of students see wealthy people out there in the media, and yes, those people were lucky or had a skill most people don't have. I also knew those were the exceptions.

"Pat, the lucky ones and the rich who got there with a special skill are in the minority. Most of the millionaires out there became rich through having a habit of saving each month. On top of that, most of these rich never had a high income. They were everyday people working in ordinary jobs. They did one thing differently; they saved 10% and invested in the stock market."

Pat looked disappointed and said, "I wanna be one of the lucky ones. I want to have all those cool clothes and cars."

"You can. First, you have to live below your means. You have to live a frugal life. You have to put money aside so you can have all those things later." I continued as Pat was nodding, "I've seen families come through this school who live a life they can't afford. Living nearly paycheck to paycheck, buying things to be happy, and impress friends. They have a nice looking house, but if their income stopped, they wouldn't have many choices."

I pictured a few of my students, wearing shoes so expensive I would shake my head, wondering how they could afford them. Often, I would talk with my students about some of the costly items they bought. They were proud of how much they (or their parents) spent on some of those items. Cell phones students didn't care if they got cracked because their parents pay extra every month so they could upgrade the phone every so often. I would tell them if an item is making you money, it's no big deal spending more to get what will work for you. If you're playing professional sports or on your feet all day at your job, buy comfortable shoes. Those shoes will make a difference in your game. If you're a real estate professional, get a great phone. You need to take pictures and make calls that will make you money. Until those items are making you money, keep things basic. I glanced at Pat's phone as he was taking notes. He had a nice phone.

Pat's Notes

On payday, before any money leaves the bank, pull 10% and invest it in an index fund following the stock market.

I don't have to be an expert to invest each month in a few mutual funds.

10% is for me. I don't have to share it. Friends who fail on their promise to pay back the money they owe don't get this money. It's for MY future.

Money buys choices. Having savings allows me to deal with problems without forcing me to make a decision based on a lack of funds.

The majority of wealthy people are not evil, greedy, or got there by taking advantage of the poor. The majority of the rich had ordinary jobs and had a habit of saving each month.

Chapter 4

What are the best investments?

Pat

Age 17, income $9,360/year; 10% fund $1,056; 20% fund $1,943; Stay out of debt fund $0

I noticed Doc looking at my phone. At the time, I had a decent phone. He had just finished saying if a phone isn't making you money, don't spend a lot on it. My problem was if you had a cheap phone, students would make fun of you. We still had a while before the first-period bell would ring. Doc started doing something else as I was putting some notes on my phone. When I finished, he was still busy. I stayed quiet. I got to thinking about how the rich didn't get there by taking advantage of the poor. I pictured my sister telling me her viewpoint, but I don't think she had all her facts straight. I also thought about my brother. At this point, he worked but never saved anything. Instead of saving, he would buy chips from a vending machine and then complain, 'I thought air was free until I bought this bag of chips.' I rubbed my jaw, looked back over at Doc with a bit of excitement in my voice I said, "You know something Doc, maybe my sister's wrong. What's the best place to put away that 10%?"

"That's an easy one. If you have a job that offers it, invest in a company-matched 401(k). The match is, in effect, giving you money just for contributing," Doc said.

I thought back to one of Doc's lessons about the 401(k), "I remember this from class. That's the one that's taxed when you retire, right? What if your job doesn't offer the company match 401(k)?" I asked. I could imagine working for a company that did offer a 401(k) match. I would contribute money to the plan, and the company would kick in a percent too. Free money for me, therefore, creating a massive jump in my savings.

"If the company isn't contributing money to the retirement plan, go for a Roth 401(k). Your money will be tax-free when you withdraw it," Doc replied. I thought back to a time in class when Doc pulled up an online investment calculator. He started with an average yearly income. Then took only 10% of that income per month and put it into a calculator. It was amazing how much money was in that investment after 35 years. I started to picture myself having that much money.

I jotted some notes on my phone then asked, "What if my company doesn't offer a 401(k) or a Roth 401(k)?"

Doc began again as I tried to put all of it on my phone, "If you aren't given choices at work, or they don't match, you'll open your own. Start with a Roth IRA."

I wanted to be sure to get this one on my phone because this is where I was today—no company match at my part-time job. I jotted 'Roth IRA' into my phone. I remember this one from class too. This one is cool because I wouldn't have tax on the withdrawals, tax-free money. I already learned how much tax is sucked out of my paycheck every other week. I earned that money, not my Uncle Sam. My thoughts got away from me. Doc snapped me back to attention.

"The government limits how much you can put into a Roth. The maximum isn't high enough to handle all 10% of your income. The max is too low. Because your 10% is more than the maximum, you can put the remaining into a traditional IRA. When you call a low fee investment company to set this up, they'll walk you through the process."

Maximum too low for Roth IRA, I have to remember that. I'll have to set up a traditional IRA as well. I guess it doesn't matter all that much that I don't understand all of this terminology. When I call one of those investment companies, I'll ask for what Doc told me to get. As he said, I don't have to be an expert to make all this happen.

I was curious but knew it was rude to ask Doc how much he had saved up. I tried to go about it a different way, "What about you? Do you have these options?"

Doc didn't fall for my trick and tell me how much he was worth.

"My options are different and not as good. Because I work for a non-profit, I would contribute to a 403(b). A 403(b) typically doesn't match, the fees are high, and the choices are limited. Because of all these negatives, the 403(b) is not worth it. For people in my place, we'll start with a Roth IRA. The government has added a limitation on those offered a 403(b). If my and my wife's combined income is too high, I can't contribute to a traditional IRA. I would have to use the 403(b) with their limited choices and high fees." Doc honestly looked a bit upset as he said this.

I gave my best-puzzled look with my eyebrows raised and asked, "If you can't contribute to a traditional IRA and your Roth IRA has a maximum too low, what would you do then?"

"A couple of choices, for those who are self-employed, have a small business on the side. We could open a 'solo 401(k)' or second-best a 'SEP-IRA.' That stands for, Simplified Employee Pension Individual Retirement Account. These both sound complicated, but when you call a low fee investment company and tell them your situation, they'll set up what you need," Doc replied.

Doc stole the words out of my mind. I was thinking, 'I would call up and ask for what I wanted, complication overcome.'

I could imagine Doc had one of those companies. I could also imagine my Language Arts teacher, Mrs. Galloway. There is no way she would go through all that trouble. I nodded to show I understood and asked, "What about those teachers who don't want to set up a small business?"

"For those who aren't self-employed and too lazy to set up their own company, they'll need first to set up and max out their Roth IRA, then deal with the extra fees and limited choices their employer offers and contribute to their 403(b) or similar retirement account. The 403(b) does have one advantage. For those teachers who started young and retire young, they can withdraw the money starting at age 55." Doc said.

I looked at Doc and saw a sly look in his eye. Like he was keeping a secret. "Come on, Doc, I know you have some sort of inside secret for teachers. Give it up."

"There is one way a teacher, or anyone for that matter, can get around those government limitations. They set up a Roth IRA. They max out their Roth IRA. They then set up a traditional IRA and roll that money into their Roth IRA. The process is called a back-door Roth. They now have plenty of money in their Roth, even the full 10%. It by-passes the limits."

I was a bit confused with all those letters and numbers. I'm glad Doc was there to give it to me straight. What was relevant to my situation was to set up a Roth IRA and a traditional IRA. I would max out the Roth and then put the rest of my 10% into the traditional IRA. Now, I needed to know which funds to put my money. "Come on, Doc, which funds for my retirement?" Every time I talk with Doc about this financial stuff, I feel better. I've never been a runner before, but I've heard runners get this feeling of inner harmony as they exercise. I guess other athletes do too. Weight lifters enjoy being in the gym; bicyclists feel at peace pedaling. For me, when I thought about finances, I was able to forget about the evil I did and the destruction I caused. One thing I was lacking, someone to share it with in the future. Maybe Lilly. I'm about to see her in Mrs. Galloway's class.

Doc

I took out a small notepad for Pat to visualize the choices and mapped out the process for him. "Here's the thing, Pat, if you're in an employer-sponsored plan, your choices are limited. You'll want to spread the money out."

I started to write a few things on a piece of paper, and I said them aloud as I wrote:

"For now and until you have enough money built up that you start feeling a bit uncomfortable, focus on two funds. Split them 90% and 10%." I watched Pat as he also typed on his phone.

I continued to write and talk:

"Top choice. You'll see an S&P 500 Index or total stock market. Either of those would be the first. The second part will go into either an International Index MSCI EAFE or world stock market fund. 90% S&P 500 Index or total stock market and 10% International Index MSCI EAFE or world stock market fund." I thought the paper would be enough. I was going to let Pat take it home with him. I paused to watch as Pat was jotting the same notes into his phone.

"Doc, what do those letters stand for?"

"I believe the E is for Europe; The A is Australasia - which is Australia and the surrounding islands. The FE is the Far East; this would be Japan."

"So those are like the major players in the world economy. With this mix, I get a powerful blend of the best the world has to offer and no duplicates. What about those other letters, M.S. whatever?

"Indexes have been around for a long time. At one point, Morgan Stanley bought a company that had created some indexes. They renamed it Morgan Stanley Capital International, but then years later wanted to spin it off of their company into a separate division. So they branded MSCI. You don't have to go with Morgan Stanley to find a fund that follows that index. All sorts of investment companies have funds that follow this type of index. Index investing lowers your costs, and as you said, you wouldn't have any duplicates."

I thought I better give him specific recommendations, so he had no excuse not to call one of these companies and start investing. "You can find your own low-cost investment company. But if you want someplace to start, you could look at Fidelity. You would put 90% into the Fidelity 500 Index Fund - Investor Class FXAIX with expense costs around 0.015%. Put the other 10% into

Fidelity International Index Fund - Investor Class FSPSX; it has a cost of around 0.045%."

I paused, and Pat was still typing. When he looked up, I continued, "If you were to choose Vanguard, you would put 90% into Vanguard 500 Index Investor Shares VFINX. That one has a low expense cost of about 0.14% and 10% into Vanguard Total Intl Stock Index Investor Shares VGTSX. Expense costs around 0.17%."

I had to wait another minute for Pat to catch up.

"Another low-cost investment company is T. Rowe Price. There, you would put 90% into T. Rowe Price Equity Index 500 Fund PREIX. It has expense costs close to 0.21% and put the other 10% into T. Rowe Price International Equity Index Fund PIEQX. Expense costs around 0.45%."

Pat put up a finger as if saying hold on. And when he had gotten my attention, he said:

"Doc, I'm still scared. I'm worried about getting into the market at the wrong time. I'm worried that I'll spend all this money and things will go down in value. I'll lose the money I could've spent on stuff I want or go out and have fun."

I could see this in his eyes even before he spoke. I also suspected he was already trying to see someone, like a girlfriend. It was also none of my business. I was just a 'financial advisor' to him—I shouldn't mingle with his private life.

"You have a fear many people have. And fear, no matter the reason, is why people don't invest. They fear they aren't an expert, but you don't have to be. They fear not asking for the right type of investment and making a mistake. They, like you, are frozen with fear because of the risk. The risk of putting money in and having it go down in value. I don't want you to lose money, and this is why you'll use the same technique the super-rich use, dollar-cost averaging," I said.

"What's dollar-cost averaging, and how would it help me? I'm not a big-time investor." Pat asked, narrowing his gaze at me.

"No matter how much money you're investing, the idea doesn't change. You'll invest the same dollar amount each month. When the price of the mutual fund is low, you'll buy a whole bunch of shares. When the price of the fund is high, you'll automatically buy fewer shares. By keeping the amount of your investment steady, you even out the price fluctuations. You average the highs and the lows. You remove some of the risks of buying at the high point of the market. Your fear is now taken care of with this automatic monthly contribution," I explained.

Pat was nodding his head and said, "With dollar-cost averaging, I don't have to worry about buying at the height of the market. All I do is figure how much I'll invest each month. Set up an automated system to send money from my checking account to the investment company each month. Set it up with the same dollar amount every month. What about being aggressive and going after those funds with the highest rate of return?"

"You can be aggressive at your age. You want a great return. The funny thing is those funds that do great for a few years, often fall short of performing as well as their peers in the future. Going after the big gains, by looking at past performance backfires more often than helps," I replied.

Pat looked at me with his eyebrows pushed together and asked a question I had never gotten before:

"Why do you think some of these high-flying funds drop in value after a few good years?"

The question astonished me. I realized Pat was going to make it big. If a student, his age, could ask a question like this, he was smart. Smart enough to follow through with my recommendations. I refocused on his question.

"When you buy a mutual fund, you're buying shares in a bunch of different companies. Each of those shares has a value based on all the companies that mutual fund owns. People buy and sell shares based on many factors. Mostly they base these buys on what they think the company will do in the future. Will the company put out a new product? Will the business earn more money compared to last year?"

"Like Apple putting out a new phone," he interjected, waving his phone in the air.

"Right, if word gets out, Apple will put out a new phone everyone will have to have, Apple's stock price will rise because people expect Apple to do well. When the price starts to go up, other people see this too and want to join in on the potential profit. They buy, driving the price of Apple stock even higher. At some point, the stock price will be more than it's worth, and Apple will see a stock price correction."

"That's fancy talk for a price drop, right?" Pat asked.

"Yeah, the price is now overvalued and will drop back to a value more reasonable, the same thing with these mutual funds. People see how great these funds are doing and want to buy in. They, too, want a piece of that great return. They initially drive the price higher to the point that it's over-valued, and the price drops. As the price drops, guess what people do?"

At this point, I knew Pat would have the correct answer. This is what amazed me about this kid over the years. He answered, "They jump out of the investment. I get it now. They were stupid. They bought at the high point. Then, when they saw a drop, they got out. They sell below the cost they purchased it. They lost money.

On top of that, as they jump out, the value drops even more, causing the fund to go down further. All these people getting out at the same time would make the fund manager have to sell shares of all those stocks to pay the people. With the drop, their fabulous return from years past is now terrible."

"I don't want that for you, Pat. For success, for you to make it rich, for you to have the options money can afford, you need to invest in two index mutual funds consistently."

Pat

Age 17, income $9,360/year; 10% fund $1,056; 20% fund $1,943; Stay out of debt fund $0

I did want options money could afford. Then, I got to thinking about how Nicole would react if I start investing. She gets mad easily, especially when people don't take her advice. I couldn't confide in Doc that I was scared of my sister, though. I thought of Lilly too, but she may not be interested. What bothered me about Lilly was the fact that she may never talk to me as soon as she learns of my past. I was terrified of someone learning the truth and hating me for what I did. I sure did like talking with her during lunch. I wanted more than just our lunch together.

"Doc, what if I'm too lazy for all that? What if I can't find those two funds?"

"Pat, I doubt you're too lazy, and almost all the plans will offer similar funds. You may have to call the investing company and ask which one is the closest match. If you really can't find them or are truly ultra-lazy, go with a Target Date Fund that has the date closest to your 65th birthday," Doc replied.

"If I go with that target-date fund, then can I just leave it there and forget about it?" I asked.

Doc stumbled out of his seat and started to walk around. He wasn't all that old, and the stumble surprised me. He then said, "I don't want you to forget about it, but yeah. You don't have to worry too much about a target-date fund. On the other approach, you'll want to re-balance the funds every May. Move money from the fund that's performing well into the fund that didn't perform as well. Get back to a 90/10 split."

"Doc, what does predict the return?" I was figuring that if I could get this inside information, I could beat the system. I could only invest in those mutual funds that would be the highest performers.

Doc had his back to me when I asked this question. The way he answered was funny. He swiveled around, pointed at me, and almost shouted, "Nothing!" Then he calmed down and continued. "But the next best thing that predicts the rate of return is the fees, the lower the fees, the better the chance at a high rate of return. Fees eat up an investment, like the students eating up the pizza at lunch. This is why I mentioned the fees earlier and why you want Index funds. Index funds have the lowest fees, lower than target-date funds."

It was nice to talk to Doc. I love my family. Talking with my brother, Chad, has always been easy. Not so refreshing to speak with Nicole. At the time, I never really saw my mom. She was constantly working. Looking back, I realize mom working was her way of dealing with the loss of my dad. Maybe it was a bit of her escape from the trouble I caused too. I know I cost the family a lot by my single, stupid action. At the time, I was still on probation, and my family had to pay some probation check-in costs each month. I wish I could've stayed and talked with Doc some more. When my mind focused on finance, I wasn't feeling sorry for myself. It brought a glimpse of hope to my dismal existence. I thanked Doc and headed out the door as other students started coming in for first period.

Doc's words made me realize a few things. When I was in juvie, I was in despair. I guess everyone was. During mandatory counseling sessions, I heard the therapists say, 'there is a light at the end of the tunnel.' I scoffed at the thought. There is no guarantee someone would make it through this hypothetical tunnel. No idea how long the tube would be. Noone had a clue as to the obstacles hidden within the tunnel's floor. But with Doc's words and the investment in my future, I was carrying a torch to light my path through the darkness. If I had an investment, it would act like a torchlight, and make the journey easier. It could afford choices for me—If I were to stumble in the dark.

'90/10; S&P, International' were bouncing around my head while I sprinted down the hallway and slipped into Mrs. Galloway's first period English class just as the door closed. She already had me marked as absent and had to change things after I walked in on time, but barely.

"Pat, please put up that cell phone before entering my classroom . . . This is a place for learning," said Mrs. Galloway.

I scrambled to finish the rest of Doc's notes as I was taking a seat. These were way more important, and I momentarily swiveled my eyes up to see the board:

LEARNING HOW TO WRITE A HAIKU

Mrs. Galloway slammed her fist on her desk and scolded me once more, "I said now, Pat!" I rolled my eyes and tossed the phone into my unzipped bag before throwing my bag onto the floor. "All done…" I mumbled as she moved from her desk and began writing on the board.

"Alright class, last night you were each assigned a three-page report on a renaissance author. Now, I want you to write a haiku about that author as I collect your papers," she said as my attention was now on Lilly, sitting next to me.

"Hey Lilly, can I call you later tonight?" She nodded yes, and my heart skipped a beat. I was going to ask her out.

Mrs. Galloway's arms were becoming filled with the papers. Through the armhole of her loose blouse, the clasp of her undone bra was sticking out. Galloway didn't notice, but all the students did. A boy spoke up and told her that her bra was sticking out of her shirt. She was mortified. She spun one way and then the other. She grabbed the white strap, dropping all the papers. Renaissance scattered in a fan-shape on the floor. Galloway blushed. She ran out of the door, leaving her class in laughter. A few minutes later, she returned. This time composed and adequately fastened. The student who told her about the bra picked up the papers and put them on her desk. She collected the rest and said, "Alrighty then, time for a haiku."

On my way home, I called Lilly. As the phone was ringing, I got scared. I was worried she would reject me. I kept thinking that after I tell her the terrible thing I had inflicted on that family, she was going to dump me. I kept trying to keep in mind what the psychiatrist said, 'let people get to know you before you confide in them.' I like this girl. I didn't want to begin our relationship with secrets, especially a secret this big.

I didn't have much time to think, she picked up after the second ring, "Hi, Pat…"

"Hi, Lilly, thought we could hang out tonight."

I said that and waited for her response. I was trying to play it cool. Act with confidence. I figured girls liked that sort of thing.

"Sure, you seem to like that one coffee place. Let's meet there around five. Surely they have something without caffeine."

"Okay, great. I appreciate. See you later."

I don't know what love feels like, but I think I was feeling love for Lilly. Who else would care enough to realize what places I enjoy, like that coffeehouse?

A few minutes after I got home, Chad came in. "Chad, you won't believe it. I've got a date."

"What, a real date? As in with a girl? A human girl?"

"Yeah, I know—a real human girl. Crazy as it may sound, I think she likes me." Chad's eyes were dramatically wide to exaggerate his surprise. I continued, half asking for his advice, "I think I'm going to tell her about the accident. We've known each other for a while. We eat lunch together every day and talk during class when Mrs. Galloway isn't watching."

Chad interrupted, "Galloway, good ole' Galloway. You know she never missed a day of school when I had her?"

I guess I wasn't going to get the advice I needed out of my brother. No way I was going to ask Nicole, luckily she wasn't around too much.

I wanted to report myself to Lilly. I needed her to know me in full before I start a loved-filled relationship with her. She may not like me after she hears I caused an accident that killed a man. I said a quick bye to Chad and hurried down the stairs past the garage doors of the mechanic's shop. I needed a lot of time to explain things to Lilly and address any of the questions that might have arisen from her hearing about my past.

The weather had been fair that afternoon, and it seemed that somehow, someone conspired with the rows of clouds straightening them into thick, firm white tubes. The clouds contrasted against the blue sky, forming a loose pattern that pointed me toward the coffee shop. My favorite coffee house was small, but with the best coffee. Tucked into a flat-roofed strip mall that's seen better days. A red and black sign, worn by the elements. Outside seating was even more uncomfortable than inside. The sign said:

CAFÉ MARZOCCA ITALIAN ESPRESSO BAR

I met Lilly sitting beside an empty seat with a stranger trying to strike up a conversation with her. She placed her hands on her jaw, listening; eyes shone studiously at him. And while I walked up, watching them, I was infected with an eerie dose of jealousy—gripped by the feeling—if I told her about my past, she may walk away from me forever and go for other guys who had 'cleaner' records. Other guys who were not disposed to using an orange barrel as a murder weapon.

I came closer to them and sat on the next empty seat.

"Hi," I said, scowling at the guy. I was nurturing a strong repulsion for him, and I wanted him gone.

It seemed for the moment that Lilly and I shared a telepathic understanding when she said, "See you later. My friend is here now."

I loved the way she skillfully arranged her words and was so direct. She smiled a beautiful smile, and I felt it rub off the gaze of disgust from my face. I looked her in the eyes and almost forgot what I wanted to tell her. I placed my hands on her palm and whispered to her in low tones.

"I have something to tell you, Lilly."

"This sounds serious. Pat, you aren't going to tell me you're pregnant, are you?"

"Pregnant, I'm a guy. How can I be pregnant?" Her smile made me realize she was joking. I guess I was coming across serious.

"I want to tell you something I did a while ago and why I went to jail. I told you I went to jail, right?"

"Yeah, you did. You never told me why."

For a moment, I thought she was not interested in the reason I went to jail. Hindsight is always clear. I should have kept it that way. My legs were trembling. The small table too small to hide their movement. I tried bopping them up and down in hope to disguise the shaking. The words of my psychiatrist now flooded my mind, especially the part where he said, 'it will be difficult to get acceptance from your new friends.'

"I'm ready to tell you what sent me to jail. I want us to have a serious relationship. You need to know everything from the get-go. If you hate me after now, I won't judge you. You need to know this before we can move forward."

Pat's Notes

Best investments in order

Company matched 401(k)

Roth 401(k)

Roth IRA with a traditional IRA

If the above options aren't available:

Roth IRA first with solo 401(k) or SEP-IRA.

Back-door Roth would be the next option

The last option being 403(b) or similar retirement account

Best funds

90% S&P 500 Index or total stock market.

10% International Index MSCI EAFE or world stock market fund.

Rebalance, move the money from the fund doing the best into the other fund to make them 90/10 again. Rebalance every May.

If I can't find those two funds, I could go with a Target Date Fund closest to my 65th birthday year.

Check the costs of the funds. Find the investment company that offers those funds at the lowest fees.

Use dollar-cost averaging, investing the same amount of money each month. This strategy removes most of the risk of buying at the wrong time.

Chapter 5

What budget is the best for the lazy?

Pat

Pat, age 17, income $9,360/year; 10% fund $1,056; 20% fund $1,943; Stay out of debt fund $0

I have heard people say the most important things are the hardest to say. I remember feeling my jaw clenching after I told Lilly about the little secret that had blighted my life. I watched how her smile melted into something that looked like revulsion and suppressed anger. I was instantly worried. I felt Lilly slipping through my fingers. I was losing her. I was losing all the good intentions I had for our relationship, the love life I could have had, those little, important things. My stomach turned. I was feeling sick. Sweats were coming to my face. It was the beginning of the end, and the thought made me sick. I had to immerse myself in my bolthole: Finance thoughts.

Two days after I had my perilous date with Lilly, I dawdled down to Doc's classroom. It was quite early; the time was edging past 6:15 in the morning. I scaled under the school's arch, and caught a glimpse of the engraved stone that said:

GREENVILLE HIGH SCHOOL

Moments later, I had lurched to the left, lumbering through the corridors to Doc's room. From Doc's windows, I got a panoramic vision of an ugly half-walled structure filled with HVAC condensers. The high school is beautiful, Doc's view, not so much.

Doc had a look on his face that said he was genuinely happy to see me. At least I had someone who wouldn't judge me like Lilly's face had done.

"Good morning, Doc. Are you busy?" I asked, with a simulated smile.

"I am here for you, Pat. Shoot."

"I thought about what we talked about with retirement funds. Since I'm not going through an employer's plan, I searched for an investment company with low costs and low fees. I found Vanguard and called. I told them I wanted to set up a Roth IRA and a traditional IRA. They started to ask me all these questions. I didn't get nervous or anything, but I also didn't know how to answer them."

Doc responded with confidence. "Let me guess a few of those questions, your age, how much money for your initial deposit, and what funds you want to invest in?"

"Yeah, I knew the age one. I felt out of my element about the others," I confided.

"These companies will want you to be 18 before investing. For now, you should save your money at a bank in a personal savings account. They'll also want a couple thousand as an initial investment. As far as which funds. Look for an index fund, S&P 500 Index, or total stock market. The other one to get into would be either an International Index MSCI EAFE or world stock market fund,"

Doc was telling me something I already had in my notes.

"Yeah, I've got those in my notes." I held up my phone. I just wanted to tell you, and I've been talking with my mom about all this investment stuff. She thinks it's good for me to talk about it. She started talking about a recipe and baking. It was quite weird. She was saying that in cooking, chefs follow a recipe. If you have great directions and the finest ingredients, you come out with the best dishes. She went on to talk about how some chefs will alter the recipe, change things up, and still come up with a fabulous dinner. If you get the main ingredients wrong, the food will suck."

Doc uttered a burst of transitory laughter. It seemed he found my analogy funny.

I continued, "I think what mom is saying is, Doc knows the recipe, Doc knows the main ingredients. If I can follow your directions, I can make something of myself."

Doc smiled and responded, "It's not complicated. Like we talked about, you don't have to be an insider, an expert, or know what R.O.I. even means for you to accumulate wealth. Save 10% of your income and invest it in an index fund following the stock market. It's that simple. If you don't believe me, go to an investment calculator online. Type in your numbers and find out for yourself how rich you could become."

Doc kept firing words at me. I was under the impression he may have thought I doubted him. He stood up and wrote on the board two words, risk and cost, "Investing in index funds reduces your risk and keeps your costs low, giving you more profit. I'm not making this stuff up."

Doc pulled up a picture of Warren Buffet and used the projector in the room. "Warren Buffet once said, 'Consistently buy an S&P 500 low-cost index fund.'"

He then pulled up a picture of Mark Cuban. "Mark Cuban agrees and said, 'If you don't know too much about markets, the best way to invest your money right now is to put it in a cheap S&P 500 SPX fund.'"

Next was a picture of Tony Robbins. It looked like he was a keynote speaker at an enormous event. "Tony here wrote investment books. He wrote, 'Index funds take a 'passive' approach that eliminates risk . . . When you own an index fund, you're also protected against all the downright dumb, mildly misguided or merely unlucky decisions that active fund managers are liable to make.'"

"So, you see, I'm not telling you anything that's not already out there. Index funds have low cost and less risk."

"Doc, I've never doubted you. Are you mad at me? Your tone gives me the impression you are upset or something."

Doc calmed down a bit. He sat back in his seat. "No, I just get pretty passionate about all this stuff."

"Yeah, I can tell. I remember, during class, we pulled up that investment calculator to see how rich we could become if we invest 10% of our income. So, I know. You're preaching to the choir here, Doc. I'm convinced it's easy; even this guy from the juvenile detention center can do it."

As I was walking out the door, I called back in:

"I guess 10% and index funds are your two main ingredients to a great recipe."

Lilly

When I heard Pat tell me about what he had done, the murder, the mischief he had inflicted on a family, it came as an assault to my sensibilities. I felt like a dragonfly with its wings ripped off. I was still alive, but could no longer fly. It's funny how no one can tell what a person is capable of. How a smiling man could be nurturing a sickening thought. I couldn't believe Pat was a murderer.

That night, I told my mom about our first and last date. Instead of just listening, like she usually would have, she spoke up. I didn't want to hear it. I shut her down.

I hadn't talked with Pat since we met at that coffee place. The weekend gave me a break from seeing him in Galloway's class. Those poor twins, no father. I looked up the news reports, and they didn't list Pat's name in the papers. The reporters just gave his age and the facts. I went to the bridge, where it all happened. I didn't tell anyone I was going. I wanted to, somehow, capture what Pat was feeling. It was no use. No one has the right to take another life.

Pat tried to call me for a few days. I refused to answer. Since Monday, I ate lunch in Mrs. Galloway's classroom. She knew something was up and didn't kick me out. It was hard sitting in the same language arts class as Pat. I changed seats. I made it obvious I was going to have nothing to do with that boy.

I finally did call him back once. I wanted him to know what he truly was.

"Pat, you acted like a wild animal. You let your anger affect your actions. A man is to act with reason, not with an inconsiderate, combative nature. You didn't let your conscience help you decide right from wrong. Instead, a beast came out of you and killed a man. I can't be with someone who lacks judgment like a hungry wolf, killing indiscriminately."

He didn't respond, but I could hear him breathing loudly, and it dawned on me that he got the message. I was clear. I didn't want to continue our relationship.

That night I called him back, I was getting ready for bed. It was my end of day ritual. I turned off the ringer and vibration on my cell phone, everything that could make noise except the morning's alarm. I placed it face down on the table next to my bed, plugged in. And I thought about my day.

I replayed things I had said and done. I brought up the good and the bad. First, I made myself face the bad. What did I do that I could've handled a little better? What am I sorry for?

I don't beat myself up over it. I agree to make it right the next day or decide not to do something like that again. After I've made that decision, I would forgive myself. I think of the good I've done. Did I take care of myself, physically and mentally?

What did I do today to become better, meet my goals? Did I focus on developing my skills?

Did I spend time with friends and family, or did I waste time on social media and gossip sites?

The day I broke up with Pat was a tough day for me. During my nightly ritual, I realized I had spent over an hour online shopping—I didn't need anything; it was a stress reducer. I had to agree to watch that behavior.

I was also shamefully harsh on Pat. I remembered some of the words that came out of my mouth, animal, wild. I felt terrible for hurting him, but it wasn't something I needed for him to forgive me. I thought long and hard and agreed if something like this came up in the future, I wouldn't be as harsh. Honest yes, but not demeaning. I forgave myself for the bad things I did and started to think about the good. Not much good that day. I went to sleep.

Pat

Age 17, income $9,360/year; 10% fund $1,056; 20% fund $1,943; Stay out of debt fund $0

Sod's law says if something could go wrong, then it would go wrong and wrong in the biggest way possible. Scary as the law may sound, it was becoming a feature of my life. Lilly's call had put me on a vicious cycle. For the first time, I understood the love that permeated my heart. I loved Lilly, and there was no second-guessing it. It seemed something was eating me up from my insides. I knew Lilly hated me at this point. I was never going to be able to forgive myself for killing a man. I felt so sorry and decided to ask Doc for advice, but then thought he might just say 'just financial matters. I don't talk 'bout matters of the heart.' Maybe it was for the best I don't talk with Doc about it. When I think about finance stuff and talk with Doc, it's like my one escape. Focus on my potential. My chance to think about the future. Dream big time. Not think about my problem time.

That night, I laid on my bed listening to Chad snore for a large part of the night and thinking of what else to do about Lilly. I remembered her smiling face. I laughed at how she had carelessly spilled coffee on me the day we first met. That day, she was all glowing with apologies and tried to make up for the coffee stains on my clothes. I remember her rubbing my chest with napkins, thinking, 'this girl can spill coffee on me anytime.' That's when I got her number and realized after several days of chatting on the phone, she lived just a few blocks away.

I didn't sleep much that night. When Chad woke, I greeted him with a "Hi," trying to get Lilly off my mind, at least for now.

"How you doin' bro?" Chad's fake Bronx dialect was pretty good.

"How's your friend? You haven't been payin' dumb guap for dates, na mean?"

I had no idea what he just asked. I gave him a puzzled look, and he translated, but this time he used a British accent, "Dear lad, you haven't been spending too much money on dates, do you know what I mean?"

My heart missed a beat. I didn't want Chad to know we've had a problem. I tried to fake it. I gave a brief response and asked him another question. "She's fine. How is your friend from work?"

"Wait…fine won't do it. Don't tell me you guys have any problem?" Chad persisted, ignoring my escape question.

I couldn't believe he noticed my pain. If he had just mentioned her and moved on, it would've been better. But he stood, walked backward, and asked, "Don't tell me you told her about the accident?"

"I did tell her, and she thinks I'm a wild animal who murders people."

I would never have expected my brother to pay much attention to how I felt about how people treated me. If my sister had asked these questions, then I'd think she would be trying to punish me further. I never thought Chad had any insight into people's feelings. Not one bit.

I was glad I told Chad. I had to tell someone. I never even kissed Lilly yet, but my heart had ripped apart.

"I want to do like you do, Chad. Ball it up. Throw it away. Pretend bad crap never happens."

"I don't do that," Chad said defensively. "I can see why you might think that. I had a coach in school back when dad died, who taught me a technique to deal with 'bad crap' as you would say. I've been using it ever since."

"I wish you could've told me," I retorted, I was nurturing some sort of anger towards Chad.

It was a wave of eerie anger, and when my dad died, I had gone through a hard-hitting time. Only, Chad seemed to get along just fine. Maybe if I had his technique, I could've, I would've, . . . I'd have choices.

Chad saw the look of interest, and inquisition on my face. He started, "Step one, breathe and recognize your emotion. Find out why you have that emotion. Step two, feel the pain immediately. Don't wait to mourn. Grieve now. Cry. Accept the sorrow as part of life. Don't try to hide from the 'bad crap' or push it down. Face it, process how it makes you feel. Deal with it. Step three, let it pass. You can't do anything about fate anyway. You can't change the outcome of history. All you can control is your reaction. Step four, focus on things in which you're grateful. Center your attention on the items and relationships you have. Things that bring you joy. Spend time doing things that make you happy and being with people who are fun to be around."

"Can't I just skip to step four? I don't want to grieve or face it. She said awful things to me."

"No, Pat, you have to face your emotions. You have to spend time sitting and thinking, even crying. It's not forever before you move onto the next step."

I could always tell when Chad was about to begin a story. He would click his tongue. Sure enough, "Dad had a friend. An older guy. I remember him telling dad this story. I don't know why I was there. Maybe I was eavesdropping. This guy named James was married. He got married young and didn't really like being married. So, he lied to his wife about the army needing him and screwing up paperwork signing him on for another tour of duty. He couldn't get out of it 'because it was the government.' While on duty, he cheated on her all the time. When he finally came home, she filed for divorce. She had found out the army never screwed up his paperwork. His staff sergeant was paying James a compliment to his wife and told her how he volunteered to serve again, 'what a great guy serving his country during this conflict.' After he got home from his tour, James had no place to go. He left their tiny apartment the same day he arrived, found a hotel, and sat there for 36 hours. He drank water and cried. No food, no sleep, just sorrow. After a day and a half, he let it pass. He knew he couldn't do anything about the 'crap' he caused, and he made the past be the past. He let it go. He controlled his emotions because he knew he couldn't control history."

Doc

I won't lie; I've always had a mix of students. Some who would pay attention. Others could care less. I was in the front of the classroom, near my stand up desk, peering down the four-column and six rows seating arrangement, and my gaze caught Pat. While other students were chit-chatting with one another and others on their phone, Pat just sat there, alone on his seat, disenchanted, and I felt there was something wrong. A part of me thought he was having a relationship problem. When boys his age looked this troubled, it was typically due to the teething troubles of a relationship. I decided not to give the lesson I had prepared for this class on the relative income hypothesis. With Pat looking sick, that lesson didn't seem like such an appealing topic anymore. Pat's welfare was more important, and I wouldn't want him reverting to his past. The computer where I take attendance forced me to notice Pat would soon be celebrating his birthday. Students always like being asked about their birthday, but never want the singing. At least they didn't want me singing. Maybe asking about his plans would help cheer him up.

"Pat, it shows you're going to turn 18 this week. What are you going to do for the big day?" I asked.

As if like a metamorphic butterfly, Pat came out of a cocoon. His eyes were no longer glazed over. His back no longer hunched like an old lady with osteoporosis. "Well, Doc, my birthday present to myself will be setting up my retirement account." I've never heard Pat talk so loud. It was as if he wanted the entire floor to listen to him. The students put down their phones. Conversations stopped.

When his words sunk into their brains, the students started to laugh. I saw a smirk come over Pat's face and knew he was going to play this one up.

"That's right, Doc. I'm going to set up a Roth IRA. I already have it all planned out. I have my minimum investment saved up. I'm splitting it into two index funds, the S&P 500 and International Index that follows the MSCI EAFE. Vanguard seemed like a low enough cost. You know, the fees the company charges makes a difference. You've got to consider the expense ratio. By shopping around, I was able to save 0.1%." The students began to laugh again. It didn't bother me. They thought Pat was making fun of me, but I knew better.

Pat let the chuckles die down and continued, "No, I did the math. If I can gain 0.1% over another fund, over 40 years, I'll have upward of $367,000 just from that one change." The students had a different look on their faces now. Some of them started to wonder if he was joking or serious.

"Doc, they've got all my information. I'm even setting up an automatic payment to Vanguard at the end of each month. That way, I take advantage of dollar-cost averaging, you know, to level out the risk of buying at the highest cost. After today, there's no going back," Pat said, vitalized, and I sensed he didn't just like finance. He was obsessed with it.

Another rush of chuckling sound wafted up from the students. They were now confident Pat was pulling my leg and just telling the financial literacy teacher what he wanted to hear, but I knew Pat was sincere.

Lilly

I came home, feeling depressed and tired. I dropped my bag on the table. The table my mom picked out cost just a little above average. The dark brown color made it look like those furnished houses where the rich men lived.

I went straight to the refrigerator, took out a coke, and sat helplessly on the chair. I was alone, figuratively, emotionally, and in the house. I thought about Pat. I thought about the pain he has to live with forever—the lives he had ruined. My thoughts started to turn to sympathy, thinking about how Pat must be lonely. When friends got to know about the situation, they find a way to check out of his life. Check out, as I did. It was tragic. I seem to live for the present, and Pat lives for the future.

I was about to sip from the bottle the third time when a call came in.

"Hello…" I was shocked I answered it. It was Pat. I took some time to process the call. I breathed in deeply. I thought I need to be straight with him.

"How are you?" Pat asked.

"I tried calling a few times, but there was no response. I hope you're okay now. How was your day?"

"Pat, we're graduating soon. I'm going off to college. Our relationship is over." These things were difficult for me to say because I liked him. "I've enjoyed the time we've had together, but now it's time for both of us to grow. You have issues to resolve."

I sensed I was selfish because I knew Pat had daily battles with demons, and I was leaving to have fun living on campus.

"Pat, I hope you understand?"

I waited. I wasn't sure if Pat was still even on the line. This time, I couldn't hear his breath.

"Yeah, I get it," Pat responded.

"I'll see you around." Pat hung up, and it was over before we had even started.

Doc

A few months after Pat's birthday, I met Pat's mom at graduation. It was sweet how she told me the impact I had on Pat and her. She first told me how he had set up his retirement accounts. I didn't let on I already knew. She told me because she was proud of him. She also told me that when Chad was in my class, soon after he joined, I gave a lesson on Social Security benefits. Part of that lesson was a survivor's benefit—people who had a spouse who died could collect from Social Security. "Having that little bit of extra money, really was a blessing," Pat's mom said.

I remembered the handout I gave the class. I made it the night before I gave the lesson, right after I learned Chad's dad had died. I figured the family might not know about that type of benefit. I wanted what was best for my students.

As I watched her talk, I could see in her eyes how her husband dying influenced Pat's decisions. She continued, "I have to say, the timing of Chad learning that information couldn't have come at a better time. I had a job, but never enough money to give my kids the lifestyle I wanted them to have. The extra money allowed me to save for a rainy day. I call it my 'stay out of debt fund.'"

I liked that Pat's mom was saving money in a rainy day fund. I started to tell her about Pat. "Pat's great. . ." then she cut me off.

Pat's mom continued to explain, "Pat got his first job at 17 years old. From each paycheck, he put away 10% of his income. My son saved up his money in his savings account. When the value reached $3,000.00, he put the money into a Roth IRA that tracked the S&P 500 Index, and 10% of it went into an International Index. After Pat had the account set up, he automated deposits from his checking into his Roth IRA, transferring a bit in the last few days of each month. I'm so proud of him for taking this step. He's such a good boy who's been through so much. I don't know if you know this, but he caused a bad accident. He hasn't forgiven himself for what he did. I don't think he'll ever stop torturing himself."

As I started to respond, Pat's mom excused herself and had to leave. I didn't take it personally. Parents act weird at graduation.

After graduation, Pat kept in touch. I learned Pat kept his monthly contributions going into his Roth IRA for a few years. That is until he got another job, where they offered a 401(k) with a company match. He wanted that company match where they would also put money into this retirement fund. Pat put 10% of his before-tax pay into the 401(k). This investment also kept the same focus as his Roth IRA with a 90/10 split between the S&P 500 Index and an international fund that tracked the International Index MSCI EAFE. Pat had to set up a different account than his Roth IRA. Pat's strategy maxed out the company match. To Pat, it was like getting a raise from work. They were paying him more, but instead of seeing it in his paycheck, he saw it in his investment.

Pat

Age 18, income $9,360-$46,800/year; 10% fund $4,680; 20% fund $9,360; Stay out of debt fund $0

Graduation was like coming in from a long voyage out at sea. Occasionally catching glimpses of new coastline. A sailor loves the sea, but a new coastline was a sign of his adventurous life. So too was graduation. Instead of coastline, I caught glimpses of friends, of Doc, of Chad, and even Nicole. Among the 350 or so graduating seniors, I saw Lilly. My graduation day showed me the promise of a new coastline like a sailor finding adventure. My life has been rough, like a stormy sea, but when that coastline came into view, like graduation day, I set my sights. I moved forward. I vowed to begin again. But on a new quest, a new adventure, I would find a new shoreline—one that would provide adventure. My troubles in life and love were like the rough seas. Although difficult, dealing with turbulence made the calm water all that much better. If I can survive the storm, the calm was going to be better than I could ever imagine. I knew life would offer its fair share of woes, but it didn't matter. It was the potential of adventure, of a new coastline in view, that erased the past and brought a tiny smile to a typically sad face.

I kept in touch with Doc after graduation, taking every suggestion he told me. I worked two jobs. Well, one and a half because one was full time and the other part-time. I made a decent wage per hour. In a way, I wanted him to be proud of me. I knew that he wouldn't be jealous of me doing well, as Nicole would. While I was working, I took advantage of on-the-job training opportunities. I didn't go to college, but I took some classes at a university in the evenings—training me for the career I wanted. It was mostly adults, and it was something that interested me. Even though I didn't get a degree, those classes paid off. At an interview, I told my future boss I'd been taking those classes. It worked. I got a new job, one with a 401(k) and a company match like we talked about years ago. I told Doc about my new job and the company-match - free money. For now, I changed my old work into a part-time job. I had big plans.

I wasn't going to mess with the recipe. I wasn't going to mess with this system. I could already see it was working in my Roth IRA and now in my 401(k). I wasn't about to buy and sell individual stocks. Things were working. I wasn't a millionaire yet, but I sure enjoyed watching that money grow.

Then the trouble started. I don't know what went wrong. I had a good job and a half. I moved out of my mom's place and got a home of my own. I was having trouble paying the bills. Sometimes I felt like my own worst enemy, especially when it comes to managing my money. I called Doc. I didn't want to talk about budgeting. I didn't want his advice about pulling money out of envelopes and eating noodles from a plastic bag. I called to check on him. I told him the balances on my investments. He was happy for me. In my gut, I knew I was living beyond my means. I'm not talking just a little bit of money. I owed a lot. Little things just added up. At first, I thought I'll pay the minimum this month and then next month, pay the credit card balance in full. When friends at the new job called and wanted to go out, I thought to myself, 'other people go out.' People my age have fun. Others, who make less than me, can afford sushi and a movie. I want that too. I put it on my credit card. Not just once.

I slipped up—one little comment. I should never have said it, but Doc heard me, "I spent a bit too much money setting up my new place. I'm having trouble paying the bills and still invest money."

Doc jumped on it and started, "Pat, you could read advice about budgeting that would help you live a financially secure life better than the advice I'll give you."

I interrupted him, "Look, Doc, I'm reluctant to talk about putting my money on a budget. I fear budgeting will take away my choices. Besides, I'm a tad bit lazy. I don't want the confines of living out of an envelope—'I don't have enough money for tonight's dinner.' If I figure a budget at the beginning of the month, I'll never buy shoes. Those shoes may make me happy, and they might be on sale that week. If we're going to talk budgets, it better be easy to follow and allow me to spend the money as I want."

"The plan I'll share is strictly for the lazy and those who want maximum choices in life. There are online tools out there that'll track your spending and help you decide if you can afford to buy coffee. But I have a feeling those aren't for you."

"Doc, you've got that right. I need simple. I need flexibility. I want choices of how I spend my money. I'm also not skimping on my coffee."

"Divide your income into three parts, 10%, 20%, and 70%. Budget to save 10% of your money for retirement, put 20% of your money away for big purchases, and reaching goals, then live off 70%. Spend 70% the way you want." From what Doc was saying, I knew there would be trade-offs. If I want to buy a pair of shoes, I'm not also going out for sushi.

Pat's notes

Wait until I'm 18 to open an investment account. In the meantime, save 10% of my income in a savings account.

Budget

10% for retirement, taken out of my pay first

20% of my earnings for big purchases and reaching big goals

70% can be spent the way I want, mostly for living expenses.

Chapter 6
What do I do if I have debt?

Doc

There were times I had doubts about Pat. Times when I traveled in a daydream, back to Maher's Pub, my mind gripped by the two-faced Frank. The way he made those eyes seem like he was really up for a change. Sometimes, it only takes a little bit of ill luck to send a person spiraling down the path of wastefulness and overindulgence. I was conscious of how easy it was for people to fall victim to this lifestyle. To protect Pat, I made a few deliberate efforts to ensure Pat could stay the course. The last time I spoke with him, I mentioned a simple budget of dividing his income into three parts. Only I wasn't impressed by the disregard he conveyed through the phone. I consoled myself with the thought that if he needed more guidance, he would call. Sure enough, Pat called again a few days later. He had forgotten to mention he had a bit of debt. It was funny because I expected it, and it seemed like the more we chatted, the bond between us intensified.

"Pat to knock out your debt, you have to hold off on big purchases and trying to reach your long-term goals," I began, and he was quiet, the soft sound of his breathing was my only clue he was still listening.

I continued, "You'll need to do some homework first. Look up the rates of competing cards. Then, call each credit agency or credit card you have debt with and ask for a reduction in the interest rate. When you call, ask to speak to a supervisor because you need your interest rate lowered. Tell the supervisor they'll need to meet or beat the competitor's rate. Be decisive and clear. Tell him or her the name of the company with a lower rate. Tell them the rate. Here, you need to make an effort to reduce the amount of money you're spending in interest, so the money you pay back goes toward the debt. Once you've reduced your rates, list each debt along with the interest rate you're paying, then pay down the debt with the highest interest rate first. All the extra money goes to this debt, and you pay the minimum on the others. You pay the debt with the highest rate first, so your money goes to the best use."

Pat responded, "I'll call. It can't hurt to ask. Not that I'm in this situation, but what if I had a bunch of debt. You know more debt than the 20% could knock out?"

"There, you'll have to stop your 10% retirement investment. Put all 30% toward the debt. If that's not enough, sell, sell, and sell!" I stopped there, hoping Pat would ask what I meant.

"What do you mean, sell?"

"I'm guessing you're talking about Chad. He probably has a car payment, credit card bills, and quite frankly a lifestyle he can't afford."

"Yeah, my brother lives way beyond his means. I love him, but he wastes money on stupid stuff. Granted, I did too."

"For someone who's in Chad's situation, he needs to sell the car. Go with public transportation or find rides until he can get a cheap, reliable, used car. He needs to sell the things that have some value. Cut the monthly expenses by going with a cheaper cell phone and mobile plan, eliminating the entertainment charges, like online movies and cable. He might even have to move to reduce his expenses."

"Move? I doubt he'll move," Pat retorted.

"If he's renting, his best bet might be to move to a cheaper place."

"What if he owns the house?" Pat asked curiously.

"Lots of factors come into play there. Like how much the house is worth now compared to how much he owes. He might be able to sell the house, move into a rental, and pay off all his debts with the money from the house sale. Here, you have to be careful. The monthly house payment might be cheaper than rent."

I waited for a few seconds to allow him to think about what I was implying, and then I continued, "People get stuck in their ways, like Chad. They think they can't move or can't give up a service they've become used to having. When they're so far into debt, they can't pay it off quickly with 20% of their income—they need a wakeup call. They need to realize the way they've been living isn't sustainable. They can't continue like this. They need a drastic change to snap them into a lifestyle they can afford to live, save for big purchases, and save for retirement."

I thought back to the first day Pat and I talked and how vital it was to realize your comfort zone and break free from that lifestyle. Chad never got out of the upper-middle class lifestyle in which his parents raised him. Now, with an income too low, he's going into debt to sustain his comfort level.

Pat sighed a disgruntled man's sigh, he exhaled loudly and gave me a bit of insight into Chad. "I can tell Chad these things, but he probably won't change. Nicole, if I were to tell her, she would bite my head off. Then she'd toss my head in the toilet and complain I clogged up the commode." Pat's dramatic flair made me laugh.

I also found out Pat had an outstanding medical bill. It was well overdue. He called the hospital billing department—it had gone to collections. He negotiated with them, saying, "I am willing to pay this today to you, not the collection agency. I am willing to pay 60% of the original charge, but only if it will be marked as paid in full and on time to the credit reporting agencies." Pat got almost everything he wanted but had to pay 75% of the medical treatment.

Later, I found out Pat wasn't successful the first time he called the credit card companies. Pat was smart. He waited until that supervisor wouldn't be working and called back, hours later. This time, when Pat mentioned transferring the money to a low introductory rate card (something Pat wasn't planning on doing because of the 3% transfer balance fee), they lowered his interest rate. He used the 20% portion to take care of his debt. He even had a bit of savings he tossed at the balance.

Pat

Age 22, income $58,800/year; 10% fund $36,562; 20% fund $40,128; Stay out of debt fund $25,480

Living on a budget can be hard, but it's worth it in the name of long-term savings. I remember calling up my creditors and asking for lower monthly payments. They said, 'there was nothing they could do' until demanding to speak with a supervisor. It's as if they don't want you to get ahead in life, or maybe those who have made it simply forgot what it's like to endure the daily struggle.

"Were you aware of the credit terms, sir?" the supervisor asked, with a condescending tone.

I muted the phone and took a deep breath before responding. "Yes . . . I knew about the high-interest rate after a year of membership, but things happen in life. Don't tell me you haven't been in a tough money spot at some point yourself?" I asked.

After a brief silence, the supervisor responded, "Alright, hold on for just a moment and let me see what I can do for you," in a chummier, considerate tone.

I was thankful for his honest change of heart. A shared understanding of one another's hardships is something most people have seemed to have lost over the years. I will admit that the troublesome debt's origin was my sole responsibility. There's no reasonable excuse for my personal inability to resist going out for drinks with friends or shopping for a weekend outfit. Thankfully, Doc's simple action plan helped me find stable financial ground without seeking out the services of money-hungry credit fixers. Regardless of Doc's simple practices, it's impossible to deny the success of his techniques. I'm not sure where I'd be in life without his help. Most people spend the majority of their lives stuck, paying an endless cycle of bills.

Pat's Notes

Steps to paying off debt

Step 1, find all outstanding debts.

Step 2, call credit companies to lower interest rates.

Step 3, pay the debt with the highest interest rate first.

Step 4, use the 20% and savings to pay off debt.

Step 4.5, if extreme debt, use my 20% and my 10% (30% of income) to pay back debts.

Step 4.75, sell, sell, sell. Sell stuff to earn money and pay back debts. Use my second 'half' job to pay back debts. Get rid of stuff costing me money, like high cell phone bills, car payments, and cable.

Step 5, stay out of debt. Then save in my 20% fund for large purchases or travel.

Chapter 7

What fund do I use for my 20%?

Doc

I was in my office taking a sip off my morning coffee, just the way I like it, black and bitter. The Portland sky uttered a shivering, chilly gust of cold air. Looking across as the students came toward the building, everything seemed foggy and turbid. And for a moment, it felt like the pallor faced sky was sneaking a sip from its morning coffee, and it liked it, cold and chilly.

I had learned that once Pat's debt was gone, he saved up a few thousand dollars in his savings account. He gave me a call so I too could be proud of him.

"Doc, are you proud of me?"

"What for? Did you do something special?" I asked.

"I did. I used my 20%, along with some savings, and got rid of my debt. All that time, I kept my retirement savings at 10%," Pat replied, in a steady, confident tone.

"That's great, Pat. I am proud of you. What are you going to do now?" I asked.

"I want my 20% fund to grow. I want a return on my investment. I'm planning on putting a good bit of money in there and then doing a few big things with it."

I knew Pat pretty well at this point, but for some reason, all I could picture was Pat buying expensive shoes with all that money.

"That's important to know because if you were planning on needing the money within the next few years, I wouldn't give you the same advice. If you're going to need the money within a few years, you'll want to protect it. Put it into a money market account that'll be sure to keep your contributions safe. A few advantages of a money market account are, it acts as a savings account, you can write checks against it, even use a debit card, and it earns a bit more interest than a savings account. On the other hand, if you have time and you want your money to grow, you'll want your contributions in the stock market. I'm guessing you aren't afraid of a bit of risk as long as the chances are high you'll get a decent return on the money."

Pat sounded excited, and I could hear his excitement popping out my phone's speaker, "You've got that right. If I invest and the stock market goes down, I'm not exactly counting on this money to pay the bills. If I need to hold off on spending some of it, I can."

I then introduced a new concept to Pat.

"If you buy a stock fund and sell at a loss, you're locking in your loss. If you buy and make money, then sell, you're locking in your gain. Either way, you get to do something with your money, but if you lock in your loss, you won't have the chance to see the market improve with that stock fund."

"I think I get it. Maybe we can talk more about that later. I need to know which funds to invest in for my 20% fund," Pat responded.

Pat was always like this, wanting the straight answer right away.

"The first thing you want to keep in mind is what other investments you already have. You don't want to duplicate those same investments. You want something different. You want to diversify."

"I have a 90/10 split between S&P 500 and an International Index MSCI EAFE," he replied.

"In that case, for your 20% fund, for a young person, I would try to find a Dividend Achievers Index. This one is diversified. It does duplicate a bit of the S&P 500 but has a great return. Another great fund with a fantastic return, but not as diversified, would be the Dividend Aristocrats Index," I replied.

"I like the idea of a high return, but you've said in class, 'the higher the return, the higher the risk.' Since I'll need the money to make these dreams a reality, I should play this one a bit safer."

"Pat, you should go with the Dividend Achievers Index. It's easy to find. Companies don't call it that, but they try to match that type of index."

"What are those 'achievers' of dividend' funds?" Pat asked, seemingly confused. I chuckled at Pat's mix up.

"Dividend Achievers Index. It's the stocks that have increased their dividend payments every year, and they've done it year after year."

Pat seemed to understand, "I get it. Since a company can keep increasing how much they pay the shareholder, they must be a great company. Even when times are tough, that company still made a profit and passed it along. Not only am I getting the best companies, but I'll also be earning dividends."

"Win, win smart Pat." I retorted.

"Call your low-cost investment company and ask which fund is closest to the Dividend Achievers Index. Go with that one. You went with Vanguard, right?" I jumped on the computer to find the name, "Vanguard Dividend Appreciation Index Fund Investor Shares, VDAIX is the one you would want." I said. "Or you could go with an Exchange Traded Fund; they call it an ETF. Invesco has an ETF called Dividend Achievers." I looked up the ticker symbol for Pat, "The stock call letters are PFM. An ETF is like a share of stock, but it invests in a bunch of different companies. It's a bit tougher to contribute each month to an ETF."

Pat had a few more questions up his sleeve, "Should I just set up these investments and forget about them? You know, only checking on them occasionally, so I'm surprised at how much return I get?"

"No. Check often. When you check, you'll be motivated to continue investing. You'll see how much you've accumulated and be happy. You'll see prices drop and realize you can buy more now while the prices are low. Checking on your investments have a positive effect in your head. Check as often as you want. No real minimums or a maximum number of times you should check."

"No minimums on the number of times to check on the investments?"

"Well, one. You need to re-balance once a year in May. So, yeah, you'll want to check at least once a year. The point is, check as often as you want. The more you check, the more motivated you'll be to keep investing."

It seemed Pat was finally content with the suggestions I had offered him. "Pat, you got time for a short story?" I asked after a momentary silence sat between us.

"I bet it's about investing, isn't it?"

"It's about this 16-year-old girl. She went to a department store to get a job. They hired her to clean up at night. Mop the floors. At 16, she didn't understand the paperwork she was filling out. Sure, she knew the form was asking for her address and stuff. When she got to the part that read, do you want to invest 10% of your gross pay into a managed account with step increases each year of 1% with a maximum deduction of 20%? She didn't know what to do, but the yes box was first, so she checked it. Each year, she got a statement as to her savings. Each year she continued to mop floors in this department store. Thirty-five years went by, checking her statement once a year. She knew she was a multi-millionaire. She was one of the richest mop-slingers, and she smiled every night."

Pat thanked me for talking. He said something about mopping a floor and had to go. I found out later Pat opened a mutual fund with his low-cost investment company for his 20%. He chose the fund that followed the Dividend Achievers Index. He set up an automatic deposit from his checking account near the end of the month.

Pat's Notes

20% fund use Dividend Achievers Index – may go down in value, so only put money there I won't NEED in the next few years.

Don't forget to rebalance investments every May.

Chapter 8
How do I set up a stay out of debt fund?

Doc

A few months went by before I heard from Pat again. This time he emailed me. He wrote:

"Doc, I'm out of debt, I've got a butt load of money in my 401(k). I'm really on a roll. What should I do now?"

I responded to his email:

"Pat, you need to save up four months' worth of living expenses. If you were to lose your job, it's because the economy is in the tank. If the economy hits rock bottom, you don't want to be in a position you have no choice but to sell your mutual funds and lock in a loss."

I didn't get an email response from Pat, but a couple of days later, he called. We chit-chatted a bit, and he brought up the four months of living expenses, "Do you mean I take my 70% and multiply that by 4?"

"That's it exactly. You need to be able to access this money quickly, within about a week," I replied.

"My mom started saving money when Chad was your student. She called it her stay-out-of-debt fund. Is this kind of what you're talking about? Set up a fund that if I need the money, I can use it instead of going into debt?"

"Yes, use the money instead of going into debt. I like what your mom called it. What was it again?"

"Stay out of debt fund—pretty smart. What do you have in mind? Where should I invest this stay out of debt fund?"

"Two trains of thought here. You know that low-cost investment company you set up your 20% with, you could open another account there, either a money market or a target-date retirement account."

Pat paused. I could tell this was his way of assimilating the things I told him.

"I know about the money market, low rate of return. Not even keeping up with inflation, but the money is sure to be there. Why would you recommend a target-date fund?" He asked finally.

"A target-date fund will have a better rate of return on your money compared to a money market. If you go with the target-date fund, choose one that has a date within the next 5 - 7 years and add 30% to your 4-month figure—in case the market goes down. History has shown that even this type of fund can see a 23% drop in value. If this drop happens, you still have 100% of the money you anticipated needing."

"I can play it safe with the money market or potentially make 7% on that money in a target-date fund. I feel pretty secure in my job, and I don't mind a bit of risk. I'll make this my priority. I was going to take a trip to some islands near Spain with that money, but this sounds more important. I already have a bunch of money in my 20% fund. I'll keep putting my 20% into my Dividend Achievers fund and move it over once I reach 130% of my four months of living expenses," he said, in a firm, calculated tone.

A few weeks later, I was nibbling at my lunch of pancakes and milk at a restaurant named: BISCUITS CAFE. Weird name, but life was strange, and the restaurant was pretty close to Maher's Pub on 4th and B. The owner was an olive-skinned, heavyset woman named Serena. I had given her advice on managing her business finances. When she saw how useful my suggestions were, she invited me down for a free breakfast. A school teacher can't refuse a free meal; it's against our state licensing. The breakfast was her gracious way of thanking me. Pat called me moments later. I swallowed the small slab of pancake I had been chewing and answered his call.

"Doc, I think I need a new car," Pat said in a quavering, worried tone. He was at the auto mechanic with a vehicle problem.

"Is it the same mechanic you used to live above, in that tiny apartment?" I asked.

"Funny, thanks for reminding me of that place. No, he was a nice enough guy, and he helped us out, but he's pretty far away from where I'm living now. Here's the thing, it's going to take more money to repair my car than it's worth. Do you think I should junk it and buy a new one?" asked Pat.

"Well, Pat, do you have enough saved up in your 20% fund to buy the car you want?"

"No, sir, not even close," he sighed.

Pat had never called me sir before. The way he said it made Pat seem like a child telling his dad something his dad already knew.

"It's simple then. You can't buy another car. If fixing your car will get you back and forth from work for another six months, it's still worth fixing the old one. You don't go into debt to buy a car. A house, sure. Don't finance furniture, appliances, or engagement rings – no, no, no. You can take out a loan for a house, and that's it," I explained, understanding it wasn't as easy as I had said it.

"But what about selling the broken down car for parts and using the money I would've spent on repairs to buy a used car?" He asked, in a child's adamant tone.

"That's a possibility, Pat. But, you're buying someone else's problems. You don't know what's wrong with a used car you buy from even a friend. On the other hand, you do know what's wrong with yours. You know that if you get this one fixed, it should last you a bit longer. If you buy something you don't know anything about, the chances are high you'll also have to put money into it too. You sell your broken down car for parts, get a few hundred maybe a thousand dollars. You add what you can to this money and then come to find out you still have to come out of pocket to get your new car running. You tapped all of your 20% funds to get that newer car. To fix someone else's problems, you have to then go into debt. People don't sell cars they want to keep. Pat, stay flexible with your goals. If something bad happens, like this, deal with it, adjust your goals to accommodate the catastrophe," I advised.

"You're right. I'll stay out of debt, get the repair done, and replenish my funds over the next couple of months."

Pat's Notes

Four months' worth of living expenses for a stay out of debt fund. Take my 70% and multiply that by 4. Use this money in case of emergencies so I won't have to sell my other investments at a loss.

Use a money market or a target-date retirement account. If I use the target-date fund, I need to add 30% and choose a fund with a date within 5-7 years from now. Target date fund has a better chance of a good return compared to little profit on the money market.

Don't go into debt for anything except a house. If the car breaks down, use my stay out of debt fund or my 20% goals fund. Once paid for, replenish the money. I need to remember, repairs are expected when owning a used car.

Stay flexible with my goals.

Chapter 9

Why should I focus on meaningful goals, things that matter?

How do I determine if a purchase fits in with what matters most to me?

What's more important to me having more or building relationships?

Why am I unhappy with my situation?

Why focus on things in my control?

Doc

I am not the kind of guy who turns down a free meal. I'm not picky either. After eating the school's cafeteria food for most of my life, I was a little happy to have someone willing to pick up the tab. When Pat called and said he was buying, I didn't care where it was, and I wanted to meet. I liked helping him out. Coincidentally, it was the BISCUITS CAFE. Pat talked about the restaurant's excellent desserts and home-style grub. Pat was already sitting at a table for two when I got there. He was on the phone, and I sat and silently mouthed hello. The cafe has mostly tables and a buffet bar. It also has covered outside seating. I've been there a few times. Don't tell anyone, but the owner makes me a Reuben with fresh avocado and bacon on top.

As I was daydreaming about my special-made Reuben, Pat got off the phone and spoke up, "Doc, I'm having a hard time meeting all my goals."

The waitress came over with some coffee for both of us. I didn't order any. I think Pat told her to bring two. He continued, "I have so many things important to me, and I want them all . . . Now. My 20% fund can't handle all of them. I've reached a point where I don't feel as if I'll ever get the things that matter to me."

It took me a minute to figure out what he was saying. I was probably still thinking about my Reuben.

"Goals?" I asked. He nodded as he took a sip of coffee that was way too hot.

"What are some of the aspects of life you see value in?" I asked.

Pat thought about it for a minute, cocking his head left and right.

"My passion and focus in life would be overall health. You know fitness, exercising, eating right, and getting enough sleep."

"Tell me a goal that doesn't align with the essential elements for your life's focus?"

"Well, I guess buying this one sports car isn't aligned with what's truly important to me," he casually responded.

"Let it go."

"Riding on a train is a goal of mine. But it too doesn't affect what's important in my life."

"Let it go. You see, Pat, if you have too many essentials that are important to you, it's hard to afford them all. If you can focus on one or two true loves and know those make you happy, you'll be able to afford them. Skip spending money on things that aren't important to you. Spend that money on important things."

Pat switched gears on me, in an eerie, inordinate fashion. Usually, he gives some indication he understands, then broaches another subject.

"I want a new mattress. I stayed at a hotel and fell in love with the mattress they used. It's expensive, so I'm thinking years into the future. Should I compromise and find a cheaper mattress? Then continue to save for the one I want."

"The first question, does this goal fit in with the focus of your life? I would say yes. A good night's sleep will help with your fitness and health. The second part would be, should you compromise? No. When you compromise, you end up less happy about the outcome, and you'll still want the original item. Instead of wasting your money on things that miss the mark, save up for exactly what you want.

Serena, the heavy-set owner, charged down to us, especially attending to our orders. She smiled, said a hearty hello, and I was quick to return the gesture. I got the Reuben sandwich, with a wink to the owner so she would know to add my two exclusive extras, and Pat got a Philly Cheese Steak.

"I feel as though I'm working to earn money, just to buy more stuff," Pat said, after a bit more coffee, that had now cooled to a temperature a human could tolerate.

Our food arrived faster than I expected. I responded to Pat's worry, "We work at a job to make money. We need to afford things in life. We all need to survive. What's more important to you, stuff, or relationships? You can have a steak with people you don't like or Steak-umms with people who love you." I pointed down at his sandwich with thin meat sticking out of the edges.

Pat

Age 22, income $58,800/year; 10% fund $36,562; 20% fund $40,128; Stay out of debt fund $25,480

I ordered coffee for both of us, hoping Doc would appreciate the gesture. I remember how I felt when Lilly cared enough to know what I liked and suggested my favorite coffee shop to meet for our first . . . and last date. I knew he liked coffee and was hoping he would want some. Something the two of us had in common, black coffee. After it cooled, he drank some. I wish I had waited to take my first sip. I continued talking about reaching my goals.

"I buy things online—stuff I want. Items that'll make my life better, and they connect with my passion. For example, I bought headphones for working out. After a few weeks, I wanted something else. I feel I'm never satisfied," I said.

"Unhappiness is brought about by a focus on gaining more stuff. Once gotten, boredom, then a desire for something even grander. Instead of focusing on the things you want, put a focus on enjoying the things you already have."

My coffee went down faster than expected. I got a refill and continued:

"Doc, the other issue I seem to be facing is how other people affect me. I was at work and got a bad review. It was so bad. I thought they were going to cut my pay."

"Some things are within your control, like doing the best work possible for your boss. Other factors are outside of it, like how other people treat you and act toward you. If you have someone trying to create a change in your life, take it seriously. Do your best to make the change, but as far as trying to control their feelings about you—well, you can't. All you can do is take the suggestions and be the best employee, husband, friend possible, and hope they see the changes and then begin to treat you better."

I slowed down on drinking the coffee. For one, this cup was as hot as the first. I took a sip after it had cooled.

"I guess what you're saying is when it comes to focusing on what we can control, the future is truly affected by our efforts. If I save for retirement, I'll have a bunch of money. If I try to be the best employee possible, the boss will eventually see this and reward me for it."

I asked Doc if he wanted dessert, and he said he would pass, firmly concentrating on the things I had to say. With our conversation, he provided me with the calories I needed to continue. I had enough fuel to refocus my thoughts and keep me from dwelling on the devil, plaguing my mind.

"How will I know when I'm successful?" I asked.

"That's a straightforward question with an easy answer. You set goals. Write those goals down. Make the goal specific with exact numbers or items in your possession; this way, you can measure the outcome. Each goal needs to be something within your power. Not like winning the lottery or marrying Helen of Troy. Those are a bit out of your control. The goal needs to be relative to what's important to you. Remember, we talked about your goals need to connect with the focus of your life. Finally, you need a timestamp. With your goal being time-bound, you'll know if you were successful at meeting that goal."

"I think I remember doing this in school. I think the teacher called it a S.M.A.R.T. goal. I don't remember what each letter stood for, but it made sense at the time. Mrs. Galloway never did explain why I should write them down."

I've never seen Doc get flustered, and it was a bit surprising to see him pulling at his hair.

"Why was Galloway trying to teach SMART goals? Forget it, don't tell me. Anyway, when you write them down, you have something concrete, you can see years later. Something specific that has all the information you need on it, like the date you want to accomplish that goal."

I was curious. I didn't know a lot about Doc's home life. I knew he had kids and was married, but he was often elusive about where he lived. I thought this might be a good time to delve into finding out more about him.

"What's important to you, Doc?"

"I found that things quickly lose their appeal. Who I become and the relationships I foster will either make me happy or miserable. The choice is mine. I can push people away and ruin relationships, leaving me brokenhearted. Or I can spend time with loved ones, building personal connections, and spreading joy from the love they show me. I can become bitter and angry with the world, altering who I become and end up irritable with life. It's ultimately my decision to make a positive change on the things I can control and let the things I can't control go."

"But surely you've wanted things throughout your life?" I asked.

"I remember my wife and our first quick goal list. We had common things on it like replacing the carpet in the house, vacations, and matching laptop computers. Sure, we wanted all those things at the time. Looking back at it, the items we bought simply went down in value. They lost their appeal or simply weren't worth the cost to maintain them. For example, after we bought the carpet, we thought we needed a $1,500 vacuum. Once we bought matching laptops. What was I thinking? Why did we need our laptops to match? Within a year, I felt the need to upgrade mine with more memory. The things that brought us closer together and built memories were moments like dancing on New Year's Eve in a hotel near Pompeii, Italy. Be careful when setting your goals, Pat. Make sure they fit the most important things that are dear in your life and make sure that getting that goal won't continue to cost you money, as our carpet did."

It made me a bit sad to think about setting goals with a wife. I had no prospects. At this point, I was over Lilly and dated a bit. Nothing serious. Chad set me up with one of his coworkers. She was cute, but after a few dates, we both realized it wouldn't go anywhere. I still had anxiety issues and flashbacks to the accident. I always thought that if I could find someone to love, she would take my mind off my terrors. Doc gave me a nudge that jolted me out of my introspection.

"It might look odd, but if you tape a visual to your bathroom mirror, it'll help. Think of a goal, come up with a visual aid for that goal, and attach it to your mirror—a reminder to focus on your goal twice a day. Do what you can to make that goal into a reality. Maybe your goal is to have $5 Million by age 55. With some of that money, you'll quit your job and buy a boat. Find an image of the boat you want. Print a quality image of it and tape it to your mirror,"

I thought about one of my goals. I could picture it in my head. I had it flagged online. I got notified when the price dropped. The cost would fluctuate a bit, but never enough.

"One of my goals is a computer. I'll find the exact one I want and tape an image on my mirror. I can see how this would guide my day. I'll feel more compelled to forego less important purchases. Alright, I can focus on what's important to me. The problem I have is, some things seem to be more important than others," I said.

"Here's the thing, Pat, you'll accomplish some goals no matter what. Other goals you have written might be nice, but in truth, you don't care much about them. Keep the goals on your list that you feel you'll accomplish no matter what. Cut the goals that don't matter. You'll feel like a failure when you don't meet those goals, even though they didn't matter to you in the first place."

I hated to tell Doc this, but I needed a straight answer. I suspected he would say no, and I should deal with it myself. I figured, give it a shot. If Doc says go for it, I'll do it.

"Doc, can I have a housekeeper be one of my goals? Someone to come by maybe every other week and clean up. I hate cleaning my place. I know it sounds childish, but I can't stand it. Dust makes me sneeze, and my vacuum doesn't suck. Then again, I didn't spend $1,500 on a vacuum." I stopped to see if Doc picked up on the joke. He uttered a brief grunt and gave a lively smile. "I'm not that good at it either," I concluded, expectant.

"Outsourcing tasks you don't like doing is okay. If you don't have the equipment to take care of your yard, someone else can do it faster and better than you. You might even make more money with your regular job or a hobby, compared to paying someone to do tasks you don't like doing."

Doc

I pictured Pat sneezing in his small apartment. I've never been to his place, but I knew he lived in those apartments a block away from Maher's Pub. Pat slowly shook his head and briefly looked down at the table before his eyes darted back up towards me.

"I seem to spend so much money on stuff. I don't think I can ever save enough to turn my dreams into a reality." I think every teen, or in Pat's case, twenty-something goes through this struggle.

I nodded my head with a sense of understanding, treading down the path of empathy.

"Spend money on things that make you happy and slash the expenses of the rest. Good coffee is important to you. Even when you were my student, you would come in with coffee. How can you make the most of something that brings such joy?"

"Guess I could look into doing some research and find a coffee maker that'll brew a decent cup. Maybe I won't go with the cheapest coffee maker, because this is important to me so I can spend the extra money if needed."

I continued on the same train of thought. "You then could order a bunch of different coffees to find the brand you like best. Maybe the best won't be the most expensive."

I knocked my knuckles on the table to indicate we were changing subjects. "Pat, you already know about setting goals, but what most people don't talk about is to list common expenses that aren't important to you. At the bottom of your list of dreams, write down things that aren't important."

"Doc, do you mean cheap stuff like bottled water or more expensive items like driving a nice car?" Pat asked.

"Both. Coming up with a complete list will help you stay focused on what's important and forgo the expenses typical people spend on items they don't even care about. These are expenses in which you'll skimp. Buy lesser quality for cheap. When you think about rich people, you imagine all the beautiful things they buy. The opposite is the truth. Most millionaires are frugal. They live in a modest house, buy used cars, and they don't have over-the-top watches. About half of the people you see buying all those things aren't millionaires at all. They have a high income, but generally lack savings and investment plans to ensure future financial stability," I said.

Pat took a few minutes to thumb at his phone, writing more notes, and then he said, "It'll be a surprise to you, but I don't care about having a nice car or having the latest cell phone. Before I thought about how indifferent I am to have a nice phone, I felt compelled to buy the latest and greatest because people looked at me funny when I pulled out my cheap phone. Now that I wrote it out, I'll resist buying an expensive phone because I don't care. I realize now, from this list, I don't need to care what people think about the things that aren't even important to me. I'll get a protective case for any phone, you know, to protect it."

"Pat, I've got a bit of a story for you. Do you have a minute?" I asked, and quickly started without waiting for his response.

"There's a Sergeant friend of mine. He would tell people, 'never buy beer, wine, or liquor, not for you, not for anyone. It's fine to accept a drink from someone, but otherwise, it's a waste of money.'"

I could see Pat was contemplating my Sergeant story when I changed the subject.

"Pat, some things in life, you just can't put a value on. Some things aren't measured by a goal, however smart you think that goal is."

He paused for a second and looked back at me with a sense of confusion. "Doc, what do you mean?"

"Pat, it might seem odd, but you need to write down the intangibles important to you. These guidelines will help direct your buying patterns."

"I don't think I have any intangibles. Do you have an example?" Pat asked.

"Finding and keeping a spouse, living near your mom, positive self-image, having life-experiences, health, and strong relationships are all intangibles."

"I'm a bit confused about how these will direct my spending habits?"

"Are you going to find a spouse if you live in a tent in the woods? You won't be able to keep a wife if you don't follow and talk with your spouse regularly about 'The Five Love Languages' by Gary Chapman."

"I've considered living in a tent," Pat responded, smiling.

I got back on the subject, "Are you going to take a job or rent an apartment, that's far away from your mom? If projecting a great self-image is important, are you going to waste your money on clothes that don't look great or don't fit well? Are you going to work 60 hours a week so you can afford an expensive vehicle when spending time with friends and family are important to you? These intangibles come down to your values. If you set goals based on other people's opinions, you'll waste time, energy, and motivation in reaching success. You'll also lose focus on your true values. If you know what's important to you, you'll direct all your goals and spending habits around what's important. You won't buy things to keep up with others. You won't waste money trying to bring temporary happiness with a bag of chips from a vending machine. This new focus can wipe out your addiction to online shopping. Scratch off goals that are interfering with reaching the most important objectives."

When I felt Pat was nearly done typing his notes on his phone, I continued, "The intangibles you no longer will live with are a bit different. Write these down too. These would be things like hanging around negative people, allowing people to say bigoted remarks without you correcting them, taking verbal abuse from a 'loved' one, and negative self-talk."

"How can I get those negative people out of my life? Some of them are very close to me, like my sister."

"People have bad days from time to time. People go through seasons of depression, hurt, and self-loathing. I'm not suggesting you drop those people because of a short time they're suffering. Help them, but if you have someone in your life who is a consistent drain on your emotions tell them, 'I don't like when you talk to me like that.' If your direct and mature way of dealing with the problem doesn't work, stop talking with them. Let their phone call go to voicemail. If they invite you out, decline and don't feel obligated to give a real explanation as to why. Give them the impression you're busy at the moment. I don't want you to hurt their feelings, but we need them out of your life," I told him.

Pat just sat there staring at me with a troubled expression on his face. I guess he was thinking about the intangible setbacks he needed to get out of his life. I waved my hand in front of his face, and he jerked out of his trance.

"Pat, you've already crossed off some goals that steer you away from your main objectives in life. Now scratch off those goals you feel will take more effort than they're worth. If you aren't determined to make a goal happen at all costs, there's no need to leave it on your list. You'll end up disappointed in not making this goal a reality. Finally, drop the goals that go against your intangibles, your life-objectives," I concluded, solemnly.

"I can see your point. If I have a goal for working for Sports Illustrated, but truly feel it's an impossible task, I won't put my heart and soul into making it happen. Also, working for Sports Illustrated might go against some of my intangibles, like being close to my mom."

Pat got a phone call and had to go. He did pay for my lunch, and it was better than the cafeteria food.

Pat

Age 22, income $58,800/year; 10% fund $36,562; 20% fund $40,128; Stay out of debt fund $25,480

I bought Doc's lunch for him. I think they messed up on his sandwich. It had a bunch of other stuff on it compared to the description. But it wasn't like Doc to complain. It made me feel a little good, trying to give back a tiny bit of what he's done for me. He stepped in where my dad would've been, and gave me advice, a reason to keep living. More than investing money, he gave me something in which to focus. When I think about the numbers, the investments, even the dates mutual funds are purchased, I get a chance to stop thinking about what I did. I've disappointed my family so many times. What I've done will never be forgiven. Nicole still holds resentment against me, not as much as the twins I left fatherless, but I can see it in my sister's eyes.

I want the good life. When I first met Doc, I wanted to be rich like the movie stars, driving fancy cars and wearing branded clothing, and all the paraphernalia of the extravagant life. As I've talked with Doc about setting goals, I realize a lifestyle like that requires a substantial monthly income, and it's wasteful. If I could invest the money instead of spending it on fancy clothes that will go down in value, I'll have more options later in life. I'm letting go of the desire to compare my situation with that of others. I dropped the sports car off my list of goals.

Pat's Notes

Goals need to focus on what's important to me. Toss out those goals that don't fuel my passions.

Save up to get precisely what I want and don't compromise on cheaper solutions.

I would rather be with people who I care about, then with people who don't care about me.

Buy Steak-Umm from the grocery store.

Focus on enjoying the things I already have instead of buying more and never satisfying my addiction to shopping. Purchases lose their appeal, go down in value, and cost money to maintain.

People affecting me: job review or people who are trying to improve me, take seriously and try to do better. People talking bad about me, ignore them. Be the best boyfriend, worker, friend possible, and trust they will see the improvements over time.

Set and achieve SMART goals to feel the success of the accomplishment. Keep the goals I have in my heart as NEEDING to accomplish and drop the rest.

Find those things that make me happy, spend money there and cut the costs of those things less important.

Having things will lose their appeal. Let go of the desire to compare my belongings with what other people have.

Building and having relationships will either make me very happy or miserable, depending on the connection I develop. Positive bonds are built on doing things fun together, like trips.

Focus on making a positive change on the things I can control and let the things I can't control go.

Hire a housekeeper. Outsourcing is OK, especially if I don't have the expertise or could spend the time making money instead of doing the task.

Write down a list of immeasurable, but essential principles to guide my decisions.

Write down what crap I'm no longer going to take. Make moves to eliminate those from my life.

Chapter 10

How can I limit my opportunity costs and invest the money?

Pat

Age 24, income $58,800/year; 10% fund $59,215; 20% fund $57,599; Stay out of debt fund $27,322

I had been busy at work throughout the morning, and it seemed my boss was especially pleased with my ability to focus on mundane, boring, repetitive tasks. I succumbed to the monotony of doing one particular thing again and again. And like Doc had implied, if you want a good name, you have to do your best. Your colleagues sure as hell won't put out a good word for you. I'm not saying my coworkers had a desperate notion of wickedness that emanated from their hearts. I'm just implying—I had to put in a lot of effort to ensure my work spoke for itself.

The time was edging past twelve forty-five when I took a long, lunch break. I had to because it offered me an opportunity to see Doc. I put a call through to Doc, and he uttered his usual, friendly, and calm tone. He said he was free and would be sneaking a few nibbles of his afternoon pizza in the school's cafeteria.

I parked and walked into the school. Now, I was a visitor. I had to check-in. I remember the school fondly. Almost all of the space in the school was for students. Teachers didn't have the teacher's lounge of days past. A copy room with mailboxes was the closest room teachers got to interact with one another. I remember going to that copy room a few times when I was a student. I didn't want the diet soda they forced us to drink. They had the good stuff in there, and it was cheaper. Mrs. Galloway almost caught me once. The memories were coming back as I walked the halls toward Doc.

The Greenville high school cafeteria was vast, large enough to fit nearly the entire town. It still had signs hanging up about clubs. The teachers still had their section for eating, away from the students. The ceilings were high with plenty of natural light. The tables had were new since I was there, sprawling, long tables with low, steady adjoining chairs. The seating arrangement was specially designated to ensure there was relative peace.

I watched an obvious freshman play with his food, forming small balls of stone. I watched as he hurled one of the granite-like chicken nuggets at a friend a table away. It missed the intended target and landed in the hair of a twelfth grader. The thirteen-year-old curled into a regretful, puppy-eyed frame, and ate his meal as quietly as he could. The twelfth grader ran a hand through his hair, spoiling the puffs, pulling the chunk of all grey-meat chicken from his head. The look of surprise on his face was scraped off as he realized who threw it. The young kid gave an 'I am sooooo sorry for hitting you with a chicken nugget . . . please don't kill me' look. The older student simply uttered a smile that said, 'it's okay, I understand. It was funny.' It was as if the twelfth grader was inhaling the glimpses of adulthood. The door teens sometimes go through and become adults on the other side. Understanding accidents happen.

I saw Doc hunkered down at one of the teacher tables, alone, waiting for his share of pizza. He waved at me, and I was soon sitting beside him. We exchanged greetings, and moments later, a tall, angular woman, Mrs. Dempsey, used her long strides to get to the table quickly. Mrs. Dempsey had been working in the school cafeteria since . . . well, before my first day. I remember the first time I saw her. That's when Lilly spilled coffee on me. I still have that shirt. The day I arrived at school, I had no student number to buy my food. Mrs. Dempsey was the one who helped me out and made sure I got fed that first day. I stood up instinctively to greet her. While I stretched my hand, she curled her arms around me in a surprising embrace.

"Pat, it is so good to see you again," she said, smiling a genuine smile. You couldn't help but love Mrs. Dempsey. I reciprocated the hospitable gesture.

She hurried back and brought two more slices of pizza, and it was funny how I never realized how friendly Mrs. Dempsey was while I was a student. And for a moment, I was transcended to the naivety that graced the life of a typical student. Life imbued with carefreeness, short-sightedness, and the one I just discovered, the tendency to miss out on the little traces of love. I was smiling when she lumbered back to her stable.

Doc kept quiet all through the ordinate show of affection, and he only expressed himself in smiles and surprised sighs. We were soon ripping off gobs of pizza, and I was telling Doc about a regrettable purchase.

"It seemed like a good idea at the time. I could use a three-bulb light in the corner of one of my rooms. It's a good looking light, but it was expensive."

"How much was it?" He asked.

"With tax, I spent $289. I'm upset with myself because that $289 doesn't even go toward one of my goals."

I was hoping Doc would make me feel better about the purchase. Maybe he would tell me it'll make a good reading light or something. Instead, he descended in a short tirade that was humbling and intensified my wistfulness.

"I think I can help you feel even worse," he started, eyes peering at me.

"If you had left that money in your mutual fund account and that fund had performed like its 5-year average, you would have over $34,000 just from skipping that one purchase. It's called opportunity cost. You give up one thing for another. Like a father who wants a relationship with his kid, but has to work to pay for a new pickup truck. He could have volunteered as a coach on the kid's sports team, but instead has to work so he can have a cool lookin' truck," he concluded, his eyes steady, and mouth nibbling on the edge of a pizza crust.

My head loomed down slightly. Before I even told Doc about the purchase, I knew he was going to be dissatisfied with my purchase, and he didn't disappoint. I guess a little bit of abuse is okay. It's Doc being honest. I needed someone to be honest with me. I took a slug off the small carton of milk Mrs. Dempsey had brought, and I started to take larger bites of my pizza, allowing silence to permeate the ambiance like a guardian angel.

I finally spoke up, "Speaking of new cars, my last major car repair got me thinking about buying a newer car. Used is fine. I'll let someone else take the majority of the depreciation. Doc, I've worked too hard to save money to waste it on a luxury car that'll go down in value."

"So, you're looking for a reliable basic car that's also safe. Good thinking. Trying to save enough for a luxury car will take longer, and that luxury car will cost more to maintain, insure, and cost in taxes. This one decision will prevent you from struggling to pay for those extras out of your 70% living expenses."

I pulled up my list of goals saved on my cheap phone.

"I can add this to my goals, right?"

Doc nodded as he finished his whole-wheat brownie.

"I'll save the money in my 20% fund," I was typing on my phone while talking. "For a used, well maintained, accident-free, reliable, and safe car," I said, writing it as I said it.

I changed some of my other goals around. As I reread them, I realized some weren't as important as others and let those drop. I changed the dates on some other goals. When I combined the private sale of my older car with the savings, and rearranging goals, I felt I could get the car I wanted. Basic was acceptable; I didn't have anyone to impress. The wanna-be rich have an overwhelming desire to impress. The truly rich don't need to spend money to impress. The majority of those people who try to impress people with their fancy car, watch, high-end liquor, and wine aren't wealthy. They're posers. The ones who have money drive affordable cars, buy affordable watches, buy affordable booze, and their wine is rarely over $13 a bottle. The majority of millionaires got that way because they were frugal. They found value in all their purchases—their house was a deal, their clothes on sale, and they didn't have to reach a shelf above shoulder height to get their liquor. They found bargains and invested, as I was doing.

It was almost ten minutes to the end of my lunch break, and I thanked Doc, scurried down to the counter to thank Mrs. Dempsey, who uttered a soothing smile. I was thinking about her when I walked down the familiar halls. It was the first time I had seen someone smile at me, in kindness, since Lilly. A grim flush of cold ran up my spine.

Doc

A few weeks after our lunch, I was putting the finishing touches to a lecture I was giving a new batch of students. It was about the relative income hypothesis. The tendency for people to take up the spending culture of their neighbors. It was precisely the first discussion I had with Pat when he was a lost, depressed boy. A few students asked the same questions he had asked:

"Wouldn't my peers laugh at me if I stop maintaining the usual lifestyle?"

It reinforced the character of people: an overwhelming desire to live according to the standards and expectations of others or the desire to look ostentatious in the eyes of their seemingly wealthier neighbors. And it wasn't just a problem in children. It was in everyone. An oxymoron, I want to be rich, but instead of saving, I'll spend to make it look like I have money. I was watching the students leave when I got a phone call from Pat.

"Doc, I got a used car last week. I probably looked at over a dozen. The first two I was seriously considering, I got checked out by a mechanic. I'm glad I got 'em checked out. Even though those online vehicle-checking sites indicated they were accident-free, the mechanic said the first one had been in an accident, and the second one had $1,500 worth of needed repairs to be safely driven. This car is great, though. It's not flashy, but I always figured that after a couple of years, it wouldn't be impressive anyway."

"Pat, that's great. How about you pick me up after school on Friday. I want to talk with you about the importance of building credit."

Pat's Notes

Before purchases, think of the 'opportunity cost' if I invested the money instead of spending it, how much would it be worth? Is it worth working for X hours for me to own that product?

Before buying a used car, have it checked by a mechanic.

Cars go down in value. Spending a bunch of money on a vehicle isn't worth it.

Chapter 11

How do I build my credit rating?
Why should I build my credit rating?

Doc

Friday at Greenville High was a smooth, less event-packed day. The students steadied themselves for the extra-curricular fun. The cheerleaders cheered, the football players played, the coaches coached.

The Greenville Titans had assembled a strong basketball team for the playoffs next week, and it was the dominant discussion in the school. A gaggle of kids scuffed away around the desks of my classroom, and they hemmed and hammed loudly, inundated by the potential excitement of watching the school team at the playoff.

The soccer team trained, in what appeared to be a well-trimmed field. In actuality, the ground was artificial turf. I was walking around the campus and was approaching Cobb field - named after Charley Cobb, a business owner in the area who specialized in golf. He loved high school almost as much as I did. Each soccer player was juggling a ball. The goalkeeper was diving left and right in the goalposts, with deft, quick feet, stopping the shots kicked by one of the assistant coaches. I watched the players drop-down, doing push-ups, drenched with sweat, succumbing to the spears of yellow light from the soporific sun that stood at an angle watching their routine. I saw a kid wearing the number ten jersey, whispering something into the ear of the head coach. It briefly reminded me of my college roommate, Eddy. Fate's best child. What would he tell these kids if he were alive?

Would he fasten his glasses over his bleary, almost blind eyes and descend into an eerie blubbering?

Perhaps he would still retain his laid-back attitude, the carefreeness that festooned his short adult life. Maybe he would stave off the bitter clarity of shattered dreams and would indulge the kids in chasing their goals no matter. Perhaps he would add that we are dead without our dreams. The kids would clap, and a few tears might well up in his eyes, reinforced by the realization that he hadn't done enough to achieve his dreams. He hadn't made concerted, calculated efforts at ensuring that life went well for him. And perhaps this realization would dawn on him, and he would tell the kids not to be complacent. He would say to them not to just believe that things would sort themselves out. He would urge them to fight to save. He would ditch out the advice he never took. And when the kids start clapping again, he would wipe off his tears and peer into his own wasted life. And how even for every man before him, death would come. Death came for Eddy, possibly too soon. It is the story that plagues us all: Death comes anyway.

The boy continued talking to the coach. Closer than most teens would get to their coach's ear. I couldn't shake the memory of my roommate Eddy this time. I stopped. I sat next to a grey brick wall with a blue metal cap. When I think of misery, my mind goes to my college friend, Eddy. Blonde, curled hair, parted at the right. Eddy was a man of faith, and he would tell me about how the Bible was a collection of witty tales. I didn't think he was wrong. Only I am not the kind of guy who forms an opinion about a person based on merely what he says he is. Words are short-lived; it's a person's action that tells the real story.

Eddy was quite popular in college, a soccer player, ambipedal, and had a striker's eye for goals. Soccer wasn't the only thing he was good at—social and intelligent. I'm sure he had other talents that the world will never see.

He had a scholarship and parents who could easily afford college. Even with all the talent he was blessed with, he lacked prudence. He would frolic late into the night, attending clubs, splashing the cash. Sometimes he would return at 3:00 in the morning, knocking ferociously at the door, drunk to stupor.

In our junior year in college, Eddy started having a problem with his eyesight. He could not see objects far away. He couldn't play soccer as effectively as he should. If you can't see the ball go past your feet, you can't play. He felt miserable, forlorn, and he decided to quit the game he loved. To leave the scene when his name was still in shining lights. The coaches didn't know about his failing eyesight. They didn't understand why he stopped. It was a secret he shared with only me. On the night he quit, I spoke to him while he lay disenchanted on his single mattress.

"I can understand your frustration. It's hard to deal with the hand you've been dealt. It's hard for a man to accept that he may no longer be able to pursue his dreams, but I think it's moments like this that you have to be strong. You have to believe in your other talents," I said, trying to console him.

"Who said anything about frustration?" He mocked. "There are a bunch of other things I can do. If I decide to follow up on just my engineering degree, I would still be a success. If I decide to go into music, I'd be a great musician. I am so damn natty; I could even go into fashion design. There is hardly a way I won't succeed," Eddy was talking fast, gesticulating, nervous. "Things will straighten themselves out. I have faith in fate."

I could sense the fear, and it got me worried. The fact that a man would go about his life with no clear, definite plan. He could be whatever he wanted to be, and that seemed to be enough consolation for him.

"So, what's wrong with your eyes?" I asked.

"Please don't ask me," he retorted.

"Okay, but are you saving for corrective lenses? Or can't it be corrected?" I asked, my eyes laboring studiously at him.

"As I said, man, chill. It's not like I'm blind. Eddy cannot be blind."

I left him alone to his thoughts and new dreams, but a part of me feared the worst. I felt it was only a matter of time before his luck and chanced progress ran out.

A week later, Eddy could barely see a textbook. The coach of the soccer team, figuring out what was going on, visited our apartment with a pair of glasses. I still remember the look Eddy gave me, once he had put them on, and could see past the blurry white fog that obscured his vision. Those eyes said, I told you so. And it seemed he was right again when he said fate had his best interest at heart. He thanked the coach and watched him leave.

Three days later, when he couldn't navigate his way from the bathroom without his glasses, I spoke to him again about his sight. I was severely concerned. It was a terrible condition, that kept me thinking: what could become of him if he lost the glasses or broke them. "Bro, I think you have to take your plight a little seriously. You can barely see without your glasses. I think since you still get a lot of extra bucks, you should consider saving towards buying another pair before those get damaged. Or better still, stop going out for parties, mate. It's dangerous for you. I've seen you trying to go without your glasses when you're out." His towel was still weaved around his waist. Eddy gave me a leery-eyed look with a dangerous combination of anger and hate. I was trying to help him. He was mad. I look back at it as an adult and realize he wasn't necessarily furious at me but upset at the situation.

I found myself cringing away from him, and this was the first time Eddy had given me such a menacing look. It unbuckled my level of comfortability around him, and it seemed for the first time, Eddy felt he had had plenty of me— enough of my caution. Fate's best friend had had enough of my reservation and how I had a pessimistic approach to the trajectory of his life. He told me things that day that he had never told anyone. And he suggested he would consider moving out of our apartment. It was a disturbing tirade. Words that threw hushed and baleful thrusts and blows. I plopped down on my bed and watched him look for his clothes with an older man's rheumy eyes. He stormed out, slamming the door behind him.

As he left, he still had that menacing look on his face. He didn't answer me as I called out, and scowled at me when his eyes did coincidentally meet mine. He wore denim blue jeans and a blue tee-shirt. I knew he was going to the club. He was going to do what he had to do because he was Eddy for fate's sake.

Fate always spared a rosy thought for the nightmares that confronted Eddy day and night. I watched him leave, and a part of me felt a danger lurked in the offing. The same piece that wrote Frank, the drunk at the bar, off before he had even begun his story. The time was drifting past nine forty when I decided I would go to the club. Eddy needed guidance, help. He needed protection from the delusion he had instilled. I stormed down in long strides across a stone-strewn trail in slacks too thin for this cold night. I remember how a rush of gooseflesh rapped through my arms, punctuating my reservation. When I got to the club, a student club that didn't have the bouncers that exemplified the more orthodox clubs, I asked for Eddy. A guy with a freckled face was laughing as soon as I had asked.

"That loser," he said.

"Where is he?" I asked

"I don't know. He picked a fight with a heavyset guy. And the guy knocked his glasses off his face. The glasses broke, still laying over there." He pointed toward the floor where high heels were dancing.

"Shut up," I bawled, a rush of anger running up my mind. I felt the bottom of my stomach go sticky and warm. I was contending with a combination of fear and anger.

"Where the hell is he?" I asked, seizing the collar of his shirt.

"I don't know," he stammered.

"He went out. It looked like he went home."

I stormed out of the club, and lumbered down the road, looking for the faintest trace of Eddy. Moments later, I heard the screeching sound of reversing tires. The car, a BMW, sped away. A body sprawled on the road. I rallied down, and there was Eddy, fate's favorite boy.

He was lying on a pool of blood, and when I got there, I raised his head and screamed for help, my voice overwhelmed by the dissenting voice of techno music.

"I am . . . I am . . . so . . . sorry," Eddy stammered, his eyes staring emptily at me.

"I thought . . . I thought," Eddy continued, as he coughed out a mouthful of blood.

"I thought . . . I would fate would be on my side," he said.

It was the final message Eddy had for the world, seemingly disillusioned at death.

It took me years to figure out Eddy's final utterances meant: fate favors those who are diligent in the things they do.

My mind raced away from my college days on the east coast. I thought about Pat. And how the memories of watching a man die from his own mischief could hunt him when no one was looking. A man plucked from his youth by a hit and run. It was a horrible memory I rarely share because I still feel partially to blame. I could have done more. I've now dedicated myself to helping young men and women beat fate because I chose not to help Eddy as he walked out that door. Perhaps unlike Frank and Eddy, I will support a golden son rise on the horizon for Pat and others.

I staggered away from the diverse frolicking on the soccer field. I was putting behind me the aptness of everyone's easy succumbing to distraction. All the distractions I too used to keep the sad memories away. For the alcoholics at the Maher's Pub, it was the strong drinks, the giant slugs that quickened an over-appropriate inebriation. For the football kids, it was football. For Eddy, it was the belief that somehow things would turn out fine. For Pat, it was finance, the desire to be prudent. The quest to lay the foundation that would cut a swathe through a moment of austerity. He may not have realized it, but Pat was trying to ensure his future so that he wouldn't end up like his father. It was an unknown force that drove him towards frugality, and the pursuit of happiness . . . maybe, someday.

A car stumbled to a halt in the coal-tarred circular driveway in front of the school. When the driver's window wound down, it was Pat. He waved his omnipresent wave, two fingers dangling in the air. I lumbered away from the arch and the memories of Eddy, from the energy of the soccer kids. Helping people was my distraction. I was walking toward the diversion that kept the stress at bay. Pat was standing outside the car when I got there, smiling in perfect dentition. It was a small, clean car, exactly what I could have recommended.

"Good afternoon, Doc," he said, stretching a hand.

"Good afternoon," I retorted, shaking his hand with a smile.

"It is a nice car, Pat. And it seems you got a bargain with this one," I said a bit too loud.

"I would say it is a fair price," he replied, smiling.

"Damn! I miss being a student," he blurted, eyes peering straight at the soccer players. "How for Christ's sake did I not partake in stuff like this?" He asked theatrically.

"Well, finance has always been your finest hobby," I laughed.

Pat accommodated a split second silence and started laughing.

Pat swerved back to the direction from where he had come, zooming off to the main road.

Pat swiveled his eyes at me, and it seemed he had only just understood what I had said earlier. He now realized that we were both alike, teacher and student, entwined together by the dictates of finance. It seemed he got it, and he uttered a quick smile, taking a lurch to the left onto Boones Ferry Rd.

"How long have you been working?" I asked, looking through the window, watching how everything along the road seemed to speed backward as we snaked down the hill.

"Since I was 17, but I got that job with the 401(k) seven years ago, pretty steady for a while now," he retorted, smiling.

I jumped right into it. It was nice to see Pat in his new car, but I didn't want this purchase to make his head big. I didn't want it to be a different distraction saddled with traces of extravagance.

"If you don't have a credit card yet, apply for one. Look for a no annual fee credit card from one of the major lending companies. Avoid prepaid cards. The major credit card companies will base their acceptance of you on a few factors. Here, you don't lie, but you also don't down-play each one, be firm, and confident about each answer. How much money do you make? How long you've lived at the same address, how stable does your job sound, how professional is your job?"

I paused as Pat thought for a moment, jerking his head as if he was trying to summon something from the depth of his mind.

"I already have one card, remember? I had some debt on it, but Doc I paid all that off already, just like we talked about."

I could see he missed having a father figure in his life. He needed someone on his side, someone who could express pride in how his son had grown up. At this moment, I wondered how much anguish Pat was living with. I knew he felt terrible about the accident, but he rarely talked about it or even his feelings. I guess this former student knew I wasn't a counselor, or maybe that's why he liked talking with me. I wasn't a counselor who would insist he atones or makes amends for his action. I was there for him to open up choices for his life, financially. As I was lost in thought, wondering what more I could do to help dispel the feeling of aloneness, of grief he mingled with, he suddenly spoke up:

"My next card, I won't lie, but instead of telling them I'm a stock boy, I'll say inventory manager."

I felt confused and had to refocus, think about what Pat was saying. I replayed the tape in my head and realized he was making a joke.

"Funny, something like that. On your first card, call the credit card company and get a credit increase even if you don't need more money. That credit increase will improve your credit rating and help you get another credit card. Use your card, occasionally put on large purchases. All your purchases, large or small, needs to be paid off when the bill comes in. Those large purchases will prove you can borrow and pay back larger amounts of money. You never want to go over 70% of your maximum. And hitting that 70% of credit card utilization would only happen occasionally, maybe once. Normally, you want to keep the credit utilization below 25%. Going upward of 70% of your available credit will hurt your credit score. But using a large amount of money and paying it off will help your score. So, on a monthly cycle, keep it below 25%. No matter what, always pay it off in full each month," I admonished, eyes fixed on him.

"Emmm . . . I am trying to digest what you just said. Are you saying if I can prove someone trusts me with money, my credit rating will go up, and more people will trust me with money?"

"Yeah, that's it. The bottom line, you want three credit cards taken out about a year apart. Each credit card will have at least one monthly bill on it, like an electricity bill. This way, the credit card stays active and continues to report to the credit burrows that you're trustworthy with money."

"Why take them out a year apart?"

"Credit card companies report the most you've ever spent with them—the more money you've taken out and paid back, the higher your credit rating. A year is a good amount of time for you to pay bills, buy gifts, live life on that card. A year will bring your maximum close to that 70% mark, proving you can borrow money and pay it back." I could picture Pat buying coffee, so much coffee he nearly hits his maximum.

I continued, "Put one monthly bill on the card you currently have. Once you get the second card, add all your monthly bills onto the new card, like gas, water, cable, cell phone. Leave just one small monthly charge on your old card. Set up with your bank to automatically pay your credit card bills in full every month."

"But what if I don't have enough money in the account before it automatically gets paid?"

"Before payment goes through, you'll get notification of the amount and be able to record it. Make sure you have enough money to pay the bill. Always pay the balance in full, everything you owe."

"Will this help improve my credit score and reduce interest charges?" Pat asked inquisitively.

"Paying your bill in full each month will eliminate interest charges. If you're ever in the situation, you didn't pay the bill in full, pay extra to eliminate that rolling interest they charge you. To eliminate the interest, you might have to stop using the card, then pay extra. You see, when the interest starts, it's added every day. If you call today and ask how much you owe, you'll owe even more tomorrow. If you keep charging on the card, those charges will also incur interest. Credit cards are a great tool. If you pay the balance in full every month, you use them interest-free. Whatever you do, never pay it late. Paying it late will surely hurt your credit score."

"What if I want to take a big trip and pay off the trip over a few years?"

I could tell Pat was serious. I've heard of young people wanting to go out of the country as a group. Spend time on the beach. I can see why people get caught in this trap. If your friends can afford a trip, why not you?

"One of the costliest mistakes people make is having a balance on their credit card. If you take a trip and spend $4,000 on the trip, pay the minimum payment, and never put anything else on that card, It'll take you nearly seven years to pay it off. The trip will ultimately cost you $6,600."

"The trip I'm thinking about isn't worth that much money." Pat was nodding and added, "I guess I won't have a running balance on my card. It costs too much interest. It'll help if I know how much I spend and still be able to pay it off each month," he said.

I wanted to stress it again, leave no stone unturned. "Also remember never put more than 70% of the maximum on your card. Getting close to 70% of your max will hurt your credit score. It's best to keep the monthly charges below 25% of the maximum. To help, you can ask for a high limit. Don't be shy at asking for some ludicrously high amount. They can always say no," I said, jerking out of a reclining position.

"I guess I can find my maximum by pulling up my account online. Is there anything else I should be doing to improve my credit?" Pat asked.

"Pull a free credit report from all three agencies. Look for negative and wrong information on the file. You might find information about people with similar names to you. You'll look for accounts marked as delinquent when you paid on time. If something is wrong, formally dispute those charges. Compare the line items against your checking account, looking for regular payments to places like rent and utilities, you've paid on time and may not be reported. Get a letter from those places indicating you've paid on time and for the length of time. Mail a copy to each agency to have that good credit added to your file. If one agency is reporting something positive about your credit, make sure the other agencies know about that too. For example, if you took out a loan for an expensive light for the corner of your room, it's listed by Equifax, but not Experian, contact Experian and be able to show them the Equifax information."

"I didn't take out a loan for that light, but it was a costly mistake. All this seems like a lot of effort. I'm starting to wonder if it's worth it," Pat retorted.

As we made a left turn to get onto highway 5, I ventured into a theatrical tirade, dilating my eyes, in a solemn sense of purpose.

"It'll be worth it. Your credit history will dictate how cheaply you can borrow money. You only borrow money on a house. But if your credit score is low, you'll have to pay more interest, even on the house, around .25% more."

"That's not that much, all this work, for a quarter of a percent?"

"Let's look at a loan comparison calculator for a mortgage." As we were now off the winding roads and on a newly paved highway, I pulled out my phone and started to type. "On a decent house in your area, you're looking at over $12,000 in extra interest payments."

Pat jerked his head backward.

"OK, you've convinced me. What else can I do to improve the records and make my credit score better?"

"Send them a letter. Tell each agency they're missing information about you and you want them to include it. You'll need to tell them your legal name and social security number. Then you add a list of items you want them to update along with photocopies of proof: date of birth, telephone number, current and past employment, and previous addresses. Your likelihood of getting qualified for a loan dramatically improves when creditors can see you won't skip town, and your life has stability," I admonished.

"How else can I prove that my current financial life is stable?" Pat asked.

"Open both a checking account and savings account. Credit unions are typically better places than banks. Creditors like seeing both a checking and savings accounts. It shows you're saving money, and if they sue you for the money you owe, they have an idea you have some funds to collect. Here's your warning, if you don't have the money, don't write a check out of your account. Bouncing a check to a creditor or utility company will show up on your credit report as a missed or late payment, negatively impacting your credit history."

"I already have a checking account at a bank," he retorted.

"Go in person to the bank. Ask to speak to a loan officer. Ask her if you can get a 0% credit-builder loan."

"What's a credit-builder loan?" Pat asked.

"Typically, banks won't offer a 0% credit-builder loan, but a credit union might. You could go to a credit union and open an account. The premise of a credit builder loan is the credit union gives you a loan. The money goes in a savings account, and each month the loan is paid back automatically from the savings account. You don't even have access to the money. The loan and consistent pay-back show you're responsible and builds your credit even further."

"Now, I like that one. Easy enough, especially if I can find one that doesn't even charge me interest," Pat smiled, winking.

Pat

Age 24, income $58,800/year; 10% fund $59,215; 20% fund $57,599; Stay out of debt fund $27,322

I was gradually becoming a man of little loopholes. I was patching things up, subscribing to the betterment of my future. It was the least I could do. Only there was an aloneness that came with this frugal life. I had a few activities I could incorporate into my schedule. If I wasn't at work, I was chit-chatting with Doc. It never really bothered me, but I had the faintest feeling that I could be bothering Doc. I mean, surely he had other things to do, and my being always there could inhibit his relationship with other people. Only the more I dallied in this introspection, the more I felt we were alike. There were times he would say something, and I would feel he had dragged it out of my thoughts. So it was easy to think if I missed him, then surely, he missed me too. It had been a while since our car ride, and I missed talking with Doc, so I called him.

"Hey, Doc, How are you?"

"I'm doing alright. Funny this year in class, I have two Pats. One Patrick and then another who likes to be called Pat. What's on your mind?"

I was glad he seemed happy to talk to me. "A buddy of mine called up and asked if I would co-sign on loan. He's good . . ."

Doc cut me off, "No! You are highly likely to hurt your credit and destroy the friendship."

Pat retorted, "What if he hates me for not helping him out."

"Then you don't have a real friendship anyway. Your buddy should understand. You don't need to give any reasons beyond 'I'm not in a position to help you out.' He should let it go, and you'll remain friends."

I didn't like Doc's answer, but he was right. I talked with the friend and just explained that I wasn't in a position to help him out. I guess that's not lying. My view is, I don't want my credit ruined, and besides, all my money is in stock funds.

My new car still smelled good. I kept it clean. I know how ladies don't like a guy with a dirty car. Nicole motivated me to keep it clean. Her horns would grow out of her head, and her forked tongue would fling spit on me as she chastised me about a dirty car. Also, Nicole tried to set me up with one of her friend's little sister, but that girl was too greedy. She put down my car for one. She ordered a Grey-Goose Martini and made me pay for it.

The next time I called Doc, I was in my car again. I had already increased my credit limit on my first card and had some automatic monthly charges. I was thinking of opening another credit card. I figured it was a good time to do it. If one card helped my credit, two would be even better. I wanted to build my credit to as high as possible.

"Hey Doc, I checked my credit rating, and it could be higher. Like we were talking about, if I can have a better credit rating, I can save on interest." I already knew the answer from our car ride, but I needed a distraction. I was feeling overwhelmed by my thoughts. I figured Doc could pull my head away from thinking about the troubles I've caused. I continued, already knowing the answer, "Will opening another card help my credit rating?"

Doc seemed a bit distracted this time. He sounded as if he was fumbling around with stuff.

"Pat, this is a great question. I'm in the middle of class and would like the students to hear your question. Can I put you on speakerphone for the class to hear us?" I was taken back. I got a bit nervous. I thought back to giving oral presentations in Mrs. Galloway's class.

"Sure, I guess," I responded, reluctantly.

"This will be great," Doc said as I heard some chit chat from the students in the background.

"Repeat the question so everyone can hear."

I was scared. All I could think about was how Mrs. Galloway used to put me on the spot. Make me do oral presentations in front of the class. I skipped school for a week because of her. I got up the courage, thinking I was just on the phone. I repeated the question. By the time I was done asking the question, I had lost my focus on where I was, where I was driving. I was cruising safely, but I didn't use my usual route. I took a wrong turn in my nervousness. Before I could realize it, I was driving over the bridge where I caused the accident. I always avoided that bridge. Thinking about it, seeing it, going over or even under it, brought back memories that were haunting. I found myself traveling in a reverie, to that fateful day. Pushing the barrel up over the wall like I didn't care what happen. I was cringing from the wild screams of the woman who first saw the dead man. I saw her point at me, and this time, her hands were different. Her fingers had become talons, long menacing talons that gently whispered the story of a devil. The light of the day faded away, and it became dark. Her teeth were long and sharp like Dracula. I had started bolting away from her, from the darkness, from the clutches of death. I fell against a wall that had appeared suddenly on the road, a retaining wall that looked like it belonged in a prison. A ray of white light flashed before my eyes, almost blinding me. I could hear platter of feet, and when the light faded away, I saw the twins staring down at me. They had bleary eyes, and I cringed away from them.

"We are now without a father because of you," they said.

The words seemed familiar. It sounded like Doc, God! It sounded like Doc

"You killed our father. Our lives will never be the same," they hollered, simultaneously.

I was jolted out of my trance by the blaring sound of horns. My car stumbled to a halt at the side of the road. I flung my mind back to finance, the antidote to my grief, and I started to think Doc would put me on the spot. Ask me questions I couldn't answer. My mind began to calm as I thought about Doc and credit cards. He never put me on the spot during class, and I knew he wouldn't now. Doc was talking, half to me, half to the class. His explanation, his voice was pushing my mind away from my bridge induced delusion.

"Getting a second credit card will hurt your credit rating, to begin with, but will help in the long run. Initially, it drops a bit, but then it raises back up. About two months before you find another no-fee card, call your first card company and ask for a credit limit increase. Having a high credit limit will help your credit rating and give you a better chance of getting another card." Focusing on Doc's voice, talking about credit cards was soothing. It was removing the pain. "When you call, you'll want to be prepared for some of their questions with true and specific answers without hesitation. For example, they'll ask you why you need the credit limit increase, your income, do you own your home or rent. The key here isn't to lie, but to have concise answers when asked."

His words calmed me down, but I can't remember how the conversation went from there. I think I responded to something that made sense and then had to go. I've had panic attacks before, but not one that made me stop driving, pull over, and use techniques I'd read about online.

I made it home, but I didn't remember the drive. I decided to focus on the credit card stuff instead of the panic attack or the bridge. It had been a while since I opened my first credit card. The holidays were coming up. I was going to spend a good bit of money out of my 20% fund. Being able to give beautiful gifts was one of my goals. I knew I could pay off a large balance. I did as Doc had suggested. I researched different no-fee credit cards. The interest rate didn't matter to me because I wasn't going to pay interest anyway. I was going to pay the balance in full each month. I liked the idea of cash back. I little perk for Pat.

Exactly two months after I got my credit limit raised on my first card, I got card number two in the mail. I transferred all but one of my monthly bills onto this new card. It's funny, and Doc didn't even suggest this, but as I was transferring those charges to the latest card, I realized I had some monthly expenses I didn't need. I canceled those services. I'm sure Doc would be proud of my frugality. I then set up another automatic payment to pay this card off in full each month. I did as Doc suggested, I stopped using the old card except for that one monthly charge. It was a small charge, about $12 a month. On that old card, I made sure the automatic payment from my checking account was still in place to pay the balance in full every month.

About 13 months went by, and I did it all over again. This time I was planning another big purchase, this time for myself. I was going to use the money in my 20% fund. My first step was calling the second credit card company and ask for a credit increase. I asked for a massive jump in my limit but didn't get it. I did, however, double my credit limit. Again, I wasn't planning on exceeding 70% of my credit limit when buying the significant purchase, and I knew I could pay it off in full at the end of the month.

After I got my credit limit raise, I applied for my third and final no annual fee card. This card had a high credit limit out-the-gate. I transferred all but one of my monthly bills onto this new card. Again, I searched for monthly charges I didn't need. I was more careful this last year about signing up for those small monthly charges but still found two. I canceled them. I had already set up an automatic bill payment on the first and second cards, so they were sure to be paid in full each month. I did a similar automatic set up for this card too.

I didn't even call Doc. I just did it on my own. I pulled all three free credit reports. This time, I didn't dispute any harmful or wrong information, but instead formally requested the credit bureaus cancel and remove any disputes I'd put into place. I started to do my own research. Online searches are fantastic. I read that removing disputes allows for more massive loans to be processed. I didn't tell Doc yet, but I had intentions of buying a house soon. I also wanted to see what was in the reports that might look negative that I could explain as I was applying for my home loan. Part of the reason I was doing research, was because thinking about finance stuff, relaxed me. I hadn't talked with Doc, and I needed more information to focus. Thinking about this stuff helped me sleep. They called it insomnia. I called it anxiety from the accident I caused.

I was still a long way out from buying the house. My big trip would come first. I was in a funk. Looking back at it, I was depressed. I didn't know why at the time. I figured it was because I didn't have a girlfriend. Now, I realize that wasn't the reason. I had the money saved—my retirement fund was looking healthy. I figured a trip could snap me away from the dark cloud over my head.

I called the third credit card company a year after I got it and asked for a credit increase. This time I was going to make one of my big goals a reality, I was traveling to the Balearic Islands off the east coast of Spain. I purposely chose this card because it had a reasonable exchange rate for the currency. The place was great. Parties at night, beach during the day.

My flight home would be time-consuming—multiple stops. The first was in Manchester, England. It felt like a short flight from the tiny airport in Ibiza to Manchester. The layover was short. The next leg of the journey would be to New York. I had boarded the plane in Manchester, and then it seemed the person who would sit by me was taking too long to come. My head was loomed down out of exhaustion when I saw a silver, soft-soled shoe standing by my side, a hand tapped me, and when I raised my face, it was Lilly. It was an emotional moment for me, and I could feel my heart speeding up in my chest. She stood there petrified, and she didn't notice I had gotten up to make room for her to pass. It felt like right there, cupid hovered above us, holding his breath, saturated by the inclinations of two lost loves, seemingly far away from the shore where they first found true love. And for Cupid, he perhaps felt it was not a moment to shoot down arrows of love. It was pointless because we already had love. So he hovered up there watching. The rest of the passengers were sure to wonder why the two of us were still standing. The plane was resolving its legs to begin his ascendancy to the sky, and we were still standing there. No one said anything, it wasn't their business, it wasn't their distraction, and it was a moment to be watched, silently, with hushed sibilant sighs, and gawks, and hisses, and resignation.

"We are to move. You should all sit down," the air hostess reminded us. On the plane, no one cared about true love, especially one that was silent, two people frozen like adventurers in Antarctica. They weren't used to the kind of love that sang its rendition with the sound of silence. It was novel. It was us.

I watched Lilly unfreeze with a smile, she made her way graciously into her seat, and once she plopped herself down, a trickle of tears welled up her eyes. Perhaps if I looked into my eyes, I would have seen the same thing. My eyes, indeed, had gone rheumy, and it resonated with the kind of love I had for her—a love that was compatible with my introversion. Briefly, I transcended to that afternoon at Cafe Marzocca. I could picture the boy she was initially sitting with at the cafe. I remembered how she excused him when I arrived—schooling the boy on the trajectory of her life. When I first joined her outside the coffee shop, she seemed mesmerized with the awkward preachment of a friend, a classmate she ate lunch with daily, a guy who she spilled coffee on . .

. minutes away from being a stranger. I could remember her eyes in the sun as columns of clouds drifted past like ships at sea. I remember that regrettable day. She saw the wild held within my mind, the noticeable fluttering in my heart. She saw all of me . . . she saw too much. As long as I was there, sitting outside the cafe with her, no other conversation mattered. I revealed my secrets, the accidental murder of an unsuspecting man, and the grief and sadness that emanated from my heart. That afternoon, we parted like two sections of a river drifting into the sea. We parted slowly, not realizing we were floating further from each other like falling leaves.

My mind snapped back into the plane, away from the cafe. I sat next to Lilly silently as I remembered how she flung me away like the specks of coffee grounds left in the bottom of a cup. The silence was better. The airplane seats were uncomfortably close. I tried to glance over and read Lilly's face. I thought I saw a mingling of disgust, revulsion, and trepidation with an undercurrent scent of love's death.

There was barely anything we could say to one another. Barely any quick antidote to the conjoined hollows of our hearts, and inadvertently, we just sat there, exchanging glances again and again. Eyes communicated, hearts bled, but mouths kept quiet. 'The most important things are the hardest to say.' The little things like I miss you, I have never been the same without you, I have not found love since you left me. The little things escaped us. The plane was wistful and flew smoothly through the rolls of blue, cumulus clouds, and it was severely silent. There was no hint of familiarity, no forced spewing of kind words, no nothing—just silence. Four eyes were looking and looking and looking at themselves, and it seemed enough.

When the plane touched down in New York, I was already mingling with a combination of sadness and anger. I was sad because I had never tried to reach out to her after all these years. Mad at myself to allow 8 hours of sitting next to her to slip by. Of course, she left me, but I could have done more. I could have tried to make her youthful heart understand. And I accommodated a wave of anger that emanated from the withdrawal of my feelings, the inability to express myself when I finally had a chance to reach out—8 hours of opportunity. I was such an idiot.

After we landed in New York, folks started getting off the plane when I gave Lilly an almost, impalpable nudge, she turned:

"I am returning from a trip to the United Kingdom," she said glibly. "I was invited to give a presentation. And I don't know how to say this . . . you . . . I don't . . . under . . ."

She went about her eerie utterances bizarrely, elliptically, fascinated by a mesmerism she could not resist.

"It's okay," I said.

"I live near North State Street," I blurted.

It seemed deep within us. We knew we didn't have to say hello, how are you, and other trivialities. Our eyes already did that.

"Oh! It is just about forty-five minutes from my place," she retorted.

"I live down Pierce Road."

The streets where we lived should be the least of our worries, but the most important things were the hardest to say.

When we were waiting for the connecting flight in New York, headed to Portland, we talked. I watched. I listened. Her adult beauty accentuated by firm cheekbones, and her hair cascaded neatly down her neck. I had fallen in love again. And it was time to be bold. I wanted Lilly back in my life. I wanted to love her and be loved. I needed courage. It was time to straighten out the mistakes of the past, and I summoned a strength both immense and frightening. As we boarded the next leg of our journey, we weren't sitting next to one another this time. I charged down to her row, and I asked the older skinny man sitting next to her if he would prefer my window seat. He peered at me, and I uttered a leery-eyed look at him, spontaneously and intense.

"Do you mind, ma'am?" he asked Lilly.

"I don't mind," Lilly retorted, smiling.

The thin man saw the need for love in my eyes and sprung up with no effort, and dawdled down to the seat I had vacated. A part of me briefly imagined what I would have done if he had refused. And it was easy to imagine myself asking to talk with him privately, explaining my situation and then handing him a $100 bill. Money buys choices.

I plopped down once again beside Lilly, and once again, I was staring at the person who continually put me in a vicious circle. At first, I was worried about starting up a conversation, thinking Lilly would bring up bad memories. How she left me in a terrible state. I was mingling with this thought when Lilly gave me a nudge:

"Pat, I've wanted to get in touch with you for so long. I'm sorry. The way I treated you was wrong. The things I said to you were a flat-out mistake on my part," she said, tears welling up her eyes.

"Wow, I didn't expect that. I don't know what to say, thanks. Why the change of heart?" I asked, curious, and happy.

"While in college, I took a psychology class. One of the focuses we had was the accidental killer. Those people who caused an accident and someone died as a result. You've probably been dealing with sorrow, shame, and even post-traumatic stress syndrome. The teacher opened my eyes as to how you must be feeling. I even went to the teacher during office hours to talk about it."

"I never thought I could be dealing with post-traumatic stress. I just felt guilty. And sometimes I would see the vivid image of the accident, and it gets fiercer these days," I explained.

"Right, that's what the teacher was saying too. I made it worse. I can't believe I said those words," Lilly stammered, dribbles of tears trickling down her eyes. Her face moved like a bar stool that could swivel. She looked out the window and tried to hide the waterworks, but I could see her emotions welling up. I could feel it because the performance of our hearts was already interwoven. I touched her hair, ran a hand through it, and she held my hand to her head, a silent gesture that spoke of acceptance, forgiveness, and the willingness to try again. There was a spare, neat, hanky in my pocket, I brought it out, and waved it to her face. She grabbed it politely, her face still staring at the clouds below. When she had wiped her face, she cocked her head forward, uttered a theatrical smile, and said:

"How have you been?"

I smiled the kind of smile Doc would use to show he cared, and I was inadvertently holding her hands when I said, "I have been fine. A little problem now and again, but I've had an indispensable company in Doc. So I would say I am managing just fine."

"Wow! Are you still in touch with Doc? I miss our language arts teacher, Mrs. Galloway. I miss The Titans. But I guess absence makes the heart grow fonder," she said, her hand looped down from my shoulder.

We talked for the entire trip home. I thought I was going to sleep after two weeks of parties, but talking with Lilly was well worth missing some shut-eye. She told me about what she did after high school and the job she now had. We exchanged phone numbers and parted ways.

The cost of the trip wasn't even close to 70% of the credit limit. I'm not trying to brag, but even with my regular expenses, my monthly bill was less than 30% of the available balance on that third card alone.

I continued to use the three cards to build my FICO score. See, having a small charge on the cards I don't use very often forced them to stay open and continue reporting positive information about me to the credit bureaus. None of the cards had a reason to close the account because they were active every month, the first two only had one transaction each, and the third was regular spending and monthly bills.

Once I got some sleep, I checked my phone. I had a text from Lilly. I didn't expect her to reach out. A smile curled around my face while I read it. She asked me out on a date. We didn't even talk about my relationship status or hers.

Lilly

I had an ambivalent feel throughout my stay at the University of Maine. I knew it was a path I had to follow, and perhaps I was happy that I was finally fulfilling a dream. Only, there were times I mingled with tinges of regret. I felt terrible about how I had ended my relationship with Pat. I had always thought he was a great guy, and I knew he loved me as much as he could afford. I saw how his eyes followed the ripple of his smile when he was with me. It was the intangible things that separated true love from ordinary love. And while I was in Maine, I realized how grave my mistake was.

I also remember talking with my mom as a teenage girl the same night Pat told me about what he did. I was venting as usual to her. Typically, she wouldn't offer any advice. That time she spoke up, and I shut her down. I got through the entire story. I told her the awful things I said. My mom's response was, 'I have a different take on the situation. Do you want to hear it?' I told her no, and she kept her mouth shut. Maybe that little comment by my mother, years ago, kept my eyes open to the possibility I was wrong.

I regretted my reactions to the news of his accidental escapade. At the time, I didn't know enough to understand how to react. And when I had known better, I wished I could take it all back. I wanted I could have empathized with him. There were times I imagined the things he would be going through, and it was in such moments I wished I could meet him again. I had lost his contact, and it was hard to tell if he still lived in Portland. I harbored the thought that he might have relocated. Portland offered him too much grieving, and perhaps I could have been the one to make him feel at home in a new city.

I wanted to take him away from the pain. Save him from himself. And when I was afflicted with this thought, how I could be an accessory to the misery he could be contending with, it broke my heart. And I had resigned myself to the possibility that I would never meet him again. I had made a few efforts to get in touch with Doc. I figured they might have had a connection, and I felt if anyone knew where he had relocated to, it would be him. Only my efforts were not successful. And since I couldn't leave Maine because of my commitments during college, I nurtured the thought of starting my adult life back in Portland.

Once I graduated from college, life started to run a marathon. I was soon overwhelmed with a job that had a lot of travel. And even though my permanent residence was Portland, I was hardly there, and it inadvertently hindered my plans of searching for Pat. When I saw Pat on the airplane, I felt my heart freeze. It was funny how the stuff of dreams had an inebriating quality, and it was what had happened to me. There was hardly anything I could say at first, and then fate offered us another chance, and there was no way I could throw it all away again. I am so glad I got a chance to talk with him.

Damn, he was good looking. His hair was still a mess. He had put on some weight and muscle. Not some muscle-rippling god, just fit. Cute. I asked him out on a date. I didn't have the guts to call him, so I texted it over. 'I want to go on a date with you. Get to know you again, rekindle our relationship. Are you free Friday or Saturday.' I've never been that bold before. It was easy to think a guy like Pat already had a girlfriend. I was going to steal him away from her. It was destiny that we met, and I wasn't going to let anything stand in my way of being with my soul-mate.

Pat responded to my text. 'Sure, let's meet on Saturday. I'll pick you up at 6 PM. Text me your address.'

I hadn't been excited like that in forever. I didn't know where we were going yet and didn't care. I had a date with Pat.

Pat's Notes

To build credit, check my credit report. Make corrections. Add information.

Take out credit card one. Add monthly bills to that card. Set up an automatic payment. Pay it off in FULL every month. After a year, ask for a credit increase. Remove monthly charges I no longer use.

Take out credit card two. Repeat the same process, leaving one monthly bill on a credit card one.

Take out credit card three. Keep using the first two cards, but only with one small bill on each. Set up automatic payments on all three and make sure they are ALL paid in FULL each month.

Chapter 12

Is homeownership a good investment?
What is the maximum house payment I can afford?

Doc

When I learned about Pat's big trip, I was indifferent about it. It had been something he'd always wanted to do. Trying to change someone's mind about something important to them takes frugality too far. If I didn't give Pat the freedom to make his own choices, I wouldn't be a good teacher. Besides, he believed he had it figured out. Only I missed his company when he was away. We had gone long spells without chit-chatting, but something is different when you know they aren't a call away. It isn't something I would readily say over dinner, but I missed him like a father would miss a son. I was proud of him. Proud of his diligent, frugal ways.

A few weeks after his big trip, on a Wednesday, I was teaching my students how poor people spend more of their money on consumption than rich people. Of course, a few students made their disagreement known by stretches of grimaces and inordinate sighs. A kid named Patrick wouldn't suppress his curiosity. He looked straight at me from the third row with an appraising eye, laboring studiously. I had intended to make things more apparent when he raised his hand. Before I could permit him to ask his question, he had already started to spew his reservations.

"Sir, I am sorry I have to say this," he started, lips quivering slightly.

"Don't worry. Go ahead," I said, trying to boost the teen's confidence.

"I think I would have to disagree with you. From where I live, the poor barely have enough money for fast food. The rich are buying steak and lobster. It's impossible to say then, the rich spend less than the poor."

I smiled my routine smile, and I noticed the furrowed brows of confusion weaved across the faces of students. Patrick had asked the question they had all wanted to ask, and now they were quiet. The underlying chattering had splintered to a trickled, hushed sound.

"Sometimes, mathematics can be confusing, and I understand why you may not understand how the poor spend more of their money on consumption than the rich. Let's say, a poor man earns two hundred dollars a month, and a wealthy man earns a thousand dollars a month, who do you think will spend more of their money on consumption? If the poor man spends one hundred and fifty dollars and the rich man spends two hundred dollars, who spent more of their money?"

The class was silent for a while, and it seemed the kids were trying to understand the puzzle. They kept exchanging glances, and it was a behavior I had expected.

"Two hundred dollars is bigger than one hundred and fifty dollars," a kid bawled from the last row.

"You're right," I replied, smiling.

"Two hundred is bigger than one hundred and fifty because you are looking at the absolute amount. The poor man, who earns $200, has spent 75% of his income by spending a hundred and $50 on consumption. On the other hand, the wealthier man had only spent 20% of his income on consumption. When we talk about stuff like this, we're talking relatively. It's why the poor hardly save because most of their income goes to consumption," I concluded, smiling my usual smile.

"Wow! That is a great way of looking at it," Patrick trilled, uttering a bright smile.

"So next time you're hanging out with your wealthier friend, and you try to match him on his spending because you don't want him to think you're inferior, remember to put this at the back of your mind. In such a scenario, you're spending more than him, and it would be stupid to buy stuff so you can look like something you're not. If you're bright, knowing this will be enough to change your spending habits and save your money. No matter how little you make, you can always save," I concluded.

The bell rang moments later, and the kids were far from reluctant to leave. The students quickly made it out the door, headed to their next class. They engaged in more exciting conversations than my lecture. I headed back to my old desk when I got a call from Pat.

"Doc, I'm doing well. I've got a bunch of money saved. I've made some of my dreams a reality, and I want to buy a house. I've heard it's a great investment," he said excitedly.

"Who says owning a home is a great investment?"

"Well, everyone. All homeowners say it was the best financial decision they ever made."

"Did you ask them what other financial decisions they've made? Did they put 10% of their income away as you did? Did they save up four months of living expenses in a target-date fund, like you? Did they set aside 20% for big purchases?" I asked solemnly.

Pat responded, "I doubt they did all that, but they seem to have a lot of equity, you know value . . . in their home."

"OK, give me an example."

Pat thought for a moment and said:

"I know this old guy. He bought his house for like $100,000 right at 40 years ago. He sold it to move into one of those exclusive retirement places. He got $480,000 for that place free and clear."

"That's about average. Most homes appreciate only slightly more than inflation. In this case, the retiree had an annual return of about 4%. Take out the extras you have to pay by owning your place, and you're likely to lose money, insurance in case of loss, private mortgage insurance (PMI), maintenance, lawn care, HOA dues, and taxes. Then we can subtract out the large repairs like a roof every 15 years, water heater every ten years, painting every seven years. Now, do you think he made that much money? How much do you earn on your investments?"

"A lot more than 4%, and I don't have all those fees either."

I could tell Pat was thinking. I didn't interrupt. He continued, "OK, I have a better example. I know this couple who bought a house. They only put down $30,000 on this $300,000 place. Within about ten years, they sold it for around $445,000. The husband called it leveraging his money. Borrowing a little and getting a huge return."

"It appears they made $145,000 in 10 years. Let's subtract the sales commission of about $26,000. That puts them at $119,000 profit. Now maintenance on a nice place runs about 2% per year of the value of the home. Their profit would be reduced by $119,000. Where are we now on this investment?"

"Zero, and we haven't even figured in taxes, HOA dues, the money they spent on PMI or homeowner's insurance."

"Here's the thing Pat, investments shouldn't require an ongoing investment of cash. Also, a house you live in doesn't generate cash flow."

"What do you mean about cash flow?" Pat asked.

"Picture some old guy in New York. He bought a place years ago and paid off his mortgage. The zoning changes, and his place is now worth a fortune. Great luck for him and by-the-way, rare. He's living in a place worth $3Mil, but he saved nothing for retirement. He gets a check from the government to buy his necessities. On the typical definition of net worth, this guy is a multi-millionaire."

"I get it. The New Yorker isn't living like a millionaire. He only has that small amount fo money to live. The house isn't generating any income for him unless he sold."

"Right, Pat. He would have to sell and use the money. An alternative, he could invest the proceeds and live on the income it produces. Then, he could live the millionaire lifestyle, or at least better than his government check. He could pull out about $120,000 a year. People make this mistake all the time, people think they're wealthy, but they don't have the income to enjoy life."

Pat soon came up with a story of his own, "I have these relatives who live in the Midwest. They own 28,000 acres with cattle. They own it all, outright. Some sort of family farm, going back generations. They have all these assets, like farm equipment and livestock, but don't have much of an income. When it comes time to sell the cattle, they make a bunch of money, but it's just enough to pay the bills and budget for the year. If they could somehow rent out the land, they could have a nice income."

"That's what you need to keep in mind. I'm not pushing you to buy a house. It's not a great investment, and it doesn't create an income."

"Why do people buy houses?"

"You buy it for peace of mind, get fixed living expenses, and make something your own. Some people have a desire for stability, and to them, a house represents this stability."

"I think I still want a place of my own. Is that OK with you?"

"Sure, it is. As I said, people buy houses for reasons other than an investment. Just keep in mind, 90% of the time, the house you live in is not a great investment opportunity."

"What would be my next step?"

"Pat, you'll want to get pre-qualified for a mortgage and find someone you're comfortable with who can explain things to you. He or she will offer a 15 or 30-year mortgage. There are advantages to both. Weigh your options. Pat, can you be honest with me? Are you thinking about buying this house because you're in love with someone?" I hadn't heard from Pat much since his trip to Spain and figured he had a good reason not to talk with me as much.

"Yeah. She's great. It's Lilly, from high school. We were almost an item back in school, but she ended it. I met her again on the flight, sheer luck. We've been chatting on the phone, texting, and going out. I've been keeping it quiet because my sister Nicole doesn't like her much, but I think I'm in love," Pat responded sheepishly.

"I don't remember her from school. I would love to meet her, but before I do, a word of caution. Don't buy a house with another person who you aren't married to. It's fine for a single person to buy a house, and you'll qualify. The problems that could take place buying a place with someone else are too huge to overcome. If you were to break up, you'd have emotional issues as well as financial issues, both a big deal. On top of those issues, you have no legal means to divide up the house. If married, a judge will legally divide up that asset."

Pat had to go. I think he was getting a call from Lilly. I was glad to know he had started seeing someone.

Pat

Age 26, income $58,800/year; 10% fund $85,686; 20% fund $63,131; Stay out of debt fund $33,686

I loved Lilly so much. I wanted Doc to meet her. I did think, initially, we would buy the house together. Although I knew everything would work out great with Lilly, Doc was right. If things didn't work out, we would be in a tough place, owning a house together. I figured we could look for a house together. Find one we both loved. I would buy it. After we were married, she could move in.

I had been working on my credit score for a while. At this point, it was pretty good, above 760. I knew this before I even started to look at buying a house. I told Doc I found a mortgage broker who went to our high school. Doc asked who he was, but didn't give any indication he knew him.

I wanted to get pre-qualified for a 15 year and 30 year fixed rate loan. The mortgage broker told me that if my credit score were lower than 760, I would've had a higher interest rate, causing me to spend tens of thousands of dollars more over the life of the loan. The loan officer said, "Yep, even if one medical bill or credit card bill went to collections, your credit score would probably drop 100 points. Not paying a $200 medical bill because you didn't agree with the charges, could have cost you more than $85,000 as extra interest on your mortgage. Furthermore, if your credit score were terrible, you would be paying 4% more in interest compared to those who have the best credit score. On a quick calculation, for a house like you want, those with bad credit would be looking at spending an additional $300,000 just in interest."

I thought back to that car ride with Doc. He told me a good credit score would save me money. At first, I doubted how much an impact it would have. He was right. It's no wonder poor people stay poor. Once you have one little problem, your credit starts to slip, and you can't recover. You can't get back on your feet because of all the money you're spending on interest.

The mortgage broker continued, and I refocused my thoughts, "Pat, I want you to buy the biggest most expensive house possible, so I make the most commission." He paused as I looked at him, bewildered. "Or do you want me to tell you the truth about how much house you can afford?"

"The truth, of course! I don't want to live in a great house, but not be able to live the way I want."

The mortgage broker began, "The first question, are you debt-free?"

"Yep, I've been debt-free for a few years now."

"Do you have a balance on any of your credit cards?"

"Yeah, I use one all the time. The other two, I only use a bit."

"Pat, this is debt, and it will count against you as you try to get a mortgage. But, It sounds like you pay it off in full each . . ."

I interrupted him, "Yes, I do. I always do, except when I was young."

"We need your credit utilization below 25%."

I remember Doc talking about this. He said that if I had a high balance on my card, compared to the amount I could borrow, it would hurt my credit report. I guess this is when all that information is paying off. "Just so we're clear, can you give me the low-down on credit utilization."

"You take the maximum you could charge and multiply that by .25 okay. If this number is higher than you owe, you have too much money charged to that card. You have to pay it down before we try to get this loan."

"Can I just pay it all off and pay cash for a while?"

"That would be your best bet, but not entirely necessary. Just get the amount owed below 25% so this loan can go through." I made a note on my phone as the broker continued.

"The second question, do you have a stay out of debt fund of 4 months of living expenses?"

"It's funny you call it that my mom called it the same thing. Yes, a bit more than four months. I put away four months of living expenses plus 30% into a target-date mutual fund with low fees. I've let it grow there and haven't needed to touch it."

I was expecting him to tell me what a great job I did. Instead, the mortgage broker continued, "The third question, besides your stay out of debt fund, do you have a 10% down payment that was not a gift from someone?"

"Yes, I have the money in my 20% Dividend Achievers fund."

"That money needs to be moved to your bank. I want that money to be 'seasoned' in your bank. It should've been sitting in your savings or checking account for three months before we take out a loan."

This guy was stern all the time, but now he pointed his finger at me as Mrs. Galloway used to when I was late to class. He demanded. "After you transfer the money from your mutual fund to the bank, don't make any large cash deposits into your account. We don't want any of your down payment to look like a loan. You know, from a relative, you'll have to pay back."

The loan officer continued, "The fourth question, will you be in this house for more than five years? If not, you're paying a lot in real estate commissions, moving expenses, as well as the chance it will go down in value."

"Yes, we're thinking close to ten."

The mortgage broker continued, "A few things I want you to think about here—the school district. If you buy a house in a school district likely to go down the dumps, so will your resale value. Think about your goals. Will buying this house interfere with the money you need to make your goals a reality? Will owning a home get in the way of your intangible goals? If you have a goal of working for a company down South, you might feel as if you can't sell for some reason, like you would take a loss. When you lock yourself into owning a home, you could miss the opportunity to jump onto that great job. You won't fulfill your goal of getting the job in California. Will this house make you feel locked-in to living here, unable to move for a better paying job or a new opportunity?"

I was confused as to why this guy was pushing against me trying to buy a house. "Are you trying to make a sale or get me to rent?"

"Hey, look, I was one of Doc's students too. Ethics is important to any business. I found that if a potential client doesn't end up using me because of one of the questions I pose, they'll recommend me to a bunch of friends who will end up using me. And also, Doc called me and told me to treat you right."

Sometimes I feel like no one is looking out for me, besides my brother and Doc, I suppose. It was nice to have Doc call and put in the right word for me. I don't want to get tied into a situation I can't afford. He brought up something I didn't quite understand, "You mentioned unable to move to a better paying job. What exactly are you talking about with that?"

The broker responded, "Doctors and lawyers build a practice and typically stay in one location their entire working careers, but corporate executives move to the next best job. They rent a nice place and move around based on where opportunity takes them. They find a job that pays more, suits their interest more, or they find some other appeal to the new situation. They never feel locked in because it's the wrong time to sell, or they would take a loss on the house. There's also a bunch of fees people pay when they buy a house. Those fees aren't there for renters. Those fees take years of house market gains to recoup. If you're thinking about moving within five years or want the freedom to move to the next big job, you can rent. You can find a great house to rent. It doesn't have to be an apartment."

I knew I wasn't a corporate executive, but I could use the same idea. I could get training and move to the next best job every couple of years. Lilly has this dream of relocating out of the country, but I couldn't imagine doing that any time soon. I want the freedom to move and make more money, but I also want to provide Lilly with a sense of stability homeownership would provide.

"You bring up some good points. I still want to move forward with buying a house," I firmly responded.

"You need to make sure the total payment, with all the extras like tax and insurance, is 25% or less of your monthly take-home pay."

The mortgage broker continued, "The first step. Take the going interest rate and add the property tax rate to that number. Where you're thinking about moving to has a tax rate of 1.3%."

I pulled up the calculator on my phone. The broker continued, "The second step, add in 1% for Private Mortgage Insurance (PMI). On the phone you said you'll be putting down less than 20%, so you'll have to pay an extra 1% until the amount you owe is less than 80% of the purchase price. That'll take about three years on a 15-year mortgage. Reason enough to consider the 15-year mortgage seriously. You're building equity faster; you're getting out of the PMI faster. PMI drops off when the mortgage balance compared to your purchase price reaches 79-80%. They don't base it on the current value of the home, but on your purchase price," the mortgage broker barely took a breath.

"Back to the 15-year mortgage. With the 15 year mortgage, your interest rate is lower, but you'll be paying more per month because of the shorter term. If you go with the 30 years, your monthly payment will be less. I'm guessing you have a family to think of, and you want a big house in a great school district. To get more house, in a nicer neighborhood, you could go with the 30-year mortgage. A 30-year mortgage keeps your monthly costs down—gets you a bigger house in a nicer area for less per month. No matter the term 15 or 30, everything together, insurance, property taxes, interest, and the principal have to be at or less than 25% of your monthly take-home pay," he said, as stern and solemn as ever.

"I don't have a family. At least not yet. I have someone, and we're kinda talkin' about it," I interrupted him.

The mortgage broker didn't seem to care about my personal life and continued, "The third step, add 0.5% for homeowner's insurance. The mortgage company will require you have it. For the area you're considering, it'll cost about half of a percent. You added up the going interest rate, the property taxes, the cost of PMI, and the cost of insurance. Use this new number in an online mortgage calculator. Choose a 15-year mortgage and how much you'll have to borrow," he paused and exhaled loudly.

I was on my calculator and had to switch to an online mortgage calculator. I was writing down some notes as he was talking.

I pulled up a calculator and said things out loud as I typed, "Ok, 1.3 for property taxes + 1.0 for PMI + 0.5 for homeowner's insurance = 2.8. I add 2.8 to the annual percentage rate and plug that number into an online mortgage calculator along with the amount of money I'm borrowing. If the monthly payment is one-fourth of my take-home pay, I should be good to go."

"Can you afford it? If the payment is more than a fourth of your take-home pay, you'll need to put down more money to eliminate the PMI or find a less expensive house," he asked, knowing he had made his point.

"I want to buy a house, but according to this, I can't afford it," I replied, disenchanted. I remember the house I grew up in, before the apartment above the mechanic's shop. I was trying to find a house similar to my childhood home. My mind flashed back to the first day Doc and I talked. It was so vivid in my mind; he was saying that people strive to keep the same lifestyle in which they grew up. They are so inclined to continue these spending habits, they'll go into debt to make it happen. That day, in Doc's computer lab, I broke free from those thoughts. I knew I was a poor kid, who screwed up, was at the very bottom. That day, my lifestyle changed. When I was sitting in front of this mortgage broker, I could have easily reverted to trying to live the same way my parents did when they had three teenagers. I shook my head no, and the mortgage broker interrupted my thoughts:

"Can you come up with more money down, let's say 20%? That extra money down will eliminate the 1% PMI and reduce the amount borrowed. Also, switching to a 30-year term will decrease the monthly payments. Let's plug in those numbers."

I wrote down some numbers, and as I did, I said them aloud, "1.3 for taxes + 0.5 for insurance = 1.8 plus the current mortgage rate on a 30 year. Reduce the amount I'm borrowing because my down payment will be 20% of the purchase price. Type in the new percent, change the term to 30, and the outcome is . . . I can do that. The monthly payment is less than a quarter of my take-home pay . . . barely" I said excitedly.

I was genuinely excited about the new life Lilly, and I were going to have in this place. The last house I lived in was with my father—a long time ago. This place would be beautiful. My father would be proud. I remember dad coming home from work, covered in cement dust. I remember mom not allowing him to wash his clothes in 'her' washing machine. I was in charge of soaking his clothes in a bucket before they were allowed in mom's washer. The cement dust had ruined one other washing machine before I was born.

"One last thing Pat, when you're looking for a real estate agent, specifically ask him or her if they'll be a buyer's agent. You want a buyer's agent. Those who can't agree to this may not act in your best interest. A seller's agent may use the information you provide, like the top price you'll pay, against you in negotiations."

I was curious why this mortgage broker was so open and honest. Someone really on my side, so I asked, "Why do you spend so much effort making sure I do the right thing with my money and this mortgage?"

"I run my business and my life the same way. I have four pillars for success. If something gets in the way of one of my pillars, I cut it out."

It was as if he needed me to ask, "What are your pillars?"

"The first one is wisdom—proper planning and good judgment. The second is fairness—includes public service and fair dealings. Along with fairness are a kind heart and benevolence. The third is courage. It takes grit to be honest, authentic, to persevere, and have confidence in my abilities. The last one is more personal, self-control. Giving in to indulgences gets people in trouble. Think about how a poor diet leads to medical issues, but also acting the fool when under the influence. Having order in my life helps me get things done without stress. Along with that, the forgiveness of those who do me wrong and humility. I don't know anything. I'm still learning, and I have to be humble. I seek the advice of those who are specialists."

I listened to this guy. I had never heard anyone living their life like this guy was. All these guidelines seemed too confining. Like he couldn't enjoy his life living within these four pillars. So, I asked, "Why do all that?"

"When I live by my four pillars, I feel joy. I do good for people, not expecting something in return, but do it for the sake of doing good for my, well . . . other people. I like to think of it as someone on their side. I like it when I have someone on my side, someone looking out for me. I feel good about the decisions they help me make. When no one is there to help me, I feel isolated. People don't deserve that type of treatment." He stopped talking. He had a slight gleam of pride on his face. I didn't feel as if he was trying to convert me to some sort of four-pillar religion. He looked happy at who he was.

"What do you do when a friend tries to force you to go against one of your virtues?"

"Quite frankly, I cut 'em out. If a friendship goes against my values, I'm indifferent to that person." He paused looked around, like he was going to tell me a secret and continued, "I had a friend. We were nearly inseparable. He was going through a divorce, and we would talk. I tried to help him. He turned to drugs, self-medicating. Whenever we got together, he would offer me this escape. Because this goes against my indulgent virtue, I would refuse. I tried to get him to stop. When he couldn't, I had to leave him. I was honest with him, 'I don't want to hang out with you when you're under the influence or doing drugs. When you clean yourself up, give me a call.' I lost my friend. It's been three years. I haven't heard from him since."

"It seems like a tough road of living correctly and breaking relationships. I mean, I can see how you could have joy from being fair, generous, having integrity, and showing self-control. But what does all that matter, besides the internal peace?"

"Character is the greatest calling card . . . no matter what."

"You have a point, I would rather do business with you, than someone who is only looking out for themselves. I would rather have a friend like you, who can be honest with me, even to the point of giving me an ultimatum, 'stop overindulging or our friendship is over.'" I was a bit worried that I misused the word ultimatum. Was that the right word?

I was driving home from the mortgage broker, and I called Doc, "Doc, I got pre-qualified for a 30-year mortgage at the best possible rate, because of my excellent credit score. All in with taxes, insurance, no PMI, principal, interest . . . everything, my monthly payment will be less than 25% of my take-home pay."

"Pat, I'm glad he recommended you keep the monthly payment low. It keeps you in an affordable house for sure, but it also does a few things most people don't realize. It puts you in a slightly more affordable house, reducing your property tax bill. A less expensive house also means cheaper homeowner's insurance. Maintenance on the house typically runs about 2% for newer homes and 4% for older homes, so a less expensive house will cost you less in repairs. You won't need super expensive appliances in a less expensive house where it might look foolish to skimp in a more expensive place. Even light fixtures, it would look foolish to go into a millionaire's mansion and see cheap lights on the ceiling. Finally, real estate commissions are a percent of the sale price. You're saving money there too."

"I get what you're saying Doc. I've got a buddy who bought a great house in a great neighborhood. The thing is, his income doesn't allow him to have any fun. It's all going to live in that place. He looks comfortable living there, but he can't afford the extras. I also get the feeling that he doesn't fit in. They have social clubs there, like senior golf, billiards, book club. Those clubs cost extra money, so he can't join. His wife wants to get involved in the neighborhood by joining the women's club, but it too costs money, and it's expected she brings wine to the events. They live in this great place, but can't socialize because they're living beyond their means."

I wanted Doc to understand that I was taking his advice and learning as I grew. He had never told me this insight. I learned it on my own as I watched my friends get married and buy houses.

"This won't be your case, Pat. You're buying a place you can afford, 25% of your take-home pay per month, all in. You'll have the flexibility to enjoy life, have fun, and find happiness."

I heard Doc say 'find happiness'; this is what I wanted more than anything. Lilly made me happy, but I still felt like a cloud was over my head. I felt worried, sadness, even a sense of dread when I thought about the future. I thought this house buying would give me something to which I could look forward. Whenever I felt anxious, I would think about finances. I would run the numbers in my head. It calmed me. Lately, I've been focused on this house buying and getting the money ready to buy it. It calmed me. It allowed me to sleep.

Lilly and I went house hunting. I learned a lot about her as we drove around. For one, she wanted something more expensive than my budget would allow. We still weren't deterred from finding a great place. As we looked at houses, we started to see features that were important to us. For Lilly, she wanted an island in the kitchen. For me, I wanted a large room above the garage. Not a man-cave, but a place where I could have a bit of a workout room. I didn't want to become one of those guys who gets married and upon saying 'I do' gains 30 pounds. Lilly was looking out for my health too. She would make my green smoothies. Lilly read online people with post-traumatic stress often had stomach issues, and these would help. She included spinach and dried dead yeast. Mostly vegetables, low carb. Occasionally, she would change up the recipe. They were all gross, but I liked the fact she was looking out for me, so I drank them.

After we found the perfect place, I put an offer on the house. As Doc insisted, I bought this on my own. My money as the down payment, my name on the title. When the offer was accepted, I took Lilly to the jewelry store. I thought, what better way to celebrate than getting engaged. The shop immediately insisted I finance the purchase. They told me that the rule of thumb for ring buying was six months of my income. When Lilly heard that, she insisted we leave.

On our car ride to the next jewelry store, Lilly told me, "You just bought a house. I love you. I don't need a huge ring. I need you. I'm happiest when we're together, and whatever we get, I'll know it's from you."

When we got to the next jewelry store, the owner was there. She was helping us. She said, "It doesn't matter how much money you spend on the ring. A woman has been dreaming of her engagement ring most of her life. She already has the desired look in her head. She already knows what diamond cut she wants. She already knows the type of metal. She even has an idea of the size of the stones. She wants something she can show off to her friends. She wants something she enjoys wearing. How about we ask?" The owner moved her attention to Lilly, focusing in on her face, "Sweetie . . ." the owner paused to make sure Lilly would look up from the display cases. Lilly began to blush a bit, just like she used to while in high school, "What style of ring do you want? If you tell us the style, I can put together the right stones to fit his budget."

At first, she acted as if she didn't know. I don't think she wanted me to hear it because when I walked away to another display case, Lilly said, under her breath to the owner, "Asscher cut center diamond, moissanite halo, all on a palladium metal band." The owner of the shop did a quick mock-up. It was perfect. It fit Lilly's finger perfectly and my budget. Also, it didn't cost me anywhere near six months of my income.

We were married within the year. Doc came to the wedding. I expected a beautiful package from Doc, but his gift was the cheapest we got. It was also the best gift we got. He got us a money belt with RFID blocking we would wear under our clothes. This thin pouch would hold cash, passports, credit cards, and tuck under the waist of our pants. We used that money belt more often than Uncle Hugh's brandy glasses. Each trip we took, we thought of Doc, right there on my ass.

Lilly

It was our wedding day. I looked beautiful in my wedding gown, Doc's wife told me. Several of the guests could not take their eyes off me. 'But, Hello… I am taken already!' my spotless gown flew very elegantly around my body, just like a waterfall of cream.

"Oh, how you look, so sweet" Doc's wife helped me with last-minute makeup and hair. I tried to force a smile. My hands were icy, and I trembled. I had been to weddings before. I never knew this was how the brides felt.

Pat's brother came in. He was the one who would lead me down the aisle.

"It is now dear, shall we?"

I bit my lip and began to feel funny in my stomach. I steadied myself and thought, marrying Pat was the best thing that could happen to me. It seemed like destiny, and for a moment, I thought it was how the script was meant to be scripted.

As Chad and I lined up outside the doors, my mind raced down an alternative path. I imagined the kind of life we would have had if I didn't break up with Pat in that coffee shop. I wondered what living near him would have done to our love life, how I wouldn't meet that college professor who opened my eyes to Pat's troubles. We needed that time of growth. That time apart. The separation was fate's way of ensuring we sharpened our respective dispositions.

The doors were about to open. I could hear the groom's men sitting the last few guests. I flashed back to how things might have gone—Pat and me together right after high school. Pat would miss me—calling me again and again and visiting me at the University of Maine. Those visits pulling at the jealousy space creates. The wonder if I would stay true. I wonder if a good-looking guy like Pat could also remain faithful. The temptation, the distance, the time. It was too much for many couples. It could have been too much for us too.

My mind came back to the church—my focus on the doors in front of me. The music for my march began. My mind kept wandering. It flickered to the airplane flight where Pat and I rekindled our relationship. Ever since then, I saw a fire in his eyes when he looked at me. I thought that if we were together when I left high school headed for the University, the heat would've incinerated him.

I held Chad's arm, and we walked together down the aisle. Pat stood on the other side of the hall, and as soon as he saw me coming, he began to smile. The guests started to grin too.

The priest said some hushed words. I had a tough time concentrating and hearing what was said. Suddenly I heard Pat say, "I do."

I held my breath and closed my eyes. I listened with great anticipation. I could feel the eyes of everyone piercing through my body. But the only eyes that mattered now were those of Pat's, and they were in the right place. When I opened my eyes, I saw him looking at my boobs.

"I do," I said after his crammed questions. There was immediate applause as soon as I responded. 'What! Did the guests think I would fail such an important question in my life?'

In the reception, the photographer took more pictures of Pat and me than all the images I've ever had in my life, and I took a lot of selfies. We sat together on a cushion of rose petals, Pat's lips pressed to mine. We broke our embrace when everyone chuckled.

I could hear, "What a wonderful couple" coming from all corners of the hall.

The DJ began to play some music, "Hope you like this, honey?" Pat asked.

"It's perfect," a smile on my face. This day was perfect.

It was perfect until I saw Chad get on the stage. I grabbed Pat's arm, "Wait a minute, is that Chad? What is he doing on the stage?"

Chad was on the stage and asking the DJ a question. Chad wanted to sing a song for us. I never knew Chad could sing. If nothing else, he would embarrass himself, and we would all have a good laugh.

Chad stood quietly on the stage, like a lonely shadow. The music started softly, it sounded like someone was playing the piano, but it was from the DJ. I shook my head in surprise and worried, for Chad's sake.

I looked at Pat, he knew from my expression—I wanted an explanation. "Hey, babe, I wanted something special for our wedding. Chad told me he could write a song and sing it. I thought, what the hell. If nothing else, it'll create the best memory for our guests. Let's listen."

Chad started singing:

Just like the sound of silence summoning

I hear your sweet voice calling

suddenly I'm falling, lost in a dream come true

Everyone suddenly turned to the stage, and the audience was dead silent. I was shocked at the quality of voice that came from him, and it seemed everyone was as captured as I was. The soft performance of Chad was a surprise. The guests couldn't resist but listen. And he was swaying, making a few, slow dance moves, and if a stranger had walked in at that moment, he would think Chad was a hired musician from a distant country.

Like the echoes of our souls meeting,

those words spoken, my heart stops beating.

And I wonder what it means.

What is it that came over me?

At times I can't find my feet to move.

People started to walk toward the stage, no talking, just nods of approval. Tears gathered in my eyes, and a wave of fresh emotions ran up my heart. I could see Pat smile, and I remembered the first time I had seen him in Mrs. Galloway's classroom. If I didn't take the initiative and ask him to eat lunch with me and then years later, ask him out, my life wouldn't be the same. Pat's brown eyes were now glowing.

Whenever you say you love me

I can hardly breathe the air

If it could be put into words

a single heartbeat in our head and hearts

Our pulse is our music in sync with the universe.

Heart beating at an accelerated rate,

my heart stops and starts again

For a moment, there's no one else alive

A pent-up kiss finally released

our kiss made of poetry.

Let me have my way with that kiss.

I kissed her softly,

I kissed her soul-fully

I kissed her, oh so bold-fully.

My kisses swallowed her moans.

I kissed some more then I heard her phone

I was about to tear up until I listened to that last line. The music stopped. The world went silent. No one moved, and then the audience went into riotous applause and cheers, even laughter. They surrounded Chad, patting him on the back and telling him how lovely he sang and how awe-struck they all were.

Pat's Notes

Homeownership is rarely a good investment. People buy houses for other reasons, like a sense of knowing you'll always have a place to live, making changes to the house, pride.

My monthly rent or total cost of the mortgage (including taxes, insurance, PMI) can't be more than 25% of my take-home pay each month.

Before I try to get a mortgage, drop my credit utilization to 30% or less of the maximum I can charge.

If I'm going to put down less than 20% on the house, I need to add 2.8% to the interest rate to find the approximate cost of the monthly payment. If I put down 20% or more, I only add 1.8% to the mortgage rate to estimate my monthly payment with the costs of insurance and taxes.

Chapter 13

Which homeowner's insurance policy do I need?
Is an umbrella insurance policy worth the money?

Doc

Pat's house buying and wedding were right on top of each other. I didn't get to see the house until after the wedding. I half suspected Pat was unboxing for a while too. He didn't want anyone to see the house until it was perfect. A few months after the wedding, Pat had a housewarming party. I bought Pat a fireproof safe for his housewarming present. I put a $5 bill inside with a note, 'This is your new piggy bank. You'll want $1,000 worth of these. In case of an emergency, you'll want quick cash, and if it was a true emergency, you don't want to have to deal with breaking large bills or have people think the large bill was fake. This safe is also to stay organized. Put important papers in here like the title of your car, sales contracts from the house, and passports.' Pat appreciated the gift, and together, we bolted it to the floor in the closet of one of the bedrooms.

After the house tour, Pat asked, "I have a homeowner's insurance policy. I had to buy it as part of the mortgage agreement. Is that all I need?"

"Do you have replacement cost insurance or fair market value?"

"I don't know, they gave me two choices, and I picked the cheaper."

"That's fair market value." I pointed down to Pat's shoes. "Right now, how much could you sell those shoes for?"

"Not much. You could probably find a similar pair of used shoes at Goodwill for less than $10."

"What if you had to replace them? How much would it cost to buy a new pair of shoes?"

"These, over $100, but I use them for running too."

"You don't have to give me excuses as to how you spend your money. Here's the point. If you lose all of the contents in your house to a fire, do you want to be reimbursed for the thrift store value or enough money to replace all your stuff?"

"If I lost everything and got the fair market value, there is no way I could replace even a fraction of what we would need to live. Can I switch this policy to replacement value?"

"Yes, and you'll also want a million-dollar umbrella policy. This policy covers almost everything, driving, the house, even some of your actions. Let's say today, during this party, we're on the back deck, and it collapses with the weight of 20 people. All 20 people are hurt. Your regular insurance policy won't be enough money to cover the medical bills of all those people. Those hurt people can then sue you."

"Oh no… I've got a bunch of money in my 401(k) that I've worked my butt off to get. I sat on my butt to get most of that money, cha-ching."

"That's why I wanted the majority of your money in a retirement account. It's safe from lawsuits there. These injured people could come after your other assets, your stay out of debt fund, the equity in your house, garnishing your wages. The umbrella policy will pay up to a million dollars for a tragedy. Better still, the insurance company doesn't want to pay that amount of money, so they'll help you win the court cases against you."

"Sold. I'm changing my homeowner's to replacement cost and adding an umbrella policy."

"When you add the umbrella policy, you'll have to make minor adjustments to your auto insurance. The umbrella insurance company wants to make sure you have at least a decent minimum on your cars before they insure you." After we talked, we went back to the housewarming party and socialized.

Lilly

Shortly after I moved into the house Pat bought, Pat had a panic attack. I had seen anxiety issues manifest themselves before, but his post-traumatic stress triggered this one. We were watching a movie. One of the characters screamed. Pat's reaction started slow and built. I interlocked my fingers with him. I forced him to slow his breathing and focus on my words:

"Pat, you can't control outside events, like a character, screaming. What you can govern is your mind and how you deal with outside forces. The anxiety you're feeling is your perception. Since it's inside you, you can choose to throw it away. These feelings and your reaction are brought on by what you're telling yourself to feel. Your thoughts are stressing you out."

Pat responded defensively, "It's not internal. The scream from the lady made me have a panic attack."

"It's easy to blame outside forces. It's your perception of these events that are causing the issue. I didn't have the same reaction you did. The conflict is in your mind. If it's within you, it's also within your power to push it out. You face joy, fear, anger, peace, regret, stress every day. These feelings come from within you. Outside events don't have power over you. You have power over the thoughts in your mind. Control your thoughts and create strength. Breath with me. Breathe in through your nose for four seconds. Hold that breath for seven seconds. Now, let it out through your mouth for eight seconds. Do it again . . . four . . . seven . . . eight. Again. Control your breathing, control your thoughts."

Pat's Notes

A top priority, $1,000 worth of five-dollar bills in a fireproof safe in case of emergency.

Only buy replacement value homeowner's insurance.

Buy an umbrella insurance policy along with the minimum car insurance to satisfy the umbrella's requirements.

Chapter 14

How much term life insurance do I need?

Doc

I didn't know this at the time, but Pat was helping his mother become financially sound as he and I talked over the years about things he should be doing. She came a long way from struggling to get by on her own with three kids. I didn't hear from Pat for a few months. During that time, I tried to reach out to him but got no response. The same week I started to get worried, he called.

"My mom died on Thursday."

"Pat, I'm so sorry. Can I come to the funeral and send flowers?"

"That would be nice. I'll text you the details. You know, I suspected something was up with my mom when I got a copy of her Last Will and Testament in a sealed envelope. I put it in that safe you got me. Can I confess something? I opened it. Inside was a bunch of information—the name and contact information for her accountant, insurance agent, an attorney. Also, she listed her account numbers and bank names. She even wrote out where she had her safety deposit box and how to find the key."

"She probably sent the same documents to your brother and sister too. This way, no one could question the authenticity of the document when you and each of your siblings had a copy."

"Doc, I've got to go, but I'll send you the information about the arrangements."

A few weeks after the funeral, Pat scheduled a meeting with me at the BISCUITS CAFE. It was great to see Serena again, and I thought her business was booming. She always kept a smile on her face whenever I visited, and it indicated her thankfulness for the little advice I had given her in running her business. I got to the restaurant before Pat and wondered if he grief-stricken from losing a mom. The thing is, a man can gain a lot of experience, ditch out advice like a talk-show host, mesmerize a few students, but there is no clear manual in consoling the broken-hearted. It's hard to find the exact words to use, and I seem to make it worse when I try to show empathy. The feeling of losing a loved one is unique to each person. And when I thought about Pat, for the first time since I had my first conversation with him, I didn't know how to cut a swathe through his grief. I didn't know how to help him. Perhaps he needed the love of Lilly more than ever, and maybe I could offer a distraction by indulging him in his financial issues. It had helped him before, and now, more than ever, I wished it would help him again.

Pat lumbered into the restaurant moments later, and his face curled up in the hangover of his grieving. He walked in the gait of a disgruntled man, and somehow, he maintained an admirable calmness, when he stopped and greeted Serena. Serena's puffy hands curled around him in a hug. She had heard about his loss, and it seemed she knew Pat's mother well enough.

Pat sat next to me. I didn't know what to say, "Pat, your mother's death was unexpected. I'm sorry for your loss." I saw Pat's quick look down; a sadness came over his face. "You never know what will happen. Like when your father passed." Oh, Christ, I didn't just say that. I didn't just bring up his father. My mind raced, and I thought of how Pat enjoyed talking with me. Maybe he enjoyed talking with me because thinking about finance took his mind off his real troubles. I built upon that idea and continued, "He didn't have disability insurance or a term life insurance policy. Not having those things, left your family in a tough situation. You need to make certain you have at least long-term disability insurance. Your stay out of debt fund will help you survive the short-term issues, but if you're out of work for the long-haul, you could be financially ruined," I was searching his face for some sign he understood.

"You mentioned term life insurance. When will I need that?" he asked.

"Term life insurance is for those who have someone else reliant on them for income, like a child needing their father to work. If the father dies, the term life insurance pays. To get it, you pay a yearly cost. By the way, the cost can nearly double if you choose to be a smoker."

"How much will it pay?"

"That depends on the amount of the policy. As a parent, you want the child to have enough money to live comfortably until they can survive on their own, let's say after they graduate high school. If a spouse is reliant on you, you'll want them to have a comfortable life as well if you were to die. You're married. Pat, if you were to die, could your wife survive on her income, without you. Could she have the same lifestyle the two of you have together? Could she afford that large house on just her salary? Could she continue to do the social things she enjoys without the dual-income? You would want a lump of money for those people you leave behind. In an example with a wife and kids, all reliant on your income, you would take out two-term policies. The first one could be for a shorter time—just long enough and enough money to get the kids through college. The other one would be for a longer period. This second one would be for the spouse you leave behind. You buy the longer policy early; keep paying on it over the years because it could be difficult or impossible to get a term policy when you're older."

"Alright, I take out a policy to take care of my wife. I assume she can still work, but I want her to have a nice life. Continue to live in our house, but never remarry."

"You want to provide for her, but make certain she's not happy?" I asked.

"Yeah, something like that. I'm just kidding. Lilly can remarry, but he has to be uglier and not as funny as me." I smiled at Pat's idea of being funny. He continued, "I take out this policy now, while I'm in good health. Since I'm not a smoker, I can get a great rate. Now, what if I'm married with kids? Do both parents need to have a policy?"

"That's a good point. Both parents need term life insurance. Even if one parent isn't making as much or any money, they need to be insured. Think of it this way. If a stay at home parent were to lose their life, how much will it cost for the other parent to slow down working and hire someone to take the place of the lost spouse."

"Come on, Doc, how much insurance do I need?"

"Pat, it isn't all that simple. I can't just give you one number. If you look it up online, it's tough to get a straight answer as well. You might read ten times your salary, but that number doesn't take into account how long the child will need to live off your life insurance money. If the kid is 17 years old and has no plans to go to college, ten times your income will be way too much. On the other hand, if you have debt, a young child, and hopes they'll go to an Ivy League school, ten times isn't enough. The other thing that these online guesses assume is that the kid will live off the interest and not take any withdrawals from the principal. No need to leave the principal in place for the rest of their lives, the money is supposed to be there until they can support themselves. Raising kids who are financially reliant on their parents while they are past the age of 27 isn't psychologically healthy for the kid."

"27, I was more or less on my own at 22."

"Pat, you're special and have an understanding of money. The age range to cut a child off, financially, can range from 18 as they graduate to 30, depending on job markets and extenuating circumstances, like continued education. The first step is to communicate with the kid as to when they won't be supported financially. Let him know what a parent will pay for and for how long. A good target to have him independent would be 25 years old would be. On the other hand, like your mom, she might opt for 22."

"My child will be financially independent at age 5. So, can we get back on the subject of life insurance? How do we figure out the amount through an annuity calculator?" He asked, smiling for the first time since he came in. It was funny how finance worked its tricks on him.

"That's right, Pat. We need to go to an online annuity calculator. Find an easy one. Input the number of years someone will be dependent on your income - this would be the length of the annuity. Next is the amount of income you have, including health care costs - you'll put this number in the withdrawals section. The annual growth rate is the percent of return you might expect from an annuity - you could even do a separate search for the rate of return. The starting principal is the number we are trying to figure out - leave that one blank."

I watched as Pat put some numbers into his smartphone. "That seems like a pretty big number, and it didn't account for the college costs yet."

I continued, "Right, now add in the estimated cost of post-secondary training - college or trade school for each child. Add any debt the parent has to that large 'starting principal' number. Another generic factor guesses don't take into account is how much you have in savings. Here, we're talking liquid assets, the money you can get your hands on within a couple of weeks, so not a house. Deduct mutual fund accounts, retirement funds, savings, even cash. Now, you have a much more accurate idea as to how much term life insurance you'll need."

"Doc, all this makes sense. Why can't other people be as straightforward as you?"

I felt I had to tell him what I thought. "I think it's out of fear of telling someone something wrong and then having that person mad for getting a wrong answer. They give these general ideas, letting people make up their minds. The problem with that approach is people get confused. When people are confused, they choose not to make a decision. They would rather not decide than possibly make the wrong choice. Didn't it seem easier taking steps to become wealthy when you followed clear expectations? Like we use to do in class, here are the directions to complete the assignment. Get it done," I admonished.

Pat smiled and responded, trying to imitate my voice, "OK class, here are the directions to becoming a millionaire. Invest 10% of your income into two index funds. The first will follow the U.S. stock market. The second will follow the foreign stock market. If you begin early enough, you can retire and live on the beach," he even threw in a double chin for good measure.

"That was a good impression of me, Pat. Don't tell anyone at the county office teaching financial literacy is that easy," I said, smiling.

It was particularly great to see Pat smiling again, and he even inclined to chip in a few humorous words. It made me remember the first time we sat and talked. He was a teen with tousled hair. A face wrinkled by the memories of his father passing. And the dread he held from being an active accessory to the death of a stranger. The version of Pat I had seen today was different. He knew how to be in control of his emotions, and perhaps it would take a while to dispel the haunting memories of the past entirely, but I couldn't be more proud. I wanted to tell him his resilience, comportment, and a refined ability to understand finance gave him an adaptability others don't have. I wanted to say to him others haven't faced horrors he's dealt with in his life. I tried to tell him he had the maturity to realize 'what is done, is done, and its time to move on.' I didn't tell him any of those things. We finished our food, paid our bills, and as we were leaving, I stopped him just outside the doors.

"Pat, It helps to have a distraction to deal with anxiety. But when you're coping with grief, you have to process those emotions. Don't deceive yourself and hide from the pain. Telling people or yourself, 'you're fine,' is a short term fix and doesn't help for a lifetime you have to spend with yourself. You've been through a lot. Each major battle you come across, you have first to face what happened—call it what it was—taking the blame or seeing it as an act of God. Next process and deconstruct the circumstances—remove expectations and your sense of being wronged by the world. Look for the positive in the situation—what good came about from turmoil. Finally, remember pain, anguish, grief, and mistakes are a part of life—we all face them. Dealing with emotions is best done sooner than later. People who run from their feelings don't get better until they face them."

Pat's Notes

Buy enough term life insurance to get a person who's dependent on you to a point they can be financially independent. A child would need enough funds to get to 21 years old with money for college. Subtract any money you already have. Add any debts, to pay those off.

Buy a separate term life insurance policy that will pay my wife if I died so she can be happy, but with someone not as fandiddlytastic as me.

Use an online annuity calculator to figure out how much money would be needed.

When I have strife in my life, face it. I need to deal with it head-on. Pull it apart and analyze each part. Decide if it was out of my control or was I to blame. If it was my fault, I need to learn from my mistake and look for a positive outcome. Realize terrible things happen in life—those are the knots that string pearls together.

Chapter 15

What do I do with an inheritance or large cash prize?

Pat

Age 30, dual-income $98,800/year; 10% fund $177,090; 20% fund $180,135; Stay out of debt fund $44,535

My mom left her three kids a chunk of money. I thought to the twins. I wondered if their father had a life insurance policy. Probably not. Newborns, expenses. He probably had a lot going on and never thought everything would end with one stupid kid doing the stupidest thing. I pictured him driving down that highway, probably going home from work. He glances up and sees this orange barrel coming at him. No time to avoid it. No time to swerve. No time to tell his family, he loves them. Too late to make certain his family would be financially set before he died.

I had to get my mind off those thoughts. I called Doc to find out what I should do with mom's inheritance. I put on the happiest tone I could, "I want to go out and do something fun. I don't want to spend all of it, but I was thinking 5% of the money. I want to remember my dad. I want to do something my parents would smile at the thought of." It was the middle of summer when the money came in.

"Right now, the money is in my savings account, doing nothing. Doc, this wasn't a ton of money, but still a good bit, I got tax free."

As I was waiting for Doc's response, I got to thinking. After my dad's death, I wasn't close to my mom. She worked so much, the three of us barely saw her. When I look back at the situation with adult eyes, I realize her working was half coping mechanism and half providing for us kids. I don't know for sure, but I think my mom was helping Nicole financially until she died. There is no way Chad and I would ever accept money from mom. She worked too hard for us to live off her. I believe parents and grandparents should predetermine how much relief they're willing to give someone. They need to base the support on their budget and how much they can afford. Parents, grandparents - they too need to live. If they decide to help a grandchild on a whim, case by case basis, their emotions will get the best of them and forego their own happiness or even well-being. They may not have enough money in their later years. I don't know how much mom was giving Nicole each month, but I'm sure my sister got all she could get out of her.

I snapped back to the conversation with Doc when he asked, "What else are you going to do with the money?"

"I don't know. What do you suggest?"

"Pull out a piece of paper, Pat . . . or, in your case, a note on your cell phone. I'm going to give you a few secrets the wealthy use. You'll want to write down some dates and months to maximize your investment's rate of return."

"OK," I said. "I'm ready for the inside knowledge."

"The stock market follows a cycle. It typically hits a low in October and builds until May. More accurately, it hits a lull November through April. The best time to buy is in October and sell in May. This cycle is true for most years, except for the 3rd year of the U.S. President's term. Then, the stock market follows a different cycle. But since this year isn't the 3rd year in the term, it would be best to start buying into your mutual funds in October."

I responded, "Leave the inheritance in my savings account for now. Pull the money out of the bank in chunks starting in October and use dollar-cost averaging to invest into my 20% fund?"

Doc had a different idea, "You might need to put more money in your stay out of debt fund. With your combined income and more expensive lifestyle, you need more emergency money. With a house, you need to reevaluate how much money should be in your stay out of debt fund."

I thought about the value of that fund. I had no reason to touch it. It had been growing at around 7% for years now. I figured it would be enough, "Since we're using the same budgeting idea you gave me years ago, I take 70% of my monthly income and multiply that by four months and add 30%."

Doc responded, "That'll do it. I bet you're not even close to your new lifestyle, Mr. Fancy pants."

I think Doc felt terrible about that fancy-pants comment because I didn't respond. I was doing the math in my head. Doc continued, "I'm not certain how much money we're talking about from this inheritance, but do you feel comfortable breaking it into four segments, October through January?"

I responded, "I think that sounds about right. I'll keep it safe for now."

We ended the conversation and agreed to meet for Halloween at Doc's house.

Doc had met Lilly before a few times. They talked a bit at the wedding and the housewarming party, but they never really hung out socially together. I was a bit worried. In a way, I wanted Doc's approval of her, but I also knew Doc would never tell me she was no good. Doc's house was beautiful. A long driveway. He had told me, in years past, he never gets any trick or treaters where they live. Doc had an old pickup truck. Doc wanted us to pile in the back of the pickup and drive around. I opted to sit in the cab with Doc while everyone else was in the back shivering from the cold. A few minutes into the drive around the neighborhood, I told Doc, "I plan on leaving 20% of my mom's inheritance in my savings account because I'm worried about losing it."

"That's reasonable. You'll always have that as a reminder of the impact you had on your mother's finances."

"Doc, I don't take that credit. I just told her the stuff we were talking about. The credit goes to you."

"No, Pat. You and your mother are the ones who sacrificed, made the right choices. Put away your money instead of spending it on things that go down in value or cost you more money."

Doc's comment reminded me of Nicole, "Speaking of costing more money. With her inheritance, my sister bought a bigger house and a nice car. Just now, she realizes she can't afford the upkeep on her new purchases. The house needed more maintenance than her other house, and the yard had to be kept nicer because of the neighborhood. She went into debt with the extra costs of the new house. The car also had more costs than she anticipated with insurance, maintenance, and a few repairs not covered by the warranty, $250 for a headlight bulb, ouch. Doc, I think my sister was almost counting on a bit of inheritance from my mom. I only say that because she moved so fast after she got her hands on the money, almost like she'd been planning on a big pay-day."

I know he wasn't, but it seemed like Doc was angry, "Don't ever count on an inheritance. You never know what will happen. The person could become sick and spend tons of money in the last few years of their life, depleting the savings. They could change their Will and cut you out or make a mistake within their Will, leaving you with less than the other people." Doc then changed the subject, "Did your brother do any better?"

"My brother used his money to pay off his debt, only to go further into debt. On top of that, I don't see he has anything for it." I could tell Lilly and Doc's family were getting cold in the back of the truck. I suggested we start heading back. Once back, we hung out at Doc's house for a while. I wanted him to get to know Lilly better, but she just sat there drinking hot cocoa and chatting with Doc's wife. At least the two of them seemed to get along. As we made idle talk, I was watching Lilly, and started to think. I was planning something big with Lilly. She was the light of my life, my salvation, a princess who could take away the darkness. There, in Doc's kitchen, I decided to use Doc's strategy of selling some of the mutual fund shares in May. I was saving up in my 20% fund, and May would be a perfect time to cash-out and make it happen.

Lilly

Pat came to me and told me about his sister's latest issue. She wanted Pat to buy her car from her. Nicole owed more money than the car was worth. She wanted him to buy it at nearly the price she bought it almost a year ago. If he folded to his sister's intentions. She would have been able to pay off the loan and have enough money left over to buy a cheap, used car. We would have had an overpriced car, not worth nearly what we would have to pay. Pat was angry, "I know it would help her out, but she's using me. I've followed Doc's advice since I was a teenager. I . . . we've skimped on luxuries so that we could live a better life. Now, she's putting me in a bad situation. I help her out and take a car I don't want at a price higher than it's worth, or I make her angry with me. She knows I'm in a situation I could pay cash for the car and would be choosing not to. She's in a situation in which she can't get out. I don't need a fancy car, and then again, neither does my sister."

"Your sister has put you . . . us in a bad situation. People make mistakes in life. The mistake she's making right now is putting you is a position to disappoint your older sister, a family member. Do you remember that electrician you hired? The cheap one. You thought since it's a simple outdoor project, anyone with experience could handle it."

Pat looked angry with me for bringing it up. Pat wasn't at fault. The guy with tattoos on his face was an electrician who didn't care to do a decent job.

"Pat, nobody makes a mistake on purpose. People do things because it's what's best for them. They don't know better. The electrician didn't know that skimping on that work would ultimately hurt him. He was short-sighted. He saw a chance to save some money, overcharge you and come out ahead. What he didn't know is we had other, larger projects he would have had a chance to do. He didn't know what was truly best for himself. We don't need to blame your sister or the electrician for their wrongdoing, but instead, pity them for being naïve. We don't blame a blind man for not holding a door open for us when our hands are full. We pity their situation. When we're in a hurry, we don't blame the special needs teenager bagging our groceries for not going faster. We don't need to blame your sister or that electrician. We need to pity them for not knowing any better. Your sister not knowing as much as you or Doc does about finances. The electrician not knowing that acting ethically in business will pay off in the long-run and not just give him enough money for another face tattoo. What did he have, a spider on his cheek?"

"No, it was an ant, crawling into his eye." I understand Pat wanting to save money, but I was just as frustrated with people not doing what was right.

Pat's Notes

Buy mutual funds in October, sell in May. Use my 20% fund to make great things happen during the summer.

When investing a lot of money, use dollar-cost averaging. Move money from a savings account into mutual funds in chunks starting in October.

When life changes, update my stay out of debt fund.

Don't get a tattoo of an ant crawling into my eye. Lilly doesn't like it.

Chapter 16

What trends do the rich follow I too could use and make more money?

Doc

A few weeks after Halloween, I was walking down the wet steps next to the press box at the field. Blue walls flanked me as I made my way to the track. Students were under the awning the press box created; talking in high-pitched gibberish, I couldn't understand. I saw Patrick, the student in my class who reminded me of Pat. He was on the field, wearing awkwardly large protective glasses. I transcended to the memories of Eddy. I thought about my stubborn late friend. Barely out of his teen years with many talents. Something eerie perpetuated this thought, Patrick, with his glasses, had taken the face of Eddy, and he was waving at me, smiling. I drew closer and closer to the field. I was aware it was an optical illusion. It had to be. There was no way Eddy was on this field playing soccer. I was soon walking on the field of play, headed toward Eddy. Everyone stopped. The coaches stared in disbelief. The mouths of a few kids were agape, and it seemed everyone was alarmed by the eccentricity of my demeanor. But I needed to see Eddy. I needed to know he was alright. That I made it to him in time. That I went with him to that club and prevented him from getting into a fight. I stopped him from walking across a street where cars were driving. Where a BMW would hit him like a wide-eyed dear trying to cross the road and drive away like his life didn't matter.

I reached Eddy. My mind jumped back to reality—I realized it was my student, Patrick. I needed an excuse as to why I walked across the field, "Patrick, I just wanted to remind you comp book test five is tomorrow."

"Yeah, Doc. I know. I'll study after practice." Patrick said as he gave me a peculiar look.

I scuffed away, half absentmindedly. I gave the coach a look that said I was sorry, but judging by the contortion on his face, accentuated by the pouches of flesh that hung down his neck, I knew he was not taking a feigned look for an answer. He kept his eyes on me, urging eyes, forcing me to further apologize for disrupting his players. The eyes won a flawless victory for the coach. I put my hands together in front of my chest, gave a bow as if we lived in Asia, and continued walking past the coach. Being a social studies teacher, he would understand my gesture.

As I approached, the coach laughed, pouches of flesh wobbled as he did. He asked mockingly, "Did you tell Patrick the opportunity costs for the purchase of his soccer ball?" His laughter infected the rest of the crew, and they joined in, chuckling as I trudged away in long strides, outwardly disenchanted.

There was no way the kid would have been Eddy. I knew beforehand, and somehow, I just wanted to know for sure. A hallucination like that had never happened to me. As I walked the track, I realized I had altered how I lived, what was important to me. All because I lost Eddy while in college. All these years of teaching were my way, never to fail another Eddy.

When I got back to my classroom, I remembered I needed to call Pat. When I had sat down, wiped off the trickles of sweat that had formed on my brow, I put a call through to him. He picked up on the second ring.

"Pat, pull out that paper, I mean cell phone notes, with the secrets the rich use. I've noticed some trends you could take advantage of." I was still having trouble shaking that weird feeling I had on the soccer field. I was hoping talking with Pat would distract me.

"Like the trend of buying more shares when the cost is low and fewer shares when the cost is high?" Pat responded.

"Dollar-cost averaging does help build wealth, but these are a bit less obvious. What day of the month do you think most young people invest in the stock market?"

It didn't take long for Pat to come up with the right answer, "Right after payday. Most of their investments are automatically pulled from their paycheck into a 401(k)."

"If we have millions of dollars dumping into the stock market the first couple of days at the beginning of the month, what will happen with the price of those stocks and mutual funds?"

"They'll jump up. More people want to buy—more demand, higher cost."

"Now, picture older people and retired people. When do they pull money out of their investments?"

"I'm guessing toward the end of the month, so they have the money to pay their mortgage, utility bills, and Metamucil."

"Pat, you're right. Because of these two factors, the stock market sees a dip in the last few days of the month and a spike in the first few days of the month. Now, this isn't always true, but it does have this ebb and flow about it. We aren't talking a huge difference, but over time buying at the end of the month and selling at the beginning of the month can make an impact."

"Doc, you're saying I should make sure my monthly investments go in around the 27 - 28 of the month?"

"Yeah, that's pretty close."

"I can't control the date my 10% retirement money is taken from my pay and put into the 401(k). On the other hand, I can control when my money is taken from my checking account and put into my 20% savings."

I responded, "Let's start there and see how you do."

"I've been buying at the end of the month for years now."

"Then, you can have a fun game. Go to your online investment and find your personal rate of return. Compare your rate of return to the published rate of return. With dollar-cost averaging and investing at the end of the month, your one-year personal return should be a bit higher than the rate the mutual fund publishes."

"Doc, that sounds like a fun game for you. I don't think most people would get much of a kick out of that one." Pat was chuckling at his comment. We finished talking and hung up.

The next time I talked with Pat, he wanted to move into a fixer-upper. He had been saving money in his 20% fund to help make this happen. He also was able to sell his house for a profit. The sale not only paid the real-estate commissions but gave him extra money to put toward the next house. We got together after school at a nearby restaurant. "Hey Doc, how are the students treating you?"

"Pretty well. I have a few who are genuinely interested in the financial literacy stuff like you were. Do you want to come by to be a guest speaker?"

"I don't know. I'm pretty busy. I'm thinking about buying a house, renovating it, and living in it. See Lilly wants a unique place, a place she can put her style into."

"Pat, it's great you want to do something for your wife, but we've talked about the house thing before. Even though you can build some instant equity in a fixer-upper, a house you live in is still not a great investment."

"I remember. I'm doing this for Lilly and me. We want a nice place, for cheap, with our style. I remember you saying something about how the rich follow trends. Is there a trend when it comes to selling large chunks of investments, pulling money out?"

"In this case, we have two trends you can follow. The first is the stock market. Over the years, the stock market has followed a trend based upon the U.S. President's term in office. The first year is usually volatile but no real growth. The third year of a president's term, late November is when you'll see the stock market reach new heights. If you're looking to sell an investment, wait until this point, and you'll see a swing upward."

Pat indicated this strategy might work, "I was initially thinking in May, as we talked about last time. I like this idea better. Timing should work out well for that to happen."

"That timing also corresponds with the best time to buy a house. You can save roughly 10% by buying between November and January, with some exceptions like Phoenix, Arizona."

Pat responded, "What about specifically a fixer-upper?"

"The smart homeowner will fix up a house to fit their needs and make a place they can enjoy for the long-term. When they redo the kitchen, the owners need it functional, but they also want the cost of upgrades recuperated when they go to sell. The smart never buy the most expensive house in the neighborhood. They let the more expensive comps increase the value of their house, not the other way around," I looked across the restaurant's table. Pat was putting notes on his phone.

I then continued after a pause, "One more thing you can do is go to the planning commission for the town and see if zoning is changing in the area, roads are being widened, new construction planned. You don't want a fast-food restaurant in your backyard."

I had to give Pat a strong word of caution about another trick the wealthy use before I would tell him about it. "This next one, I'm not recommending this because a lot of novices get burned by doing this. By novice, I mean those people who aren't super-rich. The rich have money to throw around. They can move money quickly and cover expenses. Ordinary folk, this may not be for them. Here it is anyway. When the rich feel the stock market has reached a peak, they'll take out a loan from their 401(k). The loan has to be paid back, so they elect to pay back the money within a year or two. It's paid back out of their paycheck. They slow down investments into their 20% fund to be able to pay back the loan.

On top of that, for some companies, the interest is paid to the employee as well. So, you take out a loan. You can spend the money how you want. You have to pay interest, but that interest goes to your 401(k). If the timing is right, they sell when the stock market is high and use dollar-cost averaging to buy as stock prices drop. In effect, interest-free."

Months later, I learned that even after the strong word of caution against it, Pat took out a loan on his 401(k) in late November the third year of the President's term. This loan would help pay for the repairs to his fixer-upper. Sure enough, the stock market slowed during the last year of the president's term. The first year of the new president's term was up and down because of a potential conflict overseas. The drop and volatility allowed Pat to buy shares cheaper than he sold them. One of the things going for Pat was he was confident he was going to stay at his job. If Pat thought he was going to leave, he wouldn't have taken out that loan because they would've required him to pay it back when he resigned or was fired.

Lilly

Pat was a doer. There are two types of people in the world, doers and thinkers. Pat got things done. He didn't just talk about it or dream about how he would accomplish it one day—he did it. That's one of the things I loved about Pat. It was rare that Pat would come to me with a problem. One time we were renovating this house. It had all sorts of issues. Complications we didn't foresee when we bought it. Pat came to me saying we needed to spend more money. Money out of our emergency fund. I didn't like the sound of that.

I told Pat that not having the available funds seemed terrible, but it was still a matter of perception. I related it to the time my mom and I were robbed. At the time, it seemed terrible. But on that day, I remember how gallant Pat was. Neighbors became closer, looking out for our place. We also got to replace some of our old stuff with new ones. Getting robbed was terrible, but when you change your perspective, your attitude changes too. A lot of good came out of that robbery.

Pat kept looking at me as I was trying to explain how some good came out of that day. I changed the subject to explain it another way. I told him about how it rains on a Saturday. The bride had planned her wedding for months, and now it's raining. She's furious.

The aunt, attending the wedding, is happy about the rain because her garden needed it.

I told Pat about this analogy and added, the weather isn't in our control. The termites in the house aren't in our control. Let go of the things outside of your control. Take what appears to be negative and change your perspective. How can the termite damage allow you to change the floorplan? How could a rainy wedding keep everyone inside, on the dance floor having fun?

I don't think he heard anything I said because he was so focused on the money. The money I wouldn't let him use to fix the issue. I ended with, 'ask Doc.'

Doc

Pat called me in the middle of the renovation project. The fixer-upper was nearby. I think he regretted the decision. "Doc, the 401(k) loan worked out fine for me. The house, on the other hand, didn't do as well. I thought I was getting a great deal. Termite damage. Mold. The workers took longer than expected, and they're expensive per day. I don't think I'll make as much profit as I had planned. Forget about profit. I'm losing money. To be honest, Doc, I'm out of money. I don't know what to do."

I could hear the frustration in Pat's voice. "Okay, let's look at some choices. You took out a loan against the 401(k) and can't take any more."

"Right, taking out the loan was a mistake. I used a chunk of my mom's inheritance too. The other part of mom's money went to our stay out of debt fund, as you suggested. I have to tell you. I'm taking some money out of there too, to pay the bills. I thought mom would be proud of the decision to buy a fixer-upper. Now, I feel trapped. I can't leave my company until the 401(k) loan is repaid. If I had to repay it now, I would have to sell the house at a loss."

"Alright, next, have you sold your old place yet?"

Pat took a breath, trying to calm himself, "Of course. I'm not going to have two mortgages. We're in an apartment. Before you ask, it's cheap. One of the cheapest around. We can't skimp much more on housing."

With a coy smirk, Pat couldn't see, I had to ask, "Is it above a mechanic's shop?"

"This is not a time to kid around. I'm struggling here, and it's causing a lot of stress on our marriage."

"You're right. I can feel your frustration. I'm guessing you took out a loan to buy this place."

Pat's voice trembled a bit, giving me every indication of how stressed he was. "Yeah, I maxed out the loan, so I would be sure to have enough money for the remodel. Little did I know it would take more money to remodel than I thought.

I spent a big chunk of money from our 20% fund. I have some money left in there, but Lilly won't let me spend it. I love her to death, but she doesn't know the stress I'm under here."

"When you were younger, you opened a Roth IRA. How about taking money out of that?"

"Doc, I'm not willing to pay the penalties to withdraw the money early."

"You're not withdrawing all of it. You would only be withdrawing the principal you put in. You're allowed to withdraw the principal any time you want, penalty-free. You can also pull out a chunk for a qualified purchase, like education or this house. Beyond those two withdrawals, you can't pull out the growth until you're older."

"Doc, I love it. That will be plenty of money. That fund has gone up in value like gangbusters over the years. Before I had access to a 401(k), I contributed 10% of my income into the Roth for years. I can easily pull out $20,000."

"Great, crisis averted. Aren't you glad you saved for your future?"

"You were right. Saving for my future allowed me to have choices. If I hadn't had the money, I would've had no option but to sell the house at a loss and continued to live in the apartment."

"Right, or find an auto repair place you could bunk down in."

"Thanks, Doc. Can we change subjects now?"

"Pat, I thought we could talk about the spending patterns of people and how that spending affects the economy."

"Sure, what are your thoughts?"

"Well, they aren't my thoughts at all, but I do agree with them. Harry Dent came up with the concept called 'spending wave.' He could probably explain it better than I could, but I'll try to give it a shot."

"Shoot away, Doc."

"People spend money from before birth until they die and even a bit after death for funerals and such. The time of a person's life when they're spending the most money isn't when they're kids. Candy is cheap. Isn't when they're old, they're still wearing the same shoes they had 20 years ago. The age when most people are spending the most money is 46. Picture a 46-year-old. Their kids are older. They've reached a decent income. They realize they don't have to work 60 hours a week. They want a vacation home. They want a sports car. They want a new lease on life. They want to live before it's too late."

"That's great, but how could this help predict the stock market?"

"It comes down to the baby boomers. The U.S. had a huge spike in population starting in 1946. These babies weren't spending money, but when they reached age 46, they were spending like crazy, making the stock market spike. With the baby boomers getting older, they'll start spending less money, and we have to wait for the next big wave of high birth rates and immigration to begin reaching this mature age of spending."

Pat asked, "What's the next group of big spenders?"

"The millennials are the next largest population. They will spend the majority of their money a bit later than the baby boomers, probably around age 48. This window of decreasing stock values gives a great opportunity to buy stocks as they are coming down from the high the baby boomers created. Then hold them until 2040 or 2060 as the two millennial spikes reach their mature age of spending."

"I'm scared to ask what happens after 2060?"

"By 2000, birth rates in the U.S. had a steady decline, too much for a slight immigration rise to combat. When the millennials slow their consumption as they pass their mature age of spending, the economy will slow down. The prediction is the slowdown will start in 2060."

Pat added to the prediction, "In 2060, even less money will be spent because of the rise in artificial intelligence and automation. These two factors have already changed the economy. By 2060, we're sure these factors will have an even greater impact." I wasn't surprised Pat came to that conclusion—he was smart. At this point, I wondered if he was surpassing this old high school teacher's knowledge base. Pat brought our conversation to a close, "Doc, thanks for the trends. Can we see you again at Halloween?" We agreed to meet at my place to drive around with my truck and then hung up.

Getting together with Pat and his wife during Halloween became a bit of a tradition. Pat and I would talk in the cab while everyone else was cold in the back, but staying warm, jumping in and out talking to people, and getting candy. Pat told me about how his investments were growing, "Doc, I have two funds in which I put most of my focus. I put 90% in the S&P 500 and 10% into an International Index fund. My only issue is the S&P is outperforming the world stock market fund. It's really out of balance."

"This is not the perfect time to lock in those gains. Typically, the stock market hits lows in October and highs in May. Hold off until May and rebalance at that time. Move money from your S&P 500 to your International Index MSCI EAFE to get back to the 90/10 split. You could make rebalancing fun."

Pat responded, "Actually, I do find all this fun. It's nice to have a plan in place. You know to have specific directions as to what to do and when to do it."

"Oh, I was just about to tell you that you could watch that international fund for a few days. You'll see it move up and down over a couple of weeks. When you think it's moved down, buy then. I know this isn't specific directions, but maybe it could be fun buying low and hanging onto your investment. Rebalancing is helping to lock in your gains. You've made money, now protect it by locking it down."

"Oh, Pat, I forgot to mention something. Typically, the best day to sell mutual funds and stocks is on Tuesday. Prices drop at the end of the week. For some reason, people usually sell near the end of the week, dropping values."

"Sell on a Tuesday; buy on Friday. Is there anything I can do in October?"

"The rich buy Roth IRAs for their kids in October. I know you don't have any kids, but the rich "hire" their kids to work, just enough to make enough money to legally contribute to a Roth IRA and then fully fund it for a few years. When we get back to a computer, we'll plug in the numbers to show you how much tax-free money someone would have if they left it in an S&P 500 or International Index fund from age 12 - 65."

I looked over at Pat and noticed a smile come over his face. He looked at me and confessed, "We haven't told anyone yet, you'll be the first. We're pregnant."

"Congrats. When the kid makes money from modeling, you can use that income toward its Roth IRA."

"Do you think our baby could make money modeling?"

With a sly smile, I returned, "Sure, if she gets her looks from her mom and not you."

Pat's Notes

The stock market typically dips at the end of the month and rises within the first few days of the month because of older people selling at the end of the month to cover bills and working people investing through their 401(k) at the beginning of the month.

Take advantage of this flow: buy at the end of the month. Sell near the beginning of the month.

The third year of a president's term, in November, is when the stock market typically hits new highs. The best time to sell would be November, three years into a president's term. Tuesday generally is the best day to sell high.

House buying is cheaper in the winter months. Don't buy the most expensive house. Let the bigger houses increase your property value. Check with the zoning commission to see if any changes are going to take place in the area.

Fixer-upper, make the changes fit what you need, and can get the money back upon resale.

I can take a loan out of my 401(k), but it would be stupid to use the money for consumables/living. It's still risky, but using the money for a house could work. Unsafe, because if I leave my job, I'll have to repay it immediately.

I can pull out the principal (the money I paid in) from my Roth IRA. I can also take out a qualified Roth IRA distribution to rebuild my home.

The baby boomers, reaching 46 years old, made the stock market rise to new heights.

With the baby boomers aging, you can expect a decline in the stock market.

When the millennials reach their maximum spending years, age 48, we can expect another two high stock market spikes around 2040 and again in 2060.

In 2060, the stock market will turn down unless something else happens.

Chapter 17

How do I time the market and prosper during turbulent times?
How do I create a stream of income, like the rich?
How much money do I need to retire?
How can someone who hasn't saved money retire?

Pat

Age 32, dual-income $98,800/year; 10% fund $233,315; 20% fund $116,490; Stay out of debt fund $45,907; home equity $186,690

I watched the news and saw a conflict escalating. The United States was getting involved. I had too much money to risk it in this type of environment. Lilly gave birth to a perfect little girl not long ago. We named her Alessa. I was thinking of them too. I wanted to pull the money out and safeguard what I earned. The stock market already took a dip. I was worried it would go down even further, and I would lose a bunch of money. I was going to move the money that afternoon, but I gave Doc a call in the morning, "Doc, is this conflict a sign I should move out of the stock market and focus my money into bonds?"

Doc is usually calm, but this time he seemed even more relaxed than usual, "Pat, anxiety about your money is going to make you do things that'll cause you to lose. You have a great game plan. By using dollar-cost averaging, you buy more shares as the price drops, and you buy fewer shares when the price is high. Stop the what-if game. Stop anxiety. Stop worrying about your investments, second-guessing your strategy. The way you have things set up, you only have to rebalance your portfolio once a year, in May. Besides, at your young age, I would ride it out. During the conflict, you'll see the stock market fluctuate a good deal and never make much progress. After the war, innovation and inflation will spark the economy, and the stock market will respond to the benefit of those who don't try to time the market."

I agreed with Doc and decided not to panic. Ride it out. Use dollar-cost averaging and keep buying at my monthly pace.

A few weeks later, I knew Doc was on holiday. I gave him a call. As the phone was ringing, I started to think. It seemed like teachers always had holidays. Here I was working all year 'round, and Doc was off more often than he worked.

On top of that, he never seemed stressed about going to work, as Mrs. Galloway would. Doc would bring his coffee, talk with teenagers about investing. He looked at home in that school. I guess I was a bit jealous. I had a mundane job that didn't seem to help anyone but the boss. At least Doc was trying to make young people's lives better. As soon as he answered, he asked if we could get together.

We met at a coffee shop. I ordered the darkest black coffee possible, but let it cool. I didn't know why Doc wanted to meet in person, but I started the conversation, "How much money will I need in retirement?"

"The answer is easier than you think. You already know that you can live off 70% of your income—the money you need every month. Now deduct any checks you know you'll be getting, like social security, maybe a pension. That figure is the amount of money you need to generate from savings to get by. You know, no extras, keep the same standard of living, but without the fun toys, your 20% fund buys you."

Pat added, "Let me guess, if I don't accumulate a bunch of money to fund my retirement along with social security and pensions, I'll have to reduce my expenses. Cut out my monthly fun."

"You sure would. I've known lots of people who retire, thinking they'll play golf, and they soon realize they can no longer afford the game. I had a friend of mine retire. He moved to a golf community and started to play three times a week with his wife. Just out of curiosity, I asked him how much he spent on golf. We were at a party, and he didn't give me a straight answer, but he did call me the next day. He told me he added it all up. Membership, cart fees, magazine subscriptions, a new club each year, and some miscellaneous stuff, too, all added up to $56,700 a year. He and the wife quit, except for charity games a couple of times a year."

I didn't care much about golf, but I guess Doc was trying to make a point. I need to figure out how much I'm going to spend during retirement and not over-do it with frivolous expenses. I wanted to focus more on this military conflict. I changed the conversation back to the tension the country was getting involved with and asked: "What if I was older and this conflict was about to happen?"

"Lots of factors come into play here. Where is the market now, and what type of funds you have? I'll give it to your straight. About five years before you plan to retire, you need to start using dollar-cost averaging, pulling money out of your investments, locking in those gains. First and foremost, you want to guarantee you'll have a stream of income for the rest of your life."

"Doc, I thought if I had plenty of money, I would be fine."

"The money has to finance this steady stream of income. Here's the thing. If you have a bunch of money tied up in stocks, bonds, real estate, and the economy crashes, you won't want to bail out and lock in those losses. You need something that will guarantee an income."

I responded, "Sure, I know social security will pay, but my statements indicate I won't get enough. What do you suggest?"

Doc told me, "An immediate annuity. Let me explain. You pay money to an insurance company, and they pay you every month for the rest of your life. It's like you're getting a paycheck every month. This paycheck makes up the difference that you'll need in addition to social security and any other regular payments you're getting."

Pat asked, "But what if I die early?"

"That may happen. In that case, at least you had the monthly income while you were alive and needed it. Frankly, it's an insurance policy, not a great investment. It's insurance that will give you a guaranteed payment every month. I only want you to consider a single premium immediate annuity. You'll set it up and begin getting your monthly checks within a few months. Most people start this when they retire. They want a stream of guaranteed income. They don't feel confident their investments will be around for the rest of their life."

I started to nod, "I get it. If I simply have money in investments, hoping they'll be around for my entire life, I could be wrong. I might go broke because those investments might fail. I can be victimized in my old age. I could spend all the money because I live longer than the money lasts. On the other hand, If I have a single premium immediate annuity, I'll always have enough income to survive. Enough money each month to buy food and pay the utilities."

"That's where I'm going with this, Pat. You and your wife need a secure future. The stock market can't guarantee you'll always have that money, but an insurance company can. If you set up a joint-life option with your spouse as the primary beneficiary, she will continue to get the monthly payments even after you die. If you die first, she continues to get the monthly check."

When he said that Lilly could get the money if I were to die before her, I started to think this might be worth it. I wanted more information, "What do I ask for, an annuity?"

"No, no, no. I can't stress this enough, Pat." Doc was waving his hands around, like an airline stewardess showing the exits. "There are tons of annuity products out there. You can't trust a sales agent to give you the best advice. Annuity salespeople act as though they're advisors—they're actors, like a student in the school's musical. Only consider the low-fee immediate annuity."

I shook my head to indicate I was confused and said, "I like simple. Tell me in simple terms what I need. I don't want to get ripped off. This annuity stuff sounds like I could be taken advantage of."

"You are looking for a single premium immediate annuity. You pay a large payment to the insurance company. They ask you a bunch of questions, like your age. At a certain date, within a few months of setting it up, the annuity will start to pay you every month for the rest of your life."

"That one does seem simple."

I can always tell when Doc starts to get serious. He moves his eyes down and looks at his hands. Doc continued, "I need you to keep this in mind, an annuity pays salespeople commissions. Since it pays commissions, you can imagine an annuity is not the best investment. One more thing—get an annuity only if it's a small slice of your overall assets. I'm only recommending this annuity idea because you'll have a good bit of money saved up. You'll have other assets. On top of that—only get what you need to survive. With many annuities, it's nearly impossible to get out of without penalties, so be conservative in how much money you want this annuity to pay you each month. You are using it, so you have enough cash flow to meet your basic needs—your bare-bones, basic needs."

Doc paused, I could tell he was thinking and I didn't want to interrupt his train of thought, "Another option is an investment property. I know you think you're a bit lazy, but maybe you could find a place that's highly likely to stay rented. Buy the place and rent it out."

"Doc, you're right about me being a bit lazy. Being a landlord sounds like a lot of headaches."

"It can be. Let me tell you a story about one of my students. She came to me her senior year, asking for my advice. Most students who ask my advice are talking hypothetically, they don't have anything invested yet, and they're thinking of the future. Not Laura, she owned an actively-rented office building."

"That's pretty cool. How did she get it?"

"She said it was from an inheritance. Her question was, should she sell it and have money for college or keep it so she can have the income?"

"Was it worth a lot?" I asked.

"It wasn't worth a ton. The good part, it only required yearly maintenance and to keep up with the grounds. The girl's father did the upkeep and record keeping. The girl owned it, so the dad was trying to teach her how to handle it. She had someone who had a nearby office who wanted to buy it. They wanted it so bad; they gave her a written offer for the place."

"Having the money would be great," I responded and sipped more coffee.

"Money is great, but income gives options. Think of this 18-year-old girl. What's in her future? Will she get married? Will she have kids? Will she want to stay home with the kids? Will her husband need to move around for work, like the military? Now, picture her monthly income and the options she has. If she keeps the place and continues the income, she doesn't have to be tied down to one job, one career, one location. She has choices. With income coming in on a place that requires minimal upkeep, she can choose to stay home with the kids or have a lifestyle that allows her to move around, travel."

I was thinking about other places that might require little upkeep, "Another place that requires little maintenance is an auto repair place."

"Good one, Pat. I know you're intimately familiar with auto repair places. Even the rentals above them."

"Yeah, yeah, Doc, funny. It's true, though. Landscaping is usually pavement. The walls are usually metal. They don't run the AC much because of the large doors. Plumbing is a basic bathroom without kids flushing action figures down the toilet. An auto repair place could be a perfect place for me to own. We'll still have cars in the future."

Doc added to my statement, "That's a great point. During times of recession, auto repair places usually do well because people aren't buying new cars. During good times, they also do well because people don't want to change their own oil or deal with regular maintenance issues themselves. What other properties could be a good investment?"

"How about housing?" I asked.

"People make a great living renting apartments and houses. The factors they say have the biggest impact on their profitability are the neighborhood, including schools and property taxes. Maintenance is a large expense, as we've mentioned. Crime rate increases can leave houses vacant for months at a time. Same with the job market. When investors find out about future developments of parks, malls, and public transportation hubs and they take advantage of the low cost of houses before they're built, they then can profit from people wanting to live near these areas. Another factor they look at is the number of other listings and vacancies along with the rents they charge. And the final two factors, they need to take into account - natural disasters that can leave a place vacant for months at a time and the cost of insurance."

Doc

Pat nodded his head and took some notes on his phone. "What do I do once I know how much my monthly income is from Social Security, plus rentals, plus the single premium immediate annuity?" Pat asked.

I continued to tell Pat how to fund his retirement, "After you have your steady stream of income set up through real estate and that immediate annuity, look at your investments. How much do you have in liquid funds, this is the money in your mutual funds, retirement funds, don't go into debt fund. Don't include your house or other assets like cars and boats. A safe assumption is that if 30% - 50% of this money is invested in the stock market with dividends and growth reinvested and the other portion is invested in the bond market, you can pull out 4% a year, plus inflation, for 30 years."

Pat pulled up a calculator on his phone, "For every $100,000 I have, I could pull out $333 a month? That doesn't seem like a lot. But I guess if I had a cool million dollars, I could pull out $3,333 a month, and it would still last me 30 years. What if I'm too worried about having 30% - 50% in the stock market?"

"If you feel the stock market will go down or remain level, you can buy individual bonds. If you put the majority of your money in the bond route, you can only pull out 2.5%, plus inflation, for 30 years. With your cool Mil, you're looking at around $2,080 per month. The best bet is to leave 50% in the index stock market and buy individual bonds with the other 50%. This way, you can pull out the 4%, plus inflation, per year. After ten years, see where you stand. If the markets have done well, the balance in your accounts might have remained the same, even though you've been pulling money out. In that case, you could increase your deduction by 1%. If you don't need to pull out the money, leave it in there. Let it grow."

Pat looked confident that he could enjoy retirement. He asked, "When and how do I pull my 4% out of my funds and live off it?"

I pointed to Pat's phone, "Do you remember how we want to sell in May?" Pat nodded as I continued talking, "You'll want to start with two years of living expenses, minus any regular income, like social security, pension, and the monthly annuity payment. These two years of living expenses will go into your bank or a money market. During the year, your bonds will pay their dividends. Put that into this account. Each May, look at which investments did the best. Sell the ones that rose in value. Sell enough to bring your cash balance back to 2 years of expenses. Hopefully, this is only 4% plus inflation of your liquid assets. Only selling the winners makes it, so you're never locking in a loss. You're always locking in the gains. One more advantage of selling the ones that increased in value is the re-balancing. The selling will help get you close to your mix. The re-balancing improves the investment returns over the years and reduces risk."

"What happens if all of the stocks are down?"

"Since you have two years of living expenses, don't sell. If all of the investments are down, hold tight. When you get within a few months from hitting zero, and the investments still haven't returned, sell a couple of bonds to bring your cash balance back to two years of expenses."

"I like that idea. I'll feel comfortable having a cushion of money and feel smart, only selling ones that have gone up in value. If I went this route, I wouldn't be 50/50 stocks and bonds because of the cash I have on hand. In addition to the cash, I would keep my 20% fund and my stay out of debt fund. I'll double-check, but most of that stay out of debt fund is invested in bonds at this point. All of my 20% funds are in the dividend achievers fund, so all stock. I guess I'll have to account for those when I'm figuring my 50/50 split."

"Keep those funds. Add to the dividend achievers fund as you want. Your 20% fund is where you save money to meet goals, but also making larger payments like property taxes, major car repairs, a new car, a big trip."

"Doc, speaking of goals, you'd be surprised how my goals have changed since I got married. With Lilly in the picture, our combined goals are nothing like the goals I had. It's for the better. She's right to focus on the big picture. She wants us to save up and do something huge, like retire early."

"Retire early?" I asked. "What would be your strategy? How would you change your spending habits? Would she still make you drink those green smoothies?"

"I hope not. Man, are they gross. Doc, I poop green! My poo is green."

"What makes you think I want to hear about the color of your poop?" I was laughing because it was good to hear Pat talk like we were friends. "How green is your poo?"

"I'm almost used to 'em at this point. I'm sure I'll have to drink those smoothies during retirement too" Pat shook his head. I could tell he had a plan. It sounded like Lilly, and he talked about it. "I . . . I mean, we would like to move to another country. Find somewhere with a lower cost of living and better weather. Not that Portland, Oregon doesn't have a perfect climate." Pat chuckled at his joke. "Maybe someplace tropical. I've heard of people retiring abroad, having a great life, and living a life of luxury on the cheap."

I confirmed everything he had heard was right. Then asked, "How much money do you think you need saved up to be able to retire like this?"

"I don't know. Do you have any idea?"

"A bit over 50% of the people who retire and stay local, spend more than their normal budget. They have more medical expenses, travel, and time with the grandkids. All these things cost money. Those who plan on retiring and spending like this would need to estimate 120% of their current expenses."

"I'm not in that boat. I want to lessen our expenses, live cheap."

"You are in the other 50% of the retirement population. These retirees typically spend 80% of their current expenses. These people don't necessarily have to move to reduce expenses. Simply, they don't get sick as often or travel like the others."

"Doc, you're not getting to the point. How much money do I need to retire?"

I was trying to get to the point. Sometimes Pat doesn't understand. You have to have some background knowledge and think about how much money you'll spend to come up with the right guess. I think he saw the frustrated look on my face. I tried to cover it up by telling him, "Divide the amount of money you think you'll spend each year by 4%, that's 0.04 in a calculator."

Pat pulled out his phone and started to type numbers. "If we need an additional $80,000 more a year, above annuity and social security payments, to live." He typed in 80,000. "I divide that number by .04, and I come up with a nest egg of $2Mil. I can do that."

I thought about their two incomes. "Pat, you can. You and Lilly have a high income. If retiring soon is a priority, you can focus on it. Put your savings toward it and make it happen."

I did the math in my head and figured Pat was in his mid-thirties. I wondered when he was planning on retiring early. Pat continued, "I'm worried about my brother. He keeps accumulating debt, and I know he's not saving for retirement. What can he do?"

"Lots of people are in your brother's situation. They don't have enough to retire. Step one, start a retirement fund now. Put away 15% into that fund. Even if he only works for a few more years, that money has the potential to grow for 30 or more years. If he can't start with 15%, he needs to start with 10% and do step increases each year. If he gets pay raises, all of the raise needs to go into the monthly contribution. Within a couple of years, he needs to be putting away 15%."

"Doc, that won't be enough. Saving, even 15%, won't be enough money for him to retire."

I shook my head and gave my best sympathy look, "He'll need to keep working. Move to a cheaper location to live. Sell the house and rent. Sell extra cars or even all cars and rely on other transportation. The house and cars are both money pits, and people feel they're necessities. They aren't. You can rent and live in a maintenance-free place. You can rely on other ways of getting around and free yourself from the expenses of owning and operating a vehicle. Where you live makes an enormous impact on your expenses. There are places in the United States much cheaper to live. There are places abroad even cheaper than any place in North America. Your brother needs to make some changes."

I continued, "Pat, you don't have to worry. If you follow this plan, you'll be a multimillionaire. Now for what to do with that money. Buy actual bonds and plan on keeping them through maturity. Stagger those bonds between different companies and over different years, like 5, 10, and 15. Once the 5-year bond returns your lump some money, reinvest it into a 15-year bond. Keep rotating them. This process is called a bond ladder."

"Do these bonds follow a buy/sell cycle? You know what's the best day to buy bonds?" Pat asked.

"Buy on the last business day of the month. Sell on the first business day of the month. You can put in a request to sell after the payment is made to you, so you don't have to deal with it on the first business day of the month."

"That makes it convenient," Pat responded.

"When you buy on the last business day of the month, you maximize how quickly you'll start getting payments from the bond. If you had bought it sooner, you would still have to wait that extra time before getting the payment."

Pat summed it up, "If I bought a bond in the middle of the month, my money wouldn't be doing anything for me for two weeks."

"That's right, Pat. You may as well keep it in the stock market for that time."

"These bonds are also paying me every six months or year, right?"

"It depends on the bond, but yeah. Owning individual bonds is a way for you to have income beyond your minimum needs to survive. You've been saving all your life. Now is the time to safeguard your money. Lock in your gains. Live on the returns."

Pat's Notes

Retirement savings: since we'll be retiring early, I can't figure in any payments from Social Security or pensions. Take your expenses and make our best guess as to how much we'll spend in retirement. If I'm going to increase our spending, multiply my costs by 1.2. If we're going to live more frugally, multiply our expenses by .8. Then take that number and divide by 0.04. The resulting (large) number is how much we need in income-generating assets to retire abroad. This is how much money I want in our combined 10% and 20% stock market investments before I retire.

If starting to invest late, like Chad - after 40 years old, put away 15% into an index fund. If my brother can't start with 15%, begin with 10% and do step increases each year/pay raise to get to 15% within a couple of years. Maybe Chad can get a second job?

For those who can't afford to live comfortably during retirement, move to a cheaper location. Sell the cars and use public transportation. Make money off the stuff, especially the things that cost money to maintain. Most of all, get out of debt.

Don't worry about what the news says about the economy, conflicts, or bad times ahead. Keep investing each month to take full advantage of the downturn in the economy. Leave your money in place.

Five years before retirement, begin to use dollar-cost averaging to pull money out of investments. Only sell those investments that won't work well during retirement. Sell those that made the most money first. Wait to see if the others will turn around before selling.

During retirement, you need a stream of income.

Figure how much your income is going to be from social security and pensions. Then subtract that from your bare-bones living expenses.

Create another stream of income that will give you enough to survive during retirement. This could be from a single premium immediate annuity, bond ladder, or investment property.

Investment property would need to be in a field that will continue to thrive. The building will need to be easy to maintain to maximize profit.

During retirement, keep 30-50% of my assets in the stock market for growth.

If I keep 30-50% of my assets in the stock market, I could pull out 4% (plus an increase each year to account for inflation), and the money would last me 30 years.

Keep two years of living expenses, minus any regular income, in a money market. Each May, when the stock market is doing well, pull money out of those funds doing the best to rebalance and replenish the money market. If the economy is doing poorly, wait until I need the money. Maybe by that time, the economy will recover. If the economy still hasn't recovered, sell a bond or two.

Chapter 18

When is it time to call in an investment professional? How do I choose a professional who will work for an hourly rate?

Doc

Monday at Greenville High was a long, stress-filled day. I had finished my last class at 3:30. Each course provided the grilling task of listening to the multitudes of questions hurled my way. It was how my students made their points known. If I weren't confronted with questions from expectant students, it would be pretty dull. As usual, my simple answers squashed the demystification of curiosity that plucked their minds. I enjoy the class but am relieved when the dismissal bell rings. I watched them leave. Some driving. Some on the bus. Some walking home. All were drifting off together—different colored shirts spilling from a central location, scattering outward. Scuffing away in the vitality of their age. I kept my eyes on them from the glass-paned window. Bold humans, with heads, legs, torsos, transcended into iridescent specks of dust on the horizon.

When I took my eyes off the window, I awakened to my responsibilities. I no longer could live with the shackles of regret. I needed the joys of discoveries. I needed a way to reach the youth. To inform them, like I've helped Pat, to become rich. I needed a new approach. Something never done before. Something easy, concise. Today's quick-paced working class wants clear answers to how to have it all. How could I get the word out, 'you can't have it all today and tomorrow—you have to choose. If you want choices later in life, sacrifice today.'

I was in that stage of my life where my memories hovered in my face like a madness. Ideas were capering off, replaced with an afflictive mind. It was the inevitability of growing old, and these days I am an aged man. The students would use 'old' to regard me. In their world, there were only two kinds of people: the old and the young. I would count my blessings, all the little contributions I've made to make the world a better place. And still feel I could've done more. Pat is usually the first to come to mind. I have been immensely partial to him. At this stage, it would be apt for me to earmark him as a success story. Only I understand that sometimes, one bad decision, one wrong turn, can send a man plummeting towards the vicinity of oblivion.

Serena, the owner of the BISCUITS CAFE, had paid me a visit on Monday, and she expressed her fear for the future of the restaurant. All her hairs had become gray, and she walked in the gait of a woman who knew she was close to her end. Only her eyes looked as young as they had always been. It's funny how the eyes can remain constant as the body ages. Maybe her eyes remained young by watching the vitality of life served one meal at a time. When she came to me wearing a baggy skirt and blouse, her vanity replaced with an attempt to cover, hide. Serena feared the worst for a restaurant she had groomed and nurtured like a baby. When I had helped her to a seat, she thanked me, exhibiting a social grace that valued little courtesies. Serena loved coffee just the way I loved it, black and bitter. I poured her a cup of coffee from the thermos I kept on my new office table.

As I was pouring, I told her, "Last week, the school had brought in this new table for the replacement of my old one. A replica, but they had not consulted me. I would have told them not to waste their time. The old table appealed to me. It was like me and my gradual aging process in life. Save the new table for a new teacher. Perhaps they would both start with a clean slate. These are things a younger man would have thought of quickly. At my age, a good argument comes too late, during the sleepless night. As I lay restless, there was a moment when I thought of the worst. A thought that pricked my heart like thorns. The thought infected me that someday, a younger man would clamber up the flight of stairs, accompanied by the principal, and perhaps the mayor. And it made me fear the worst. The realization that someday the principal would slap me on the back and thank me for my services. He would speak of the immense help I had offered, and he would try to festoon his good words on my head like a crown. It was the hypocrisy of routine words and behavior. The lauding of a man they cannot wait to replace. It was how the world worked. The propensity to offer one last, appealing set of words before giving them a kick in the ass."

With Serena's coffee cup in hand, I cringed away from the new table. The school didn't listen to me. The principal didn't care about my preference for the old table. The custodian did as instructed and cast the memories the old table held into the dumpster.

"I just liked the old table, and it seems good enough for me," I had said.

What I was saying shouldn't have set Serena to tears, but she now had rheumy eyes. It gave the illusive impression her eyes were getting used to an inevitable end.

"I am sorry I had to come at this time Doc, I'm sure you're busy. But thank you for making time for me," She said, uttering a hearty smile.

"It's okay. It is my job, and feel free to call me any time," I retorted.

A brief silence permeated the ambiance of my classroom, and Serena heaved a heavy sigh, shook her head, grimaced, head swooped up, eyes stared at the ceiling.

"I thought I had to meet you because your help has been instrumental to the success of my little restaurant. But as you well know, and as you can see," Serena paused and took a dutiful look at her wrinkled, tanned arms that now looked soft like chocolate. "I am not as strong as I would like to be these days, and I am afraid that all my efforts to make my restaurant a success would come apart once I am gone," she said, somberly.

"Why would you think that?" I asked.

"I just have a strong feeling about it. The thing is I have two children: a son and a daughter. My daughter has been indispensable in helping me manage the business. And apart from this, she is also quite frugal, and when I think about a more deserving successor to the business, it is only her that comes to mind," she paused again, and this time she feigned a smile.

"But my boy . . . well, now a man needs me more than ever these days. Things have been hard for him. He has continually failed in everything he tries. I don't think he's frugal, but there is a tenacity about him. He wants to do better, but I think he wouldn't sacrifice his standard of living. Also, he has had a failed marriage, and I can't trust him with the business. But he has nothing, and I cannot think of the possibility of giving everything to my daughter. My boy loves me so much, and it would seem like I betrayed him. It is a dilemma I have had for some time now, and I don't know how to go about it," she concluded. I looked at the expression on her face. It was hard to tell if tears lurked in her eyes, or if it was just the eyes of an older woman.

I understood why it would be tough for her to make a clear-cut decision. Humans are mostly sentimental. It's hard to be fair when torn between your intuition and rationality. And when it came to the management of business and finance, one has to trail down the path of rationality. A very sentimental man would not make a successful businessperson.

"I understand why it's difficult to make a decision," I said, empathetically.

"You love your son, and I think it's okay to love your son despite his extravagant life. He's your son, and family comes first. But on the other hand, I think you have to be more selfish about the future of your restaurant. It's your legacy. If you give it to your son, your legacy has a strong chance of coming apart. "

"I know Doc, but what am I going to do?" she asked, curiously.

"You have to understand your son offers no tangible managerial skills. He has continually failed, but that is not the problem." She jerked herself forward from a reclining position, and I could see she was immensely attentive. "The problem is his inability to learn from his mistakes. If you gave him the restaurant, you wouldn't be helping him. From what you've said about your son, he seems like a very emotional man. I want you to imagine how he would feel when he finally crumbles the restaurant, goes bankrupt. He would be sad. When he remembers that it was your legacy, he would not only be sad, but he would hate himself. Giving him your restaurant might be your way of making things harder for him. Trust me; you don't want your son harboring suicidal thoughts because he feels he's failed his mama."

Serena jerked back when she realized she could be an accessory to woes of her son, and she sighed a deep sigh, fingers interlocked.

"So should I give it to my daughter? "

"You should Serena. State expressly in your Will you want her to be 100% responsible for the management of the restaurant. Leave your son with 30% of ownership. In your Will, you want to explain everything is even. When one child receives less, they feel betrayed. List the hours your daughter will have to work over the next two years to make this restaurant successful. Multiply that figure by a typical wage, and that's how you explain the difference in percents. I have known you for a while, Serena, and I feel your daughter is a reflection of your virtues. She loves her brother as you do."

Serena's long face tapered into a hearty smile. In that smile, I could see the younger, healthier Serena.

"Thank you, Doc. I think I know what I'm going to do," she said, stumbling out of the chair. Instinctively, I stretched my hand towards her, helping her up.

I escorted her outside, and helped her down the run of stairs, watched her enter her car, and zoomed away into iridescent dust.

And when I cringed out of the window on that Monday, it was the thought of helping Serena sort out the future of her restaurant that comforted me.

But you couldn't help Eddy Doc. You know you could have gone to the club on time. You know this, Doc. You can try to find consolation somewhere else, but you failed Eddy when he needed you the most.

The thought of Eddy capered around my heart, disengaging me from the calmness I had earned from helping Serena. I staggered away from the slanting light of the sun, plopping down on a chair, and while I tried to stave off this thought, I got a phone call from Pat, and it seemed like the constant story of my life. Whenever a negative thought lurked, finance in the form of Pat, came to the rescue. At this point, Pat had accumulated a great deal of wealth. I wasn't sure exactly how much, but Pat felt as if it were a lot. He confided in me on a phone call.

"Hello, Doc. I hope you are doing well?" He asked, more formally than usual.

"Yeah. I'm fine, Pat. I am fine."

"Doc, you know how the stock market took a downturn this week?"

"Sure, I saw it, but we all know this will happen from time to time. With our strategy, we ride it out."

"Well, the money I lost in that one little down-turn was a lot. I can't take that kind of stress."

"Pat, time to be honest. We both know the stock market will have difficulties. You've dealt with similar situations before."

"I know, and at the time, I knew that dollar-cost averaging would have me buy more shares as the price was low. But . . ." Pat paused as if he didn't want to tell me something. "Lilly wants to move. She wants us to, in essence, retire abroad."

"That is a big deal. I'm assuming you repaid the 401(k) loan already?" I was worried about Pat. I wondered why Lilly would want to move away. I suspected they weren't very close to Nicole, but Chad and Pat seemed to get along well. "How do you feel about this move?"

"To be completely honest with you. I'm struggling with it. It might help with my real issue. I don't like to talk about this problem, but I'm depressed. I still think about how I took that father away from those twins. Do you know I avoid driving over that bridge? I drive 15 miles out of my way to avoid that bad memory, but it can't escape me."

"Pat, maybe Lilly has a good point. Finding a place outside of this country can have a lower cost of living and even offer a better standard of living with housekeepers, gardeners, chefs."

"You know I like the housekeeper idea. Maybe Lilly has a point, and if I can get away from here, I can leave my struggles behind me."

It was time he got the advice of a professional financial consultant. I told him, "Pat, you need to talk with a professional. Once you reach a point that you feel as wealthy as you feel, you need some professional financial guidance."

"I don't know Doc. We've been doing pretty well. You know the two of us talking. Can't we keep going like we are?"

"You run a risk of losing. You are NOT as diversified as you should be. You're still relatively young. You've got a wife and kid to think about now."

"But how do I choose someone I trust, as I trust you?"

"First and foremost, you want someone who won't take a percent of your principal, but instead just pay for the advice."

"I should call around and just ask?" Pat asked.

"Yes. You'll ask, 'Will your advisor work for an hourly rate?' Once you find a few, ask them specific questions over the phone. 'Are you a CFP - Certified Financial Planner?' Or 'Are you an RIA - Registered Investment Advisor?' Both of those could work well for your needs."

I figured Pat was still typing RIA into his phone, so I continued, "Now this last one sounds over-the-top, but I promise you, Pat, it's not. For you to find the right person, they need to be willing to look out for you. You have to ask them, 'Will you sign a contract that gives me assurance you will work to the fiduciary standard at all times, with my situation?'"

A few weeks later, Pat called me back, "I called around. I found 15 who met the first few criteria. When I asked them if they would sign a contract assuring me they'll work to the fiduciary standard at all times, with my situation, three of them pretended not to know what the fiduciary standard was. I let those people go. Four more acted insulted and claimed they don't need to sign an agreement. I told them that if they change their mind, they can call me back. I found three who said, 'yes, I would be happy to sign that type of agreement.'"

Pat continued, "Only one stood out from the others as someone I seemed to relate to and trust."

Pat and the financial advisor agreed to meet and talk. After a few hours of meeting and a dozen or so emails, Pat had a clear direction to move forward with his money. Pat paid the financial advisor (a lot) and set out to roll over his 401(k) into four different segments. The advisor considered many things, like Pat's age, his risk tolerance, what has done well for Pat in the past, and Pat's goals for the future.

Pat

Pat, age 33, dual-income $98,800/year; 10% fund $296,626; 20% fund $136,536; Stay out of debt fund $49,227; home equity $220,315

The financial advisor gave me specific mutual funds with low fees, bonds, and some individual stocks. All these combined further diversified my investments. I paid him an hourly fee. Dang, it was a lot per hour. I was in the wrong business. I suppose having the peace-of-mind I was doing the right thing was worth it. The financial advisor said, "Pat, we need to simplify things. If you have more than one retirement account, we need to pull them together into one IRA. If you have more than one Roth, we need to pull them together into one Roth IRA. When you get to the age of retirement, you need things simple. If you forget to pull money out, you can be penalized. Having multiple accounts sets you up for that type of failure."

I tried to sound younger than I am, "Dude, I'm not that old. You make it sound like I'm decrepit. But in all fairness, Lilly wants me to retire and for us to move away."

The advisor tried to apologize, "Sorry, Pat, I'm so used to talking to old, really old, people I kinda forgot. Still, no need to have multiple accounts, OK?"

I took notes as the advisor continued, "The first thing is. I don't want you to pull all of your money out at once to go into these investments. You used dollar-cost averaging to put the money in. Now we'll use dollar-cost averaging to pull it out and diversify it more than it is right now. Pull money out of the funds that are doing well. This locks in your gains—you've made money, now protect it. The other funds might turn around. If you pull money out of those funds that aren't doing as well, you'll be locking in losses. You diversified so you wouldn't have to sell when funds went down. Because you're using dollar-cost averaging, you have time before you would be pulling money out of those funds that could have been doing better. Pat, you're retirement accounts have done well with the S&P 500 and international index funds, but now that you have a substantial amount of money and you're thinking of retiring, we need to protect it. I want you to move your retirement money into four equal parts."

"45% Dividend Aristocrats Index

10% 'foreign' or 'international' fund, the one you had is good.

25% Corporate bonds, laddered.

20% industrial REIT stocks that focus on warehouses and electric companies that pay dividends."

"Find a fund that tracks the Dividend Aristocrats Index. Put 45% of your overall balance in there. Also, each month you contribute, put 45% into that fund."

I retorted, "I've been following Index funds for so long. I have friends who have funds that are doing much better than mine. I want the type of returns like they have."

The advisor responded, "Don't let greed or fear dictate your investments."

The financial advisor continued without letting me put up an argument, "I want you to put 10% into a 'foreign' or 'international' fund. Avoid those funds that say 'global' or 'world.' You are looking for a stock fund that doesn't have any U.S. stock—investing in this type of fund safeguards you against a drop in the value of the U.S. dollar. Here if you want to go risky, take a chance, and go after those high returns. If you have a liking for a specific culture, consider investing in those countries."

I asked, "For my peace of mind, should I invest some money into a few different bond funds?"

"No. Those bond funds are for schmucks. Both bond mutual funds and ETFs are highly likely to go down in value. When the economy crashes, people pull money out of their funds, including bond funds. When enough people pull their money out of bond funds, the manager is forced to sell its bonds at a loss. On top of that risk, those funds are traded like stocks, going up and down in value. The returns are typically low, and they have fees eating up part of the return. Now, I'm not saying bonds are bad. I am saying bond mutual funds are a poor choice. Bond mutual funds are NOT where I want your money."

The advisor continued, "These last two investments aren't going to make you a bunch of money, but we need them in case the stock market drops. I want you in bonds, but I want you to buy the bonds directly. This way, you know what percentage you'll get as a return, and you'll be nearly certain to get all your principal paid back."

I assumed bonds were risk-free, but I thought I'd ask, "Is there a risk with bonds?"

"There is a risk with bonds, but you'll minimize your risk to a small portion of your investment. Decide on a number, 10 thousand, 15 thousand, maybe 20 thousand. Invest in different companies that offer bonds that payback at different times, 5, 10, 15 years. Divide your money up between those bonds."

"Should I go after a high rate of return?"

"Pat, you know better. Don't let greed or fear dictate your investments. The bulls and the bears make money, but the hogs lose their ass. Choose companies that are highly likely to pay you back. Choose companies you feel will be around for a while. Choose companies that a competitor couldn't undercut and steal their business in a blink of an eye."

The advisor continued, "The last piece is 20% invested in individual stocks. I want you to do some research and find companies you think will do well in the future. But these companies will only come from two segments. First, industrial REIT stocks. Find a few stocks that are industrial REIT stocks that focus on warehouses."

I felt Doc would have talked about REITs in class. Maybe he covered it during the week I skipped when Mrs. Galloway tried to make me give an oral presentation. She's probably still looking for me to show up and present. I asked, "What's an industrial REIT?"

The advisor responded, "REITs are a way of investing in real estate without the headaches. R.E.I.T. stands for Real Estate Investment Trust."

"But what's an industrial REIT?"

"Industrial means any real estate for businesses, but I don't want you to focus on just any industrial REIT. I want you in a REIT that focuses on eCommerce by investing in warehouses."

"Why industrial REITs that focus on warehouses?"

"First, I can tell from your personality—you want to manage a part of your money actively. You get a bit of a thrill from buying stock. Here's your chance. You can self-manage this portion of your portfolio. You finding and buying REIT stocks will keep you active and engaged in your investments, without messing with the system."

I wonder if this guy knew that I focused on financial stuff in an attempt to calm my anxiety? This was going to be perfect. I could follow these stocks and think about them to help me sleep. He continued as my mind wondered, "You and Doc set up a great start. You and I will take it to the next level. We'll diversify more and give you a portion to manage." The advisor continued without me having a chance to interject, "Pat, let's look at the future of real estate and take our best guesses as to what will happen. With more and more people doing online shopping, what will happen to malls and shopping centers? What will happen with REITs that have some of their focus on malls and shopping centers?"

I responded, "I've already seen stores closing and vacant shops."

"With the increase in people renting out their houses and spare bedrooms to travelers, what will happen with REITs that focus on hotels?"

"That too could crumble."

"Now, let's look at student housing. With more students doing online college, college classes while in primary school, going to trade schools, and going to local colleges for two years, then transferring."

I interrupted, "Yeah, I see what you mean. Student housing could fall too."

"How many people do you know who now work from home? Traditional offices are becoming a thing of the past. We are in a global marketplace, where office buildings aren't needed as much."

The advisor didn't give me a chance to interject, he continued, "There is another industrial REIT segment I want you to avoid, apartments. Sure more families are splitting up and temporarily moving to apartments, and apartment REITs are great during times of inflation because they can increase their rent each year. The downside is when interest rates are low, people buy houses. People still strive to have a place of their own. Also tons of overhead. Always repairs to be made."

"Are storage units, industrial REITs?" I asked.

"They are, but think about how disposable all your belongings are. You might have a couple of heirloom items from a relative, but most of your stuff is better off tossed than stored. When things get too crowded or old, people are tossing the items instead of storing them. When families split, they divide the items, with no real need for storage. Avoid storage unit industrial REITs."

I wanted to make sure I got it right, so I summed it up, "Find a few REIT stocks, but ones that don't focus on office, storage, malls, shopping centers, student housing, apartments, lodging, mortgage, or self-storage. Focus on warehouses. Got it, thanks."

"I couldn't agree more. The second type of stock I want you to buy is in electric companies. Companies that create electricity and pay a dividend."

Pat asked, "I know what a dividend is, but why do you recommend electric companies?"

"Right now, would you buy a gas station?"

"No, not with all those electric cars coming on the market . . . Oh, I get it. You feel that electric power will be the new fuel for cars, and these companies will be in the perfect place to take advantage of this trend."

"That's it, Pat. Also, the dividend they pay can be right at or more than your 4% withdrawal." The advisor smiled and nodded, making me feel like I was smart. "So, 20% in warehouse REIT stocks as well as electric companies and find a few, not just one or two."

I was jotting down some notes on my phone. I could tell he waited for a second to let me catch up before he asked his next question, "What are you using for your 20% fund?"

I responded to the advisor, "I have a mutual fund that follows the Dividend Achievers."

"Great fund. Who told you about that one?"

"My finance teacher, Doc."

"Well, you are about to have a bunch of money in there. If you continue with your current plan and want to retire early, this is where you're putting your money. You won't be able to touch your 401(k) for a while. You'll need a bunch of money to live off of in that 20% fund. Keep saving in there, but you need to diversify more."

I responded, "Yeah, diversify. I spread my investments over a few funds. I sure don't want the money just sitting there, making barely any interest at all. Here's my concern. Lilly, my wife, wants us to move out of the country in a few years. I need to protect a chunk of this money so we can make this happen."

The advisor looked concerned, "Pat, I can't guarantee a date you'll be able to move. I'll give you the best strategy possible to make this work for you, but you might have to be flexible with your goal. If the economy keeps on doing well, you might be there at age 44. If not, you might have to wait until 47."

"Pat, like life, we have to do our very best and know the results are not in our control. We have to accept what happens, what fate does with us. Did you ever play any sports?"

I didn't want to admit it, but I hadn't played organized sports since I was a kid, before my dad died. "Yeah, I played soccer for a few years." That sounded convincing. It was a few years—I just didn't want him to know it was ages 4-8.

"Well, you can practice. You can kick with the right part of your foot. You can aim. You can take into account the wind and the length of grass, but what you can't predict is how the other team will respond. We have to accept what the other team did and adapt our next movements to make for the best outcome. Winning doesn't have to be the ultimate goal. Using your training, preparation, and skills to have the best game possible is a more realistic goal, and you leave happy no matter the outcome."

"I guess what you're saying is, we'll try our best with the information we have, but not beat ourselves up if nature changes things and has a different plan." I pictured a gust of wind, blowing some of my savings away, and understood it's better to deal with what happens than get upset with an unexpected outcome.

"Yeah, it's like hitting a target with a bow and arrow. I'll teach you everything you need to do to pull the arrow back, aim, steady your stance, and shoot with the best possible outcome. It's up to outside forces how close you come to hitting a bullseye. You can only account for some of the wind. We can't determine every possible thing that might happen to your savings. We use our knowledge and base our decisions on research and history. We don't just hope it will turn out great, we prepare. Like you wouldn't show up to an NBA basketball game, ready to play center without first going through the process to become one of the best."

"I get it. I'll let the family know. What's the strategy with my 20% fund?" I wanted straight answers. I was used to the way Doc talked with me, and this guy was blabbing about warnings. Each warning was taking up time. And for this guy, time was money . . . my money. I needed him to get to the point.

"If you are going to retire early and live off that 20% fund, you need that money diversified." He finally started to tell me where to put my 20% portion, "When you sell your house, you'll take the proceeds and dump it in this section too. If you are moving out of the country and sell your belongings, that money also will go here. We need to be conservative with this money. Your 20% fund is the money you'll be living off of during your early retirement.

"30% Dividend Achievers Index, you already have your money in that one.

70% Corporate bonds, laddered. Again, don't duplicate the same bonds as in your retirement account."

The advisor gave an indication he was wrapping up the conversation and concluded with, "Keep investing 10% of your income into the four investments for your retirement. Also, invest your 20% into those other two investments. Each year, in the middle of May, balance both of these portfolios. You'll typically see, the U.S. stock market does better than your other investments, move money to get back to the correct percents every May. You'll also see the REIT and electric stocks paying dividends during the year. Use that money to help rebalance the funds too. This rebalancing will lock in your gains. At first, it might seem contrary to pull money out of a fund that's doing so well, but you are doing two things, locking in the gains and leveling the risk. Portfolios heavily invested in one type of fund have too much risk of dropping in value."

As I was thanking the advisor for his time, the advisor said one last thing, "Pat, this is very important, When you are first setting up your new retirement funds, make sure you are 'rolling over' your retirement money."

Pat's Notes

When finding a CFP - Certified Financial Planner or an RIA - Registered Investment Advisor, find one who will work for an hourly rate and not a percentage of my investment.

Have the advisor sign an agreement that reads, _____ will work to the fiduciary standard at all times, with my situation.

Use dollar-cost averaging to lock in the gains as I pull money out of my investments into one ordinary IRA "ROLLING OVER" the savings into four diverse segments. Keep investing 10% of my income into these investments.

45% Dividend Aristocrats Index

10% 'foreign' or 'international' fund, the one you had is good.

25% Corporate bonds, not a bond fund.

20% industrial REIT stocks that focus on warehouses and electric companies that pay dividends.

To retire early, invest my 20% into two parts

30% Dividend Achievers Index.

70% Corporate bonds, bought directly and not the same bonds as in my retirement account

Chapter 19

Should I move to a place with a lower cost of living?

Doc

Loneliness laid siege to me like a condemned prisoner. I stayed in my room, overlooking the air handlers. The thinning number of people who would stay after school to talk was a reflection of my age. Sometimes, I would hear students whisper to one another in hushed, sibilant sound. They are under the impression I am slower, dragged a few words, older. I can understand their reservations. Fellow teachers were becoming younger and younger. A fresh batch each year. I lost interest in Maher's Pub. It was increasingly difficult to conjure up a new bolt-hole.

Routine activities would temporarily retract the talons of my hidden anxiety. But the pain would fly back out and swipe at my flesh. The shackles of the past knew how to win eventually. I had not done enough to make the world a better place. I was still dealing with my own silent demons, wishing I could save more souls. Hoping I could make up for losing Eddy. Surely, there is only so much a man can do.

Serena died two years after I last talked with her. I had met her daughter for lunch soon after the funeral. She thanked me for all the things I had helped her family with. She asked if she, too, could talk with me like her mom did. She looked like her mother, and I thought she would be a success. I never got to meet Serena's son. I was told he had felt his mother's decision was fair and moved to start anew someplace else. I hope he would because I could imagine Serena staring through the tenuous blue rows of Portland's clouds, with pride and happiness curled around her face.

Also, I had not heard from Pat for a while. My boy had become a family man with varying waves of distraction. There were times he would come around to my place, accompanied by his wife and kid, and we would have fun, like extended families. Halloween offered the peak of this joy that remained in my heart when I thought of the tousle-haired boy with a look of disenchantment on his face, hunkered on a chair, twiddling with a computer keyboard. And look how much he had grown, how he not only catered for himself, but a daughter, and a wife. Seeing them wear masks on a Halloween night was amusing. Seeing Pat care for and love on his family made me better understand how the success of a man is a reflection of the little decisions he made and how he made them.

I began to realize, as I missed Pat, I was reliant on him as he was on me. I needed his success to make me feel better. To make me feel as though I've contributed to society. Selfishly, I saw his family life had created a hole in my escape.

I was hunkered down on a chair in my office, thumbing through papers on my new table when I got a call from Pat. He had a tone inflicted with suppressed sadness and anger.

"Hello, Doc. I hope you are holding out fine. I would love to see you. Would that be possible today?" he asked, in a formal, business tone.

It was funny how he always asked if it were possible to meet me when he already knew the answer to the question.

"After lunch, I have a planning period. How about we meet at school. We'll eat cafeteria grub and then have a while to talk before I go to class," I suggested.

"That sounds good." He responded in a flat voice and hung up without saying bye.

When we met, Pat had a visitor's badge on and a polo shirt. He seemed down in the dumps as he shook my hand without his usual firm grip.

"Doc, I've been depressed for a while now. I've never really gotten over killing that guy and leaving a mother with two infant twins to survive on their own, and my sister Nicole never lets me forget it. I know how they feel. I'm angry at the doctors for not saving my dad. I'm always thinking about how we could have handled my dad's illness better. I can't get over what I did to that family by accidentally killing that guy. I have plenty of money, but still, I'm not happy. Lilly and our daughter, Alessa, are so great, they don't deserve me."

I had not expected his litany of remorse and regret. It left me momentarily confused as to what to do for him.

"Pat, what are you getting at?" I asked

"Lilly thinks we should move. A change of scenery will make a difference and snap me out of this funk," he replied.

His reply had come as an assault to my sensibilities, and I had not expected it. A brief silence wafted off my end, and I had my eyes on him, fearful his absence would worsen my state. Of course, it would be selfish to say it would not help, because, sometimes, distance helps us eliminate the embraces of our demons.

"Doc? Are you all alright? "

Pat waved his hand to my face and jolted me out of my introspection.

"Sure, that could help. Maybe Lilly's right. You've been talking about it for a while," I responded wistfully.

"Then it's settled, we're moving to Máncora."

"Máncora as in Peru, below Ecuador, Máncora?" I asked, my eyes wide with surprise.

"Yep, that's the one. Perfect weather, fantastic sunsets, great people, and a perfect cup of coffee. Low cost of living. That's where I'll find happiness. Speaking of happiness, I've noticed something."

"What have you noticed?" I asked

Pat looked around like he was going to tell me a secret only spies could hear.

"The people who spend beyond their means don't seem happy. I'm talking about those people who buy stuff to make themselves look rich when they aren't all that rich." Pat leaned in closer like he was going to tell me the exact recipe for Coca-Cola. "Those people who make a good living and live in a neighborhood they can easily afford, don't drive over-the-top cars, or spend a ton of money on top-shelf liquor, seem to be the happiest." His voice came back to a reasonable volume, "Like why go to all this effort to go to a fancy meal and try to impress some people? When hangin' out, grillin' hamburgers brings more happiness. I see those people who live below their income also have a better chance of traveling and spending time with loved ones. I'll stay in touch with you, Doc. This whole living in a house you can easily afford and skipping the luxuries in life is what I want in our new life in Peru. I've always been frugal," he said, smiling.

"Except with your coffee," I interjected, with a wink.

"True. I don't skimp there. Here's the thing, Doc. I desperately want happiness. Lilly wants me to be happy too. I think living in paradise, frugally, will bring me joy. I figure every four years, two years into the U.S. President's term, in early October, I'll schedule a meeting with the financial advisor. I'll show the advisor my portfolio and ask for suggestions. I'll even see if you can't be a part of the conversation."

"That's a good idea, as long as you rebalance on your own each May. And you know each time you meet or do a video chat, you'll pay the advisor," I paused, and added, "a lot."

"Oh, I know how much he charges, but it's worth it. Each time I talk with him, immediately afterward, I make the changes we agreed to, in anticipation of the upswing in the stock market the third year of the president's term would likely bring."

Sometimes it's the little things that send tears trickling down our eyes. I could not remember crying for a long while, and I intended to keep it so. Only, the news of Pat's imminent departure knocked on the threshold of my tears. It felt like such a vacuum had been created in my social life. Except, I had to give him the requisite advice. Portland continually reminded him of his past, the glitch, the little mistakes he had made. It was okay to run away from the remembrance. It was okay. I had left Maine because of the same reason. Existing there, my senior year reminded me of Eddy, and all the little demons I could not dispel. Leaving Maine had been helpful, and immersing myself in finance had been instrumental. Pat was moving to save his head, to chase away the embraces of his demons. Similar to the reasons I left Maine. But I have been down this trail for a long time, and I still felt the loose clutches of life's choices.

Lilly

It's hard to see the one you love lick closer and closer to depression. It hurts, and the thought twined around me like a snake. I knew I had done my best to stop Pat from reverting to the memories of his past mistakes. But it was not working, and Portland connived with his past to continually reiterate the errors he had made.

I was concerned about my husband. His depression seemed to get worse and worse. I was adamant I could save him. That's why I insisted, years ago, we have a master plan of moving away. Get away from this place that reminded him of the pain. Every turn he took, he would have a trigger. Most of the time, he would pretend nothing was bothering him. I could see his muscles twitch. Sometimes, when he realized I noticed the muscle spasms, he would pretend he was coughing or choking on nothing. I let him think I was fooled.

To show him I cared, I made smoothies. I would look up new recipes, trying to get them just right. You couldn't even taste the essential ingredient, fermented yeast flakes. I think he started to like these low-carb, green smoothies. They were supposed to help him with his post-traumatic stress and anxiety. I think they worked. We are finally in a position to retire and move abroad. Retiring and getting a change of scenery would be healthy for Pat and the family. Alessa will get her dad back.

Pat

Age 45, dual-income $139,800/year; 10% fund $1,630,990; 20% fund $661,844; Stay out of debt fund $113,749; home equity $373,732

I couldn't believe we were moving. Wow, a permanent change for us. We started to sell everything. We put the house on the market. I put one car up for sale and planned to sell the other one to a friend who already agreed to buy it on our way to the airport. We had a few items to store, things we couldn't take with us, but also couldn't bear to sell. I first asked Nicole if we could use her place. After all, it was big enough. She was willing to but insisted we pay a yearly fee to keep it there. Nicole had been a thorn on my flesh, and she simply did not know when to stop. Her mien frustrated the hell out of me, and it seemed she had no care whatsoever for the rehabilitation of her brother. Here we were, trying to make our lives better, trying to escape the depression, and the painful memories of the past, and yet, every step of the way, she was fighting us, making sure my ambitions were futile. In her world, only one person mattered, and it wasn't me. It wasn't anybody else.

I asked Chad if he would help out. His place wasn't as big, but he agreed. He was so gracious about it. I couldn't help but agree when he asked if he could use the coffee table we were keeping. We moved a few things into Chad's place, boxes, the table, clothes that we couldn't sell in a garage sale, but knew we wouldn't need in South America.

Things were going as planned. Chad and Doc saw us off, but Nicole had to work. My friend bought my car and then used it to drive the three of us to the airport. We had a few suitcases and no place to live. It felt liberating.

We arrived to sunny skies, and the cloud of depression was already lifting. We initially got a hotel. Something affordable but clean. The three of us started our house hunting. I wanted to rent. I wasn't sure of the area and would hate to buy something, not knowing the best places yet. Besides, Doc always said that homeownership isn't as profitable as people believe. Renting will be fine for us.

I wanted to be right on the beach, but the cost was much higher. We got a great place. All white. Lots of windows with views of the ocean. The central living area was downstairs. It came furnished too. It had a courtyard with a tiny pool, really just a spot to cool off. The upstairs beds were simple, but the view was terrific. . . if you could look past the power lines.

Our new life began. I didn't have to work, but I got bored. I found a part-time job, just while Alessa was at school. Alessa was learning Spanish, but it was different from the Spanish I was used to hearing in the United States. Being able to order at a Mexican restaurant helped, but I had to learn an entirely new dialect and slang. They also talked faster than a Mexican rapper. Alessa helped me with the pronunciation.

It was the second year into a new President's term when I did a video conference with my financial advisor. Usually, I would try to include Doc in on the call, but I couldn't work out a time for all three of us to meet. I wanted his advice on what I should move around to take advantage of the upswing in the economy, as Doc predicted. Still, the advisor was elusive about telling me to do anything different. He kept insisting that I was on the right track to take full advantage of any movement in the stock market.

The advisor did bring up a different point. He told me I wasn't taking advantage of reducing my tax liability as much as I could. He told me there were legal ways to reduce how much I was paying in taxes. He agreed that living abroad was one of the best ways, but I would still have to file tax forms in the United States because that's where my income was generated. He suggested I spend less than $200 to set up a limited liability corporation, an LLC. This type of company would shelter some of the money from lawsuits and reduce my taxes. He also suggested I set up an HSA – health savings account and take it near the max allowed by the government. The HSA would be money used for medical expenses that wouldn't be taxed and could grow tax-free. He said the uber-rich setup HSAs and pour a ton of money into them in anticipation of when they get older and need more medical care; they'll have the money. One more thing Doc never mentioned in buying bonds, but the advisor did tell me. He said he ran some numbers and found that in my tax bracket, it was worth it to buy some state-issued bonds that would be tax-free. With the tax savings combined with the interest, it paid better than a highly rated corporate bond.

Even though I had money to spend, great coffee, and a beautiful family, the depression began to sink back under my skin. The newness of living abroad wore out pretty fast. I love where we were living as much as my wife did, but even with all that sunshine and perfect sunsets, I still wasn't happy. When I would call my brother, I would perk up a bit. He's was like a familiar teddy bear you can say anything to, and he wouldn't judge you. He was easy to talk with, and I missed him.

Doc

At one point, as Pat was living abroad, the economy was acting crazy. Pat emailed his financial advisor and copied me so I could be a part of the conversation. The advisor responded to both of us to stop worrying. He wrote,

"You have a great strategy in place, Pat. The economy is going to act crazy from time to time. Just keep doing what you're doing now. Leave your Roth IRA alone. Leave your 401(k) alone.

"I know you don't have as much income as you're living abroad, so your contributions are low. If you want to take advantage of these falling stock prices, you could use your stay out of debt fund. Sell part of that mutual fund and buy investments in your 20% funds. This way, you'd be investing while stock prices are falling.

"The people who panic and get out of the market, lose. The ones who persist and keep investing during the downturns, win. If you panic each time you hear of a big event, you'll end up selling after the market has already gone down. If you do that enough, you end up losing. Those who ride it out and keep investing during these 'bad' times, end up winning. Don't think of these as 'bad' times. These are great times for you. You are buying more shares each month compared to last month and the month before. These are the times, people like you look forward to. Pat, I want you to win. Keep your monthly contributions going.

"With your lower cost of living and being retired, you don't need as much money in your emergency fund the one you call stay out of debt fund. Consider using some of that money and buying more shares in your 20% fund – the one you used to retire early. The Aristocrats are down, the REIT and electric company stocks are down. Now would be a great time to buy. But above all else, remember what I told you a few years ago, don't let greed or fear dictate your investments.

"Do you ever drive in bad weather?"

Pat responded to the odd question emailed to him, "Not now that I live in Máncora. But sure I have. I've been in ice, snow, nasty rain. Why do you ask?"

The advisor responded to both of us again the following Monday. "Picture yourself following someone, at a safe distance, in icy conditions. They hit an ice patch and panic. Spinning the wheel and slamming on the brakes puts them in a ditch. You, on the other hand, saw their mistake, kept calm. You didn't slam on the brakes. You didn't twist the wheel. You may have slid a bit, but you steered through it and got to the other side. Your training took over, like a policeman or fireman at the scene of a rescue. You did what you were trained to do. You stayed the course. You didn't panic like the other people who sold their investment at exactly the wrong time."

"Thanks for the advice. I'll follow it. Do I owe you for the time you spent emailing?"

"No, Pat. This one's on me."

Lilly

I sat crying all afternoon. I wanted to call Pat on his phone but decided I'd rather talk with him in person. Pat finally came home from his part-time job.

"Pat, do you know the single mother who lives next door? Her little boy died. He drowned in the waves."

Pat grabbed me and held me. He could tell I was upset. With a quiver in my voice, I continued, "They were at the beach. You know, where we normally go. The boy was playing, scooped up water for a sandcastle, but went too deep. A wave knocked him down. The undertow pulled him out. His mother ran to get him, but by the time he surfaced again, he wasn't breathing. They tried to do CPR. It was no use." Pat was tearing up.

"I spent the day thinking about losing our daughter, losing you, losing what we've built."

"Lilly, don't be ridiculous."

I cut Pat short, "No, Pat. It made me thankful. I was happy at where we are in life. Happy to have our daughter, to be living here." I paused and thought for a moment. "It also helped prepare me. I spent the afternoon imagining all these terrible things that could happen."

"Lilly, I don't want you doing that. I won't let anything happen to you."

"No, it's okay. Thinking about the what-ifs gave me power not to be caught off-guard. Not to be surprised at adversity. I feel I can better take whatever fate hurls my way, calmly. I no longer feel vulnerable to bad situations."

"To me, it sounds terrible. Not uplifting."

"Imaging bad things happening in my life and how I can overcome them, prepared me. I know, I can't think of every scenario, but at least I can use the thoughts to assess the situations better as they arise. It also made me thankful

for the things and people I do have around me." I hugged Pat in an embrace—
I didn't want to let go.

Pat's Notes

Those who spend all their income on stuff aren't happy.

Those who have a lower cost of living and willing to pay for experiences (like travel) and spending time with loved ones are happier.

Don't panic when the stock market changes. Keep to my game-plan, keep investing, don't pull money out.

Take into consideration taxes when deciding what to invest in and for how long to hold those investments—longer is better.

Chapter 20

Should I branch out into riskier investments?

Doc

The third time the financial advisor and Pat talked, Pat wanted to talk about some investment options he'd been reading about. This time, it was through a video chat. They let me sit in on the conversation, and Pat was helpful enough to arrange it during a school holiday so I could listen. Pat first asked about leveraging. The financial advisor told him that buying his house with a mortgage was leveraging. Pat used other people's money in hopes an investment would go up in value, and it did. Pat thought, why not use the same principle and leverage other investments? The advisor's short answer was "risk." "Why take the risk of losing that money and the money you've built up over the years? For your house, you needed a place to live. You needed a place to raise your family. Your mortgage is all the leveraging you need to take out in life. Flipping houses is a typical way people are using leverage. Flipping houses is riskier than they let on. It's also time-consuming and frustrating."

As I listened to Pat and the advisor talk, I remembered going to investment 'opportunities' before. They push this idea of flipping houses on young people. Use just a little bit of your money, along with your good credit, and score big. The advisor must have known about these as well. He's probably even seen how people have gotten burned using them. The investment doesn't work out. They lose that money. Then comes the leverage part, pay up son. You borrowed money, and the investment is near worthless now.

Pat's next question was about hedge funds. The advisor answered, "Hedge funds are the same as leveraging. These risk-taking managers are taking out a loan to buy more shares of stock. If they make a bad decision, they lose not only the money invested but also the interest they have to pay back."

Over the years of teaching finance classes, I've had students want to get into hedge funds. Young people want them because they do great for a few years. For whatever reason, the stocks those funds were invested in dropped in value. Overall the hedge funds my students wanted would fall 12%, but when you factor in the money the hedge fund borrowed, they lost an additional 5%. Down 17% was severe for my students to deal with and why I too wouldn't recommend them.

Pat's friend told him he needs to buy on margin some individual stocks. The investor responded, "Your strategy has worked nearly flawlessly, and you are a multimillionaire because of it. Buying on margin is again, taking out a type of loan to buy more shares. What if you pick the wrong stock? You'll lose money on the stock and lose money borrowed. Chances are slim you can pick a winning stock. I'm in the business, and I only get about 40% right."

I felt a little odd, sitting there, listening, and not adding anything. I didn't want to take away from the advisor's responses, and I didn't want to cost Pat more money by spending the advisor's time. Talking with the advisor on an hourly basis was worth it, but expensive. When I've spoken with other financial planners over the years, they always seem to recommend exchange-traded funds (ETF) and mutual funds. I think they recommend these because they don't want to admit they can only pick a winning stock 40% of the time. Another reason is the blame game. 'Not my fault, the manager of the ETF didn't pick the right stocks.'

Pat saw an online video about Forex, and it seemed like an exciting idea. The investor agreed, "It's exciting. It's like going to the ultimate casino with cash. You are putting cash up against other cash in hopes their value drops so you can make a profit. There are so many elements at play in currency exchange rates; even experts can't predict how things will move. Currency exchange is not a way to make a consistent profit. This falls into that class of investments you've heard of before. If it looks too good to be true, stay clear."

My Uncle Bill tried to get yours truly, a high school teacher, involved with Forex. I was barely in my twenties at the time. I seriously considered it. I thought if the value doesn't jump up, I'll hang onto it until the rates change in my favor. Then I started to look at the fees. The fees were so high—I would have to be investing big money to overcome those fees. I wasn't willing to risk even a small portion of my money on something that had such high costs.

"I've heard I can make money on commodities," Pat mentioned.

"Sure, people make money on commodities, but what most of these investors are doing is buying and selling contracts that promise a specific commodity, like oil or corn, to be delivered at a certain date at a specific price. As time gets closer to the delivery date and someone can buy the commodity cheaper, your contract will be near worthless. It's only if the commodity goes above your contract price that your contract would be worth money. Do you have intimate knowledge about pork bellies?"

I liked the sense of humor this finance guy had. I love bacon, but I don't know why people trade pork bellies.

The video chat ended soon after the pork belly comment. Pat did have to pay for that call. Near the end of the conversation, Pat got my attention and asked if we could talk after I had gotten some sleep. "Hey Doc, tomorrow morning, can we video chat again. I need to talk with you about something big."

I got some sleep and then set up the computer again to video chat with Pat. Ten or so minutes before we were scheduled to talk, I started up the computer. When he connected, it looked like Pat was at a seaside cafe. "Where are you, Pat?"

Pat

Pat, age 46, part-time income $10,000/year; 10% fund $1,764,136; 20% fund $1,073,693; Stay out of debt fund $121,972; home equity $0

"Hey, Doc. Thanks for meeting me again. I'm in my favorite coffee shop. The food is great. The coffee, dark and rich. Amazing view of the ocean. Some people would call the service poor, but if you look at it another way, they leave you alone—allowing me to connect with people in the U.S., like you. The place is amazing." I turned my computer around to show Doc. He could see the blue water of the ocean and the umbrellas on the beach. Mostly open-air with wooden tables and chairs. Doc could see I had a coffee already. "Here, I can talk freely."

"What's the name of that place?"

"Green Eggs & Ham. Isn't that a hoot? We don't live too far from it. I would've never found a place this great without some help. From the outside, you wonder how great this place could be. Once you get inside, fantastic."

I refocused the camera on me again as Doc brought up the conversation we had with the financial advisor, "Are you going to go through with any of those risky investments the advisor warned you against?"

"No, he made a lot of sense. That's not why I wanted to talk, though."

I took a sip of coffee to give Doc a chance to ask, and he did, "So, what's up?"

"I want to move back home. Máncora didn't help. Even though I'm thousands of miles away, I'm still depressed. I thought living in paradise, retired, would do it for me. I still can't wrestle the devil inside me and forgive myself for what I did. Maybe being near my brother would help."

"What does Lilly say about all this?"

"I haven't mentioned it to her. That's why I'm calling. How should I ask her?"

"Pat, I teach finance. How am I supposed to know?"

"Well, it just seems like when we talk, things work out."

"Pat, you've got a big one on your hands here. Be straight with her. Tell her the whole truth."

"Ok, as soon as I finish my coffee and get back home, I'll talk with Lilly. Can we chat again, same time next week?"

"Sure, until then, enjoy that coffee. I'm a bit jealous." Doc gave me a smile that always made me feel like he was on my side. Someone who was there for me. Besides my brother and Lilly, no one else has been closer to me.

The next time we video chatted, I was back at my house. "Doc, you there?" the computer's video came up.

"I sure am. Can we talk freely?" Doc responded.

"Oh yeah. I'm at home and came to a decision. I'm not leaving Máncora because Lilly won't leave. She loves it here, and our daughter, Alessa, is in school. She's made friends and becoming part of the community. Lilly's not here right now. Therefore, I can call it what it was. She gave me an ultimatum. She didn't call it that, but we all know what it was."

"How do you feel about the decision?"

"I feel like a piece of me is dying. I love my wife and kid, but can't find happiness. Surely it will come. Hell, I'm in paradise, right?"

We talked a bit further about investing in Peru and ended our chat.

Doc

I was worried about Pat. I guess he had always been a bit depressed. But this time, it was seen through the calm tone that wafted off his mouth when we talked. I had obliged myself to help him out in his finance, but I felt a little sad that I couldn't help him fight his demons. I had my share of woes I had become accustomed to fighting. Perhaps, I could tell Pat there was no way he could entirely forget about what he did in the past, and maybe get better if he embraced it. Only, it could be risky to make such a suggestion. I feared it is how psychopaths are undetectably created. I was usually reserved when he hurled his personal issues at me. There was no clear-cut strategy in tackling the shackles of the past. People who are dealing with internal conflict need to find a healthy distraction. Some turn to self-medication, they can't find a healthy diversion.

It was rare for Pat to call me on my cell phone from Peru, so when I got the call, I answered it. I was concerned about him. The last call we had, he seemed hopeless. Like he had no way of crawling back to happiness. He had no one who would help, and this concerned me. Living away from family and now, even his wife was working against him. I wasn't teaching at the time, so I had no problem spending time talking. Pat started right away,

"Lilly and I are getting a divorce."

"Why the divorce?"

"My sister, Nicole, thinks it's for the best. I'll be moving back home in August and staying with my brother for a while. After that, I'll file the divorce papers and send them to Máncora for Lilly to sign."

"Pat, I don't know what to say. I don't know how to help you in this situation. I feel for you, buddy. We all want what's best for you and your family."

"Yeah, I know. I'll still come back to visit my daughter, Alessa. She can come to stay with me during the holidays. I figure I'll video chat with her once a week or so. Back at home, I'll start over. A fresh start. Something new. Kind of a rebirth of Pat."

Sure enough, Pat moved back in August. I saw him a few weeks after he arrived.

Pat's Notes

Meet with my hourly paid, financial advisor every second year of the President's term in office. This way, I can take advantage of the upswing in the economy the third year will likely bring.

Don't let an uncertain economy influence my financial decisions. Keep to the game plan to maximize profits and minimize the chance of selling at the wrong time.

Don't go after risky investments. Even if the thrill would be like a game of roulette, stick to the plan.

Chapter 21
How do I leave a legacy?

Doc

We met at a coffee shop. As Pat looked around, he said, "This is nothing like Green Eggs & Ham back in Peru, but I'm sure I can find a good cup. Doc, part of my plan is to set my sights on a select few charities. Besides my own money, I want to do fundraisers for charities. Back in Peru, I showed Alessa how important it is to care for people other than ourselves, and doing so felt good."

"Pat, that's a great idea. I'm guessing you don't need to work anymore?"

"Right, I could work. I'm able. I have enough saved up, so I'm not worried about getting a job. My financial planner took into account my age and the goals I have with seeing Alessa and suggested I keep the mixes we set up a while ago, still re-balancing every May. For me, the rebalancing is pulling money out of the stock market and putting more into the bond ladder. I'm reinvesting the dividends from the dividend achiever's fund, but spending the dividends from the REITs. With that money and the interest from the bonds, I'm living pretty comfortably. Not extravagant. I'm not buying a jet, but I can afford to buy your coffee. What will you have?"

"Same as always, just like you. Black and bold."

After I had found us as quiet a seat as possible, Pat handed me my cup. He opened up, "I miss Lilly and Alessa. It's been a few weeks. I've talked with them, but it's not the same."

"Are you and your brother getting along?"

"Chad is great. He can tell how much I miss Lilly. I've also met up with my sister a few times. She's been pushing me to meet with a divorce attorney she knows. She's worried about Lilly taking all my money and thinks I should meet with this lawyer guy. He's supposed to be an expert at protecting men's assets in a divorce. Nicole set up an initial meeting the first week in September."

"Are you going to meet with him?"

"I love Lilly, and I don't think she'll take advantage of me, but Nicole might be right. I'll see what this lawyer has to say and take it slow. Being a quarter way around the world from my estranged wife allows me to take my time with this."

We both finished our coffee and headed out. Pat was going to check out a charity, and I was going back home.

Pat

Pat, age 46, part-time income $0/year; 10% fund $1,764,136; 20% fund $1,070,693; Stay out of debt fund $121,972; home equity $0

Doc seemed surprised to see me poke my head into his classroom, as I used to when I was a teen. There he was, right after school at his desk as usual. "Hey, Doc, what's up? I see you got new computers. These look great."

"Since you've been in school, we've replaced the computers a few times. Pat, you're an old man now."

"I am not, but I can see you've got some grey coming in Doc."

"I sure do, each grey hair represents a student, just like you . . . trouble."

"I was no trouble. You loved it." Pat sat down and pulled out his phone. "I was looking over some of my notes. With October coming up, I want to set up Alessa with a Roth IRA. I want her to be independent, able to survive on her own. I don't want to subsidize her income and have her reliant on someone's generosity to pay the bills."

"You have a good point, Pat. It's one thing to give adults meaningful gifts and even cash, but nothing extravagant that would change their standard of living."

"Believe it or not, Alessa has been doing a bit of modeling in Peru."

"She did take after her mom, after all?"

"Well, she didn't get her looks from me, that's for sure. Anyway, I still have my Roth IRA I set up when I was 18. I only contributed to it a few years before I got that job that offered the 401(k) with a company match. When I left that company, I started investing in the Roth again. It's grown pretty well. Even after all these years, do you think I should set Alessa up with a Roth 90/10 split between S&P 500 index fund and an International Index MSCI EAFE fund, like mine?"

"Yes. Even after all these years, that's still the best bet. If not the International Index, look for a world stock fund. Since you're contributing money Alessa has earned, you'll be able to put it in a Roth, and it will grow tax-free. At retirement, she can withdraw the money tax-free. Max out the contributions to the Roth IRA for four years while she's young. This money will grow and be worth millions when the child retires."

"I want to set this up to ensure she'll be financially set even if I was no longer around. I want to leave a legacy."

"This is a great way to influence multiple generations. Think about how she can help her kids from this investment you set up. One more thing you can do when she's older."

"What, buy her a car?"

"No, but about the same age. Add Alessa to your credit card. She'll build her credit rating and will be able to qualify for a better loan because of her good credit. Even if she doesn't use the card, you paying it off each month will benefit her."

I agreed, "Sure, that seems like a long time from now. To change the subject, what about Halloween? Can I invite myself over and hang out?"

"Yeah, that sounds good to me. I still have that old pickup truck." I couldn't believe Doc still had the truck. It was old when we first went out trick or treating. I was surprised it even ran.

"We'll pile in and cruise the 'hood." I felt a ray of hope, something to look forward to. I was hanging out with my former teacher and now friend.

As I was leaving the classroom, I called out, "I'll see you at 7 PM on Halloween."

It was Halloween night. I got to Doc's house a few minutes early. "Come on in Pat. We still have a few things left to do before we can leave."

"Over all these years, have you gotten any trick-or-treaters yet?"

"All the years we've lived here, we've only gotten two, a grandfather and his grandson. That was years ago. Nonetheless, we leave a bowl of candy on the front steps. We don't need any tricks because they didn't get their treat," Doc laughed at himself. "Here, take this bowl out with this note and leave it near the door." I read the note,

You climbed up the hill.

It is time to trick or treat.

Candy at your feet.

"Hey, is this a haiku?" I asked.

"Yeah, I made it up myself." Doc seemed proud of himself.

"Mrs. Galloway taught us about haikus. How's she doing?"

"On time every day.

She did a good job teaching.

And now she is dead."

"Doc, you're terrible, but nice haiku."

As I took the bowl of candy out, I looked in the driveway and screamed. I ran down the steps toward the truck. In the back of the truck, wrapped up in blankets, were Lilly, Alessa, and Chad. "Why are you here?" I called out with tears starting to form in the cold October air.

Chad started to explain, "I knew how miserable you were without your family. So, I contacted Lilly and convinced her to leave Peru and be with you."

Lilly jumped out of the truck, tossing her blanket to the side and hugged me, "We are a family, and we need to be together. Living in Máncora was essential to me, but I could see how it wasn't helping you. If you need to be here for your happiness, then we'll be here with you.

I began to cry as I thought how much I loved my wife and child. Lilly was my princess. She always knew what was best for our family and me. I picked up my daughter, "Oh, how I've missed the two of you."

Lilly started to explain, "You would be so proud of Alessa. She found some needy families and donated all our stuff to them, her bike, most of our clothes, nearly everything."

I then asked, "Did you get rid of our Inca Cross collection?"

Alessa spoke up, "No, dad. I couldn't get rid of those. We did come home with only two suitcases. Are you proud of me?"

"Yes, very proud and thankful my family is home."

"Pat," Lilly started, "You need closure on that accident you caused years ago. I've found the twins—the babies of that dad you killed. We're meeting them tomorrow. I don't know how it'll go, but you need to talk to them."

"You're probably right, Lilly. How did you find them? They must be adults by now."

Lilly looked up at the house, "Doc gave me the name and number of this guy, Henry Townsend. I thought he was an author, but Doc said he was some sort of investigator. I called him, mentioned Doc's name, and gave him as many details as I could remember. He texted me back within an hour with names, addresses, phone numbers, where they worked, how many kids they had, and even where their kids went to school."

"That's kinda scary." I thought about what information is out there about my daughter.

Lilly responded, "I know, right? I asked him how much I owe him for all that information. He told me he owed one to Doc and wouldn't charge me. I guess who you know pays off. Anyway, I contacted them, and they're willing to meet."

"Chad, can you watch Alessa while Lilly and I meet the twins?"

"Sure, I need more time with my niece anyway. I need to hear all about Máncora and your modeling career." Chad was poking Alessa in the ribs, making her squirm.

Alessa acted coy and played off the modeling career comment. That night I rode in the back of the truck as Doc carted us all around the neighborhood. Alessa and Doc's wife would jump out and get candy while Lilly and I snuggled under the blanket.

I met the twins at a coffee shop. It was odd seeing them. I still pictured them as infants, but here they were, adults. The first twin explained, "When we were about five years old, we had a lot of questions about our dad. At first, we were upset. Our mom explained it to us this way. She told us we could go through life being dragged by a rope or run along, dealing with the terrain. She gave us an example of a dog tied to the seat of a bicycle. The dog has two choices, he can be upset, fall to the ground, and be dragged, or he can run along, keep up with the bike. Deal with the obstacles as they come. Jump over hills along with the rider. Not having a dad growing up wasn't easy. It was a major obstacle."

"Wow!" I said in amazement. "With that attitude, nothing can be so devastating that you give up, become jilted, or angry."

The second twin added, "One way is exhausting and miserable. The other has joy in it. Check out your surroundings, enjoy the journey, learn along the way."

The first twin started back, "That accident changed who we are. For me, not having a dad growing up, I was sure to be there for my kid." The second twin was nodding. "I passed up a promotion because of the extra time it would take away from my family. I want to coach little league. I want to be there for all the bumps and bruises my child goes through. If I had a different upbringing, I wouldn't have the same attitude."

With some tears forming, I responded as best I could, "Don't go to battle because of what's happened; things happen for you. Accept it. Run with it instead of against it." We continued to talk for a while. I learned about their lives, who they became.

A week after Halloween, I stopped by Doc's house unexpectedly. He was doing yard work. "I met the twins."

"How did it go? Were they mad at you?"

"Actually, no. The twins weren't mad. Their mother taught them to forgive, and they told me they never knew their dad, but had heard of the accident and forgave me when they were young children."

"Did they have a lot of questions?"

"After we talked about them and how the accident affected their upbringing, they had questions about me as a person, my family, and such. They don't know a ton about investing and never really had a bunch of money. I'm going to meet with them once a week and teach them about investing. I'm going to set them up a few funds with my own money—a small one for their retirement. I'll teach them to put away 10% of their income into those funds. Doc, I'm going to do one more. They each have a kid of their own. I want to start a college fund for their kids. I figure if I put $15,000 into a college fund for each kid, it should be enough to pay for their tuition when they're 18 years old. Doc, I've learned a lot over the years, and I want to pass along that knowledge, not only to my kid but others as well." As I said this, a look I've never seen came over Doc's face. I've never seen someone's spirit lifted before, but I think it did that day. Something changed in Doc's eyes. It was almost as if the color changed in his eyes. Like a dark shadow left him as we stood in his yard.

"Pat, passing knowledge along is the most generous gift. You have a knack for simplifying things so people can understand them. You'll be a great mentor to those twins. Funding a college fund with set limits is a great way to help out. This way, it's not an open checkbook, and it won't be quite enough. They'll have to come up with some of the money themselves—putting their skin in the game. Giving them a better reason to do well in school."

I responded, "I don't know if I have some gift of simplifying things. I know that investing in your future isn't as complicated as people think. I've learned you don't have to be an expert to begin an investment. You don't even need a financial advisor. All you need is to realize you can live off 90% of your income, invest in the stock market, and your future self is worth the investment."

Pat's Notes

To leave a legacy, focus on charities that make a difference in areas of people's lives that matter to me.

Set up and contribute to my kid's Roth IRA so she can have a great retirement, even if I'm not around.

Invest in education to make a lasting difference in people's lives.

Don't give over-generous gifts that could change a young person's standard of living. Let them earn their way through life.

Pass along knowledge to the next generation.

Chapter 22

How do I teach someone all the investment strategies to become rich?

"Doc, I've created a kind of lesson for the twins. It's not everything we've talked about, but it's the part I found to be the most helpful. I wanted to begin teaching these concepts to the twins. Would you mind looking over it? Tell me if I should present it to them."

"Sure, I will, as long as I can take it too. You know for my class."

Day 1

You want to be wealthy. You have two choices, you could appear to be affluent, but owe a lot of money, or you could be debt-free and have a bunch of money saved up.

Debt can break marriages apart. Owing money can be stressful. Living paycheck to paycheck is nerve-wracking.

Simple steps are outlined to get you out of debt and begin to invest in your future. The first step is to realize: you won't become wealthy when you take on consumer debt.

Consumer Debt is Too High

Do not purchase goods and services you cannot pay for immediately. Those who are self-indulgent and spend more than they earn, learn quickly of the trouble, worry, distress, and shame debt can bring. Pay for the merchandise when you buy it, not on credit.

A slave works for others. If you are spending everything you earn, you are working as a servant to consumption. Instead of paying someone else interest, let that money work for you in your investments. All of your income does not have to go toward goods, services, and debt. Keep for yourself at least 10% of what you earn. Invest that 10%. With compound interest and time, each dollar will multiply, gaining even more dollars. The ability to earn money from investments, whether you are working, traveling, or retired, will make you wealthy.

You can be Debt Free and Rich

Financial prosperity is within your grasp. Utilize your source of income to finance your fortune. To create financial freedom, keep a portion of what you earn. Following this simple guideline can make you debt-free and prosperous. You can get out of debt, learn how to invest, cut your living expenses, and make your dreams a reality.

Use this one fundamental to your financial benefit. Learn how to keep part of what you earn. It's many people's dream to be making as much, if not more, from investments compared to what they earn each month working. Most other people's aspirations are also dependent upon money. Having money can make those dreams a reality. With enough money in investments, you could live off of the income investments produce and be able to afford the luxuries in life.

It is best to start today—don't wait. If you're young, you have time on your side and can accumulate your fortune that much sooner, possibly retiring early and having the financial life people dream of having. If you are older, do not hesitate to begin. No matter what your age, your time is now. Do not drag your feet.

There are three simple steps to reach your financial goals. The uncomplicated, quickly understood steps to becoming rich make sense. The guidelines are clear. Within the first month, after implementing the world's most simple budget, you will know if you are on the right path to your financial wealth.

Day 2 The First Step to Becoming Rich

The below plan has worked a countless number of times for millions of people throughout history. It is simple and utterly brilliant. Anyone can live on this simple budget, no matter your income or education. Even a vagrant, living on the street "makes" money panhandling. Putting away only a few dollars a day isn't going to make someone a millionaire. On the other hand, if that panhandler saved away part of what he was given each day, he could consider himself wealthy after a few years. You, with your job and source of income, can become very wealthy following this time-tested, simple budget.

Divide your Take Home Income into Three Parts

10% = Pay yourself first. Keep a portion of what you earn; 10% goes toward your LONG TERM, DO NOT TOUCH INVESTMENT PORTFOLIO.

20% = Pay off your debt; 20% of your income goes toward DEBT REPAYMENT.

70% = The remaining can be used for everyday expenses; 70% of your take-home income will go toward LIVING EXPENSES.

No need to stuff an envelope full of cash for entertainment. No need to put off that purchase of shoes your child needs. It's your money, and you know best how to spend the 70% of your income on living expenses. A small portion set aside to pay off your debts. An even smaller part will make you well-off.

No matter what your occupation, no matter what schooling you have had, you can become a millionaire.

This strategy is not some gimmick or paid-for advertisement you see late at night. It has been proven time and time again to work, no matter who you are, no matter how bad off your finances seem to be. This simple division of your income has taken people from living in poverty to living better than kings and queens. For this to work for you, all you need is time and the determination to be successful.

Living on a fixed income is hard enough, but living on a traditional budget feels inflexible. The majority of people have a difficult time accounting for every penny spent. Living on a budget similar to one that regulates how much you can spend on food and entertainment, causes more problems and grief than its worth. Some months, you may want to go to a couple of movies. In another month, there may not be any good movies, but you'll need to buy new shoes. With these proven wealth-building guidelines, you are dividing your money so that you can live a financially correct life.

At first, we are not going to worry about our living expenses. The way our "budget" works is:

1 Use 10% of our monthly income toward your LONG TERM, DO NOT TOUCH INVESTMENT PORTFOLIO saved away in the stock market. Choose two index funds. One that invests in the top companies in the United States and another one that has a focus abroad.

2 Use 20% of our monthly income to take care of your DEBT REPAYMENT. When you have no debt, you can use this money for large purchases and making your dreams a reality.

3 The remaining 70% is for LIVING EXPENSES. Your living expenses will take care of themselves with the money left over.

10% LONG TERM, DO NOT TOUCH INVESTMENT PORTFOLIO

Pay yourself first. Take 10% off the top and put it toward your LONG TERM, DO NOT TOUCH INVESTMENT PORTFOLIO. You have worked hard for this money. You do not need to work as a slave to consumption. Put some of what you earn, 10%, away for yourself—for your future. Paying yourself first is a sure way for you to save money. Before you pay the bills, buy groceries or a new pair of shoes, take 10% out and save it away. You could put it into a savings account, money market, mutual fund, or employer retirement fund. Out of all of those choices, the employer retirement fund is your best bet—look for a 401(k). The main strategy is to get it out of sight. If you leave it in your checking account or keep it as cash in your underwear drawer, it is more likely you'll spend it. Use stock market index funds to ensure you are putting the money to its most effective use and to put you safely on your road to financial success. 90% S&P 500 Index; 10% International Index MSCI EAFE

20% DEBT REPAYMENT

Use 20% of your take-home pay as the DEBT REPAYMENT portion. Ultimately pay all your debts in full, but if this is not possible, pay the ones with the highest interest rate first. Credit card companies do not want you to be able to pay off the balance in full. Creditors are out to take your money. Credit card companies make a substantial amount of income from people not being able to pay the full amount and therefore having to pay the high levels of interest they charge.

Once you have paid off all of your debt, you'll be able to set this 20% aside to pay for large purchases. Maybe you need to save up for a car, TV, or family trip. Putting this money in a separate account will help prevent you from pulling money out for everyday expenses.

70% LIVING EXPENSES

Spend 70% as you see fit. Pay those services you know will come due each month, such as utilities and insurance. If you know a bill comes due at the end of the month, write the check early. Write the check at the beginning of the month, so you see exactly how much money you have for everyday living expenses. It is the second day of the month, and you've paid all your monthly bills. You have written the checks for the mortgage/rent, insurance, utilities, and all of those troublesome bills. Spend the remainder of that 70% as you see fit. If you feel food is essential, go to the grocery store.

By using the strategies of saving 10%, paying off debt with 20%, and living off 70%, you will put the fortunes of capital on your side, and relieve some of the stress associated with paying the bills. You will not be caught off-guard by a hefty charge. You will know where your money is coming from and where it is going. If a bill does come due unexpectedly, pay it as soon as it comes in. Deduct the cash out of your checking account immediately.

Do not go further into debt. Like a black hole, it pulls you further and further from your goal – wealth and financial security.

The biggest asset to building your fortune is your job. With a job and time, you can become a millionaire.

Excuses

Many people who start the 70-20-10 plan feel as though it's too difficult to achieve. Then, they realize their lives are not much different from those people who have found it easy and have realized their dreams by following the 70-20-10 plan. There are all sorts of excuses:

"I have children."
Children are expensive, but yet costs can be cut, and money saved. You've seen other families survive on less income or with more children. They may not buy name brand shoes, but there is the same potential for love in either household.

"I spend every penny I make."
Currently, most people spend everything they earn. It is a learned behavior to reduce costs. It will take time to reduce your spending. It takes a realization of what expenses will most positively affect your life. Will you get the same amount of entertainment value if you rent a movie compared to going to the theater? Will you become just as full fixing dinner and eating at home as you would by going out? If you are spending everything you earn, cut your expenses.

"My bills are too high" or "The house payment is too high."
Many people have outrageous bills—owing tens of thousands of dollars toward credit card debt. There is a way out of these bills—a change in lifestyle. The fuel for this lifestyle change originates from your desire to become wealthy because even those with extreme debt have a chance to succeed. The first change is to stop going further into debt. Stop charging things on the credit card. Do not finance those large purchase items. Work your way out of debt. Pay your creditors more than the minimum balance owed.

"I don't make enough money for saving to make a difference" or "I'm too young."
Over time, your income will increase. By starting now, the 70-20-10 process will become so routine that as your income increases, you will be saving more and growing your wealth to generous portions.

"I need to look cool in school."
Young people will use the excuse of their bills or desire to be social (going out with friends or buying the right clothes), and again it takes a commitment. Do you want to be a millionaire? The earlier you start, the easier and sooner you will become

wealthy. The sooner you begin, the more time you'll have to take advantage of compound interest, the wealthier you become.

"I heard that investments are risky – I don't want to lose my money."
Yes, investments are risky, and you may lose money. In a way, it is like betting in Vegas, but unlike Vegas, the odds are in your favor. If you continue to spend everything you make and not put money away, the chances are working against you becoming wealthy.

"I have always managed to get by. Why change?" or "I'll start saving later."
As a person just getting by, you can see the advantages of having money. The rich can afford the luxuries in life: the larger homes, the fast cars, and the nights out on the town. Getting by is one thing, but experiencing life as a wealthy person gives another perception of the world altogether. If you ask someone rich as well as poor, he or she would tell you, rich is better. Most people know the limitations of being poor, and the rich have their share of problems as well. There are differences in the types of difficulties these two groups have. While the poor are trying to get food on the table, the rich are trying to find a cleaning service that will do a decent job.

People will always have excuses. You may come up with one not listed above. No matter what the justification, it's still possible to save money. Even if the amount protected is small, you will be on your way to becoming wealthy. You can prosper using the 70-20-10 plan.

Day 3 You Can Succeed

You can overcome any excuse for not following the world's most simple budget. It starts by paying yourself first. For you to become wealthy, invest at least 10% of your take-home pay. Merely putting away 10% of your monthly income can take you past the barely-getting-by stage, to the status of a millionaire. A couple from Virginia used this 10% method on an annual salary of $36,000 and is now worth over $4,000,000. Thousands of others have done the same. Keep in mind, the more you make – the more you put away into your LONG TERM, DO NOT TOUCH INVESTMENT PORTFOLIO – the faster you become rich.

At first, some people are skeptical. They feel as though they cannot put away 10% of their monthly income. Most people can't even put a finger on why they don't want to save a portion of their income. Every culture in the world has people who feel the same way. They fear what they will 'miss out on' by not spending all of their income. These people want to succeed. They think if they don't spend every penny earned, they may not have such a high quality of life. Will they miss a great movie at the theater? Will they have to miss going to the baseball game with their friends? The amount of money saved is substantial. Yes, you could buy quite a few meals or have a great day out with the kids with that money. It's also enough to make you stinkin' rich.

You will be able to put 10% of your monthly income away into an investment without noticing a drop in your standard of living. Anyone can accomplish this savings plan. Take a look at your neighbors or acquaintances. Other people make less money and are still getting by. Those neighbors and acquaintances are always seen at the grocery store, even going to the movies. Their standard of living is not much lower. Some people make less money than you and have more children, a more expensive mortgage, more ex-wives, and they still get by. Whatever your extenuating circumstances are, you can live within the 70-20-10 plan. Realize today you can adopt this savings program; put at least 10% of your take-home pay into two index funds at a low-cost investment firm. Divide the money; 90% goes into the S&P 500 Index and 210% into an International Index MSCI EAFE and expect wealth. It may take a couple of months to get used to it, but you can do it. The emotional and monetary rewards are well worth the wait. You can become a millionaire.

As soon as you're paid, while you are depositing the check, put your 10% away into an investment—pay yourself first. You are paying yourself before you spend any other money.

Now you are no longer working as a slave to consumption, spending everything you earn—time to pay back your debts. Use 20% of your take-home income for debt repayment.

Day 4 Debt

Debt can be your worst enemy. It can eat up your income like a drug addiction. Owing money can tear a marriage apart and keep you up worrying at night. You want a simple budget, and you want to become wealthy. Going into debt to buy consumables does not work in your new plan.

Think back to the last time the economy took a nosedive. Those people in debt were hurt the worst. Those who didn't have obligations weathered the storm. The economy is in a constant cycle, going up and down. There is no stopping it. During inflation, recession, and depression, those with debt are more likely to become the losers than those who are debt-free. Reduce your monthly commitments to survive any economic change.

Why is it so easy to go into debt? Your wants exceed your limited income. Why do so many institutions loan us money? It is incredibly profitable. Don't let others make money off you for sitting on their butts. That's what you're supposed to be doing.

Credit card debt is the worst of them all. Most credit cards are charging outrageous interest. Even more upsetting than paying that monthly bill is there is little to show for the debt you incurred.

Paying Off Your Debt

Use 20% of your monthly income to pay off your debts.

If you are deeply in debt, just using 20% of your income won't be enough. You'll have to add money to it to get that debt down. Use the 10% that is set aside for your LONG TERM, DO NOT TOUCH INVESTMENT PORTFOLIO, along with your 20% DEBT REPAYMENT portion to begin to pay off your debts. It is so essential to get rid of your obligations that it may be necessary to use both your 20% portion along with your 10% portion to pay off your debts.

If you are spending money as interest to our creditors, you'll need to pay off your debts (besides your house) before you can save up and enjoy your 20%.

Some debt is understandable—a loan out to buy a house. It is not advisable to take a loan out (credit card use) to buy groceries or a television.

Once you have paid off all of your debts (excluding your house payment because that is under the heading of living expenses), you will have the 20% DEBT REPAYMENT amount to spare. With this spare money, you can begin to make your dreams become a reality.

Which debt do you pay off first? Target the debt charging the highest interest. These creditors are taking the most money from you. These creditors are taking away your ability to buy new furniture or to take a trip. These creditors are ripping you off. Put a stop to this madness of giving your money away. What is your strategy to begin to pay off your debts?

Write down the minimum payment of every loan you are responsible for paying. Do not include your house or apartment. Next to each loan, write the percent of interest you pay. If it is a credit card, you can call the credit card company and ask them. While you are talking with the credit agency, ask them for an interest rate reduction. Add up the minimum payments and subtract that amount from your DEBT

REPAYMENT amount. Pay as much as possible on the debt with the highest interest and the minimum on the rest.

How much debt is too much? Any liability, beyond your house, is too much debt. Your home is supposed to appreciate. Taking out a loan to buy a house is understandable. The bottom line to figure out if you have too much debt – if your minimum monthly payments are more than 15% of your take-home pay, you have too much debt. At that point, you have to use your 10% LONG TERM, DO NOT TOUCH INVESTMENT portion along with the 20% DEBT REPAYMENT portion to knock down your debt.

Using the 70-20-10 plan is a sensible and realistic method to build wealth, pay off debt, and live within your means.

Don't go further into debt. Instead of using credit cards, pay in full for the goods you want the same month you buy them.

Extreme Debt

First, determine how you created this sizable amount of debt. Then realize the majority of that debt was unnecessary. Learn from those mistakes, learn what items are necessary, and learn how to maximize your bang-for-the-buck. If you want entertainment, find an activity that will fulfill your wants at the lowest price. Some people feel as though expensive and excessive dinners at restaurants, jewelry, movies, trips, or indulging their children's every whim are necessary living expenses. They are not required. If you go out to dinner a lot, you probably can't remember every dining experience. A fur coat will keep you warm, but so will a jacket from a thrift store. Shopping at the mall for things is fun, but look around your house, you have enough. You have clothes to wear already. Not every item you bought and went into debt for was necessary. Stop living above your means.

If your debt is so extreme that your 10% and your 20% combined will not cover the minimum monthly payments required by your creditors, contact your creditors and explain to them what you have planned. Ask them to lower your interest rate. Explain exactly how much you can pay them each month. Explain how you are utilizing a total of 30% take-home income toward paying off your debt. Do not continue to go into debt by continuing to use your credit card or spend unwisely.

Write everything out. Write out how your income is going to be spent. Write out how much each creditor is going to receive and when. Make a list.
1 Which creditors will be paid?
2 How much will each creditor be paid?

3 When will each creditor receive their check?

Write down the names of the people you speak with at each agency. Write down what they tell you. Document everything, in case the matter goes to court.

Keep to your word. Pay the amount you told the creditors you would pay. Get your payments in on time.
For you to become a financial success and to accomplish your dreams and aspirations, you must pay off your debts.

Once you have paid off all of your debts (excluding your house payment because that is under the heading of living expenses), you will have the 20% DEBT REPAYMENT amount to spare. Use this 20% to create a cushion of money to fall back on in case of an emergency. A self-created insurance plan, if you will. Once this emergency fund is established, save for the luxuries in life, save up over a few months for a large ticket item. Enjoy your new-found freedom.

Before the luxuries, you need an emergency fund. To figure a minimum emergency fund, add your 70% monthly living expenses, and any monthly minimum loan repayment you still owe and multiply that figure by four.

Set up a money market for this emergency fund. Automatically transfer money from your checking to the money market after each time you get paid. If the cash is automatically deducted from your checking account, it is more difficult to spend it on frivolous, unnecessary trinkets. Before the money comes out of your checking account, record the amount to be withdrawn. Record the amount well before the withdrawal to prevent overdrawing your checking account.

When you have no debt, and you have a cushion of money, have fun with this 20%. Your 20% fund, saved up, is money for you. Achieve some of your dreams. Determine how you can start to save to make your dreams a reality. Once you have four months of LIVING EXPENSES, plus any monthly minimum debt repayments, begin to put your 10% into a high return, low risk, index fund investments.

Index Funds

Keep your cost low with index funds. Creating a portfolio of differing mutual funds is a smart move toward your financial success. One of those mutual funds should deal with the American stock market, so that when the stock market rises – and it usually does – your mutual fund will also grow. Each night, on the news, the Dow Jones Industrial Average is reported as a rise or a fall. The S&P 500 (Standard and Poors 500) is also reported. These are market guides called indexes. The rise and fall of the

S&P 500 indicate the top 500 publicly traded companies in the U.S. went up or down in value.

The value of an index fund is figured by the rise and fall of stocks of many different companies. These companies have to meet specific guidelines to be part of the index.

Investing in an index fund can, on average, create a better return than other mutual funds because the cost of managing an index fund is lower than managing most other types of mutual funds. With an index fund, there is very little guesswork for the person buying the stocks, the names of the companies that form an index are published, the only management costs are deciding how much of a company to purchase and the transaction costs of buying and selling. Also, once a company gets its name added to an index, the price of its stock almost always rises. This happens for three reasons:
1 Index funds immediately buy into the stock, raising the price.
2 The company is noticed because it is now all over the news. People start to buy into it, again increasing the value.
3 People see the price going up, and want to jump in on its rise, so for the third time, the stock value rises.

70% Is Not Enough

If you try this plan for a couple of months and find living off 70% of your income is not enough to cover your living expenses, you have two choices.
1 Create another source of income.
2 Reduce your living expenses.

People in other countries work three or more jobs six days a week. In Egypt, you'll see people working through the night just like it was daytime. Fly in to view the pyramids at 2:00 AM local time and get a haircut on your way to your hotel. East Asian employees work far more hours than Americans, French, and Germans. Back in the 1950s, the average American worked 13% more hours than they do today. A part-time job might be just what you need to make things work.

Look at your current bills. Which bills seem to be higher than they're worth? If your cell phone bill seems high, drop the carrier, stop using it so much, and use a pay as you go phone. If your rent or house payment is too high for you to afford, move. If the cost to repair or pay the monthly note on your car is high, sell it and get a more affordable vehicle. You can quickly think of solutions.

For some odd ideas: Electric bill – use closed-cell foam to insulate your roof. Cable bill – drop the satellite or cable and use On-Line TV as your entertainment solution.

Home maintenance bills – mow your grass, trim your trees and shrubs, clean your own house, watch videos On-Line about how to repair small problems. Grooming – have a friend cut your hair and only go to a professional once in a while. Bad habits – stop smoking, stop drinking, stop buying stuff from the vending machine.

What it all boils down to is you have created a lifestyle your income can't afford. Cut the bills and start living within 70% of your take-home pay.

Day 5 When to Invest

What day of the month is best to buy low and sell high?

The stock market runs in a constant cycle of ups and downs. Studies have shown the stock market follows a cycle up and then down within each month. Typically, within the last couple of days of the month, the stock market will see a rise in value, usually rising through the fourth day of the next month. After the fourth day, the stock market takes its turn downward. The best day to buy low, when the stock is typically at its lowest cost, would be near the end of the month. Usually, the best day to sell high would be the fourth or fifth day of the month.

This cycle happens for a variety of reasons. Most people are paid at the end of the month and automatically invest at the beginning of the month. The other reason is people pulling money out to pay the bills that come due at the beginning of the month. Retirees typically make an automatic withdraw at the end of the month to pay the mortgage. Take advantage of this cycle and make your contribution near the end of the month, when stock prices are typically low.

The U.S. Department of Labor will tell you, "Start now, set goals, and stick to them. Start early. The sooner you start saving, the more time your money has to grow. Put time on your side. Make retirement saving a high priority. Devise a plan, stick to it, and set goals for yourself. Remember, it's never too late to start. Start saving now, whatever your age."

John Steffens of Merrill Lynch and Co., Inc. advises, "...begin an investment program early on. As he/she earns money, he/she should look for a good long-term growth fund with an excellent record, and use dollar-cost averaging over some time."

Your keys to success: starting early, long-term, and dollar-cost averaging.

Starting Early

Start your program as soon as possible. The longer you have your money invested, the more likely you are to reap the benefits of interest.

Long-Term

Keep your money invested for as long as possible. The 70-20-10 plan is extremely effective at building wealth. It works because cash is regularly and consistently invested (every month), and this money remains in the investment for a long time. Markets fluctuate. You are likely to see ups and downs in the market, with your principal varying with it. Take advantage of this flow with dollar-cost averaging.

Dollar-Cost Averaging

Invest the same amount of money at the same time each month to achieve dollar-cost averaging. When the price of the investment is low, you will be able to buy more shares with the same amount of money. When the price of the investment is high, you will buy fewer shares. Over the long-run, you will spend less money than the average cost per share over the same time. Dollar-cost averaging will work to your advantage over a complete market cycle when the price goes down as well as up. This strategy will have a small but positive result.

Warnings

Jonathan Clements, a financial columnist for The Wall Street Journal, warns, "Stocks are a long-term investment, and if you don't have a long time horizon, you shouldn't own them." Here, you are looking at five years. If you don't need the money within the next five years, invest in the stock market. If you are trying to save your babysitting money for college and you know college is only five years away, you can't risk it in the stock market.

Risk

How much risk are you willing to take? If you are a conservative investor, not wanting to risk your money, you'll invest a portion in the bond market. By examining the risk vs. reward factors, decide how much risk you can handle.

My investment risk tolerance is . . .
- Conservative, stock / bond mix.
    - When will you need the money?
        - 0-5 years. Don't invest in the stock market. Use a bond ladder.
        - 6-10 years. 50% in the stock market.

11-15 years. 55% in the stock market.
16-20 years. 60% in the stock market.
21-25 years. 65% in the stock market.
26+ years. 70% in the stock market.

Risk Taker, stock / bond mix.
When will you need the money?
0-5 years. Don't invest in the stock market. Use a bond ladder.
6-10 years. 90% in the stock market.
11-15 years. 93% in the stock market.
16-20 years. 95% in the stock market.
21-25 years. 98% in the stock market.
26+ years. 100% in the stock market.

Bond Ladder

As time goes on and your lifestyle changes or the market changes, you will want to add a bond ladder to your investments. A bond ladder is buying a few bonds over different years. When the bond reaches maturity and pays you the principal back, you buy another bond. The new bond you buy will be further out in time. Buy the bonds directly, not a mutual fund of bonds.

Show Caution

Your biggest asset is your job. You have an investment in working for your company. That is as much an investment as you need in your company. Do not pick a mutual fund that invests heavily in the same company where you work. If you have a 401(k) or retirement program that your company has set up, make sure all of its capital is not reliant on the company's performance or stock value. If the company goes out of business, you would not only lose your job but also your money for retirement.

Advanced Bond Investments

The day of the month to buy bonds is very similar to stocks but for different reasons. The issue date of the bond is recorded as the month and year of purchase, not a specific date. It is best to buy bonds late in the month. Reap the benefit of the interest from your money market by holding onto your money. Buy the bond(s) at the end of the month and sell them at the beginning of the month, and the interest paid to you will be the same.

When interest rates are high, and on their way down, it is best to invest in long-term bonds. Bonds will pay the most interest during this time of an economic cycle.

Day 6 How the Economy Affects Investments

Like the stock market going up and down, the economy goes in cycles too. These up and down cycles can produce fluctuation and even turmoil in the economy. During an economic crisis, people are most likely to go broke. It is more probable for an individual without investments to go broke than it is for one with investments. The wealthy take advantage of economic change. The rich are not the only ones who can take advantage of the ever-flowing economic cycle. Anyone can move their investments around to maximize their profits.

Inflation

Some will argue that during times of inflation, one should not invest at all. However, some investments are most robust during times of inflation. During inflationary times, your best investment is your house. Take good care of it and be careful where you buy your home. You want to be sure the property value will not drop. During times of inflation, prices of goods and services go up (including your home), the stock market falls, interest rates for loans go up, interest rates on bonds go up. Take advantage of these situations to make money.

You don't have to worry about your house because that is paid for, or you have a fixed-rate mortgage on it. Take advantage of an inflationary period by:
1 Not selling your home.
2 Buying long-term government bonds.

Bonds

To avoid paying commission, buy bonds directly. Use a broker to find bonds that suit your needs. Bonds issued by the United States Government have an advantage. The government is the only institution that can print its own money to pay its debts. For a slightly higher interest rate, you could buy AAA-rated corporate bonds. Do not purchase anything rated lower than AAA. During economic change is when most companies go bankrupt. If money is invested in a company of compromising financial strength, there is a chance you may never see your money again. Any company could fail. Those companies rated AAA are the least likely to default on their bonds.

Gold

During inflationary periods, a good alternative is gold. The two economic conditions that can increase the price of gold are inflation and a political or military crisis. The trouble of buying, storing, and selling gold is reason enough not to bother with it, but even more objection is the value of gold has been unpredictable. The main reason gold goes up in value is that someone wants it and is willing to pay for it. Stocks, on the other hand, have consumers buying the company's products and employees adding value by working.

End of the world dooms-dayers advice buying gold and silver. They think that if the economy crashes, the government is overthrown, or we're hit by an electromagnetic pulse (EMP), precious metals will be the best method to trade for goods. What they aren't figuring is no one is going to have change for a brick of gold. No one will even want a small silver coin because it can't feed their family. During an actual economic disaster, precious metals will be worthless. During these awful times, people will value canned goods, cigarettes, alcohol, coffee, guns, ammunition, and above all else, seeds – the value of seeds will be worth more than platinum.

If you do invest in precious metals, make sure you have a safe place to store it. There are some banks and foundations that will house your gold for you. These places will charge you money to stock your gold – taking a bite out of any profit you could gain. Since we are creating a long-term, do not touch portfolio, it would not be in your best interest to pay someone else what you have earned over the long term. A safety deposit box or fire-proof safe bolted to your closet floor is an alternative. When you are looking to buy gold, look for the best price, there will be a markup from the published price per ounce for minting.

Make sure your gold is pure and certified. Do not buy jewelry, thinking it is worth what you are paying for it. If you were to melt a gold necklace down, you would be surprised at how little it was worth. Stick to the gold that is easily exchanged and recognized as being certified: American Eagle, Canadian Maple Leaf, and Krugerrands. Try to keep premiums for both minting and the selling of gold to a minimum. If you can buy the gold in person, you will not have to pay postage, handling, and insurance. Do not buy stocks or mutual funds that invest in mining speculations. They are risky ventures. Mining speculations are not the same as buying gold. Do not assume mining speculations have a direct correlation to the price of gold.

Prosperity

In times of prosperity, stocks perform at their best. When interest rates are below 9 – 9.5%, and at the bottom of their curve, the stock market performs at its best.

Recession

In times of a recession, it is wise to have treasury bills. If you use a money market, look for a money market that invests in U.S. Treasury Bills or short-term U.S. Treasury Securities.

Depression

In times of depression, it is wise to have long-term (25-30-year) treasury bonds. The value of stocks will drop, but the rate of return on bonds will increase. If you invest in bonds from a company, you will be taking a chance that the issuing company could fail. During a depression, a company is more likely to fold, taking your money with it. The U.S. Government, on the other hand, is highly unlikely to fold. A company cannot legally print cash to pay off its debts as the government can.

Doc looked at my explanations and responded, "The student now becomes the teacher. Are you trying to take over my job?"

"It's about time you retired, Doc."

If you enjoyed or got something out of reading this book

Thank you. You had plenty of choices, but you picked this one. If you got something out of it, please recommend it to friends and on social media. Please leave an honest review at the store or online vendor where you bought this book.

Made in the USA
Middletown, DE
27 October 2020